Ross Macdonald

# The Ferguson Affair

Ross Macdonald's real name was Kenneth Millar. Born near San Francisco in 1915 and raised in Ontario, Millar returned to the United States as a young man and published his first novel in 1944. He served as the president of the Mystery Writers of America and was awarded their Grand Master Award as well as the Mystery Writers of Great Britain's Gold Dagger Award. He died in 1983.

## Also by Ross Macdonald

# THE FERGUSON AFFAIR

## Ross Macdonald

**Vintage Crime / Black Lizard**
*Vintage Books*
*A Division of Random House, Inc.*
*New York*

To Al Stump

FIRST VINTAGE CRIME / BLACK LIZARD EDITION, DECEMBER 2010

The Library of Congress has cataloged the Knopf edition as follows:
Macdonald, Ross.
The Ferguson affair [by] Ross Macdonald.
New York, Knopf, 1960.
p. cm.
PZ3.M59943 Fe PS3525.I486
60009990

**Vintage ISBN: 978-0-307-74079-3**

www.blacklizardcrime.com

# The Ferguson Affair

## chapter 1

THE CASE BEGAN QUIETLY, on the women's floor of the county jail. I was there to interview a client, a young nurse named Ella Barker who had been arrested on a stolen-property charge. Specifically, she had sold a diamond ring which was part of the loot in a recent burglary; the secondhand dealer who bought it from her reported the transaction to the police.

Our interview started out inauspiciously. "Why you?" she wanted to know. "I thought that people in trouble had a right to choose their own lawyer. Especially when they're innocent, like me."

"Innocence or guilt has nothing to do with it, Miss Barker. The judges keep an alphabetical list of all the attorneys in town. We take turns representing defendants without funds. My name happened to be next on the list."

"What did you say your name was?"

"Gunnarson. William Gunnarson."

"It's a funny name," she said, wrinkling her nose.

She wasn't intending to be rude, but she was suspicious of me. Fear made her stiff and stupid. I wished we had a better place to talk than the visitors' compartment of the jail.

"It's an old Scandinavian name. Barker's an English name, isn't it?"

"I guess so. Does it matter?"

She was trying hard to be blasé, to find some armor she could put on against her surroundings. She looked around the room, at the steel-paneled door with its reinforced-glass peephole, the bars on the windows, the table and chairs bolted to the steel floor. Her dark eyes strained wide, trying to take it all in and realize her predicament. She had been in there one night.

"You want to get out of here, don't you?"

"No, I want to set up housekeeping and live in here the rest of my life. Wouldn't anybody?"

"I was going to suggest that the quickest way out would be to tell the truth. Tell me how you got hold of the diamond ring you sold to Hector Broadman."

"So you can broadcast it all over town?"

"I'm your attorney, Miss Barker. What makes you think I'd break your confidence?"

"I know about lawyers," she said cryptically. "And there's nothing you can do to make me talk, so there."

She looked at me with a kind of bleak pride. In her thin, dark way, she wasn't a bad-looking woman. In decent surroundings, properly groomed, she could be a handsome one —the kind of girl you'd want to give a ring to.

"Who gave you the ring, Miss Barker? I'm certain you didn't steal it. You're not a burglar. Even the police don't think you broke into the Simmons house yourself."

"Then why did they arrest me?"

"You know the answer to that as well as I do. We've had a number of burglaries recently. There's an organized gang at work in this area."

"You think I'm a member of it?"

"I don't. But your refusal to talk leads the police to that conclusion. They know you're covering up for criminals, and as long as you persist in that, it seems to make you one of them. You're doing yourself a grave injustice."

She moistened her dry lips with the tip of her tongue. I thought that she was about to tell me the truth. But her dark gaze flickered down and away.

"I found that ring," she said tonelessly. "I picked it up on the sidewalk on the way home from the hospital. Just like I told the policemen."

"You're lying, Miss Barker. Somebody gave you that ring. If you'll confide in me, and let me handle it, I'm practically certain I can get you probation. But that means making a clean breast of everything."

"All right." She touched her breast. "It was given to me, like an engagement ring."

"Who gave it to you?"

"A man. I met him on my vacation in San Francisco."

She was a poor liar. She spoke in a hushed voice, as if she could somehow avoid hearing herself lying.

"Can you describe him?"

"He was very good-looking, tall, dark, and handsome like they say. Only he wasn't so tall. He was about your size. About your age, too," she concluded lamely.

"What was his name?"

"He didn't tell me his name. I only met him the once."

"But he gave you an engagement ring—a diamond worth four or five hundred dollars."

"He probably didn't know how much it was worth. Anyway, it was love at first sight." She tried to look pleased and proud, to make the fantasy real for herself.

"If you're going to lie, Miss Barker, you might as well stick to the story that you found it on the sidewalk."

She plucked at her skirt with fingernails from which the

polish was flaking. "I don't see why you want to give me a bad time. You're worse than Lieutenant Wills. Why don't you leave me be?"

"I will when you tell me the truth."

"Say I do tell—tell you all about that fellow in San Francisco. His name, and everything. What happens then?"

"I think I can get you off. He's here in Buenavista, isn't he? Are you in love with him?"

"Don't make me laugh." But she was far from laughing. "Say you do get me off. What happens then?"

"To you, nothing. The worst you can expect is a couple of years on probation."

"You think so, eh? I bet I wouldn't last a couple of years."

"Probation isn't so bad."

"I don't mean that. I mean this."

She drew her finger across her throat, and sucked air audibly between tongue and teeth. Her violent gesture surprised me, and disturbed me. It seemed to frighten her more than she was already frightened. The blood rushed to her heart, and left her face sallow.

"Have you been threatened?"

She fingered her lower lip and nodded, very slightly, as if there were spies at the barred windows.

"Who threatened you?"

She was silent, her eyes on my face.

"If it was a member of the burglary gang, you'll be doing us all a favor by naming him. You'll be helping me, the police, yourself. And doing the community a service."

"Sure, and end up in the cemetery. Why don't you go away and leave me alone, Mr. Gunnarson? You just don't understand. I want to help you and all, and get out of here. But I want to go on living, too."

"Who threatened you?"

She shook her head twice, fiercely and stubbornly. She rose and went to the window. Her hospital shoes were quiet on the steel plates. She stood with her back to me, looking out across the courthouse grounds at the tower with its clock.

I sat and glared at the back of her sleek dark head. I couldn't guess what secrets lay coiled inside of it, but I was morally certain that they weren't criminal secrets. Ella lacked the earmarks of the type: the dull-eyed resignation, the wild flares of rebelliousness, the indescribable feral odor of sex that has grown claws.

The harsh rasp of a turning key cut into my thoughts. The matron who had let me in opened the heavy door. "Lieutenant Wills would like to see you, sir."

The girl at the window started visibly, then got herself under control. She remained staring out through the bars as if she was mesmerized by the clock in the tower. I went out into the corridor.

Detective-Lieutenant Harvey Wills was leaning on the balustrade above the spiral stairwell. He was a man in his fifties with nearly thirty years of law enforcement extending like an uphill road behind him. He had short gray hair, a pugnacious prow of a nose. His coloring and his bearing went with the steel-gray angularities of the jail.

"I don't like this," I said when the matron had closed the door. "It's hard enough questioning a client in these surroundings without the police department horning in."

"That wasn't my intention. Something came up, I thought you'd like to know." Wills added in a mildly questioning tone: "Is she giving you a difficult time?"

"She's frightened."

"Then why doesn't she break down and give us the facts

we need? This is a big case, Bill—seventeen burglaries with
a total take in money and property close to forty thousand. I
got my first break in five months on it when that little client
of yours walked into Broadman's store with Mrs. Simmons's
diamond ring."

"She doesn't deny that she sold the ring. But it doesn't
prove that she's involved with the burglary gang."

"It does when you put it together with certain other facts.
I'll tell you something, because I don't want to see you
climbing way out on a limb. There's one outstanding fact
linking more than half of these burglaries together. In nine in-
stances, nine out of seventeen, one or more members of the
victimized family were in the hospital at the time the burglary occurred. The other members of the family, if any,
were visiting the hospital. It's pretty clear that someone inside the hospital tipped off the gang each time that the coast
was clear."

"Why blame Ella Barker? There must be two hundred
people on the hospital staff."

"Two hundred and forty-seven, we've been checking them
out for months. But only one of them sold a diamond ring
from the Simmons burglary. Only the one had a platinum
watch from the Denton job hid in her bureau drawer."

"What platinum watch are you talking about?"

"This one." With a slight conjurer's flourish, Wills produced an object wrapped in tissue paper. He undid the
wrapping and showed me a wafer-thin ladies' watch. "We
found it in Ella Barker's apartment this morning. Mrs. Denton has identified it as hers."

I felt an emptiness at my back, as though the room where
Ella was waiting had gone down like an elevator. I realized
that I had invested fairly heavily in the girl. Perhaps my

belief in her innocence was mistaken. Perhaps her unrespon-
siveness was sullen caginess, her fear a natural fear of what
she had coming to her.

"All I want to do," Wills said, "is ask her how she got hold
of it. Surely you don't have any objections to that."

"I'll ask her."

But before we could summon the matron, a man called up
the stairs: "Lieutenant? You up there?"

Wills leaned over the balustrade. "What is it, Granada?"

"Trouble on Pelly Street."

"What kind of trouble?"

Sergeant Granada thrust his dark, saturnine face up
through the curved shadows in the stairwell. "Somebody
tried to knock off Hector Broadman."

chapter 2

WILLS LET ME RIDE along in the back of
his black Mercury. Granada drove, using the siren. In the
streets behind us another siren was howling contrapuntally.
Before we were out of the Mercury, an ambulance pulled
in to the yellow curb behind us.

Broadman's store stood in a poor neighborhood between a
tamale shop and a run-down hotel. Its windows were obscured by hand-lettered signs: WE BUY AND SELL EVERYTHING,
INCLUDING KITCHEN SINKS. OLD GOLD BOUGHT: HIGHEST PRICES.
The interior resembled the nest of a giant magpie, choked
with the debris of people's lives. In the dusty gloom halfway
down the store, a white hat hovered like a puff of ectoplasm.

A dismal voice called out from under it: "Here he is, back here."

Wills and Granada strode toward the white hat and the voice. They moved as policemen do, with heavy purpose carrying a hint of menace. The ambulance men, a tall one and a short one, trotted behind them light-footed as shadows, and I brought up the rear.

A bald man with a bright wig of blood was sitting up on a couch. He was supported by a brown, thin man who wore the white hat and apron of a short-order cook. The bloody man was breathing loudly, gasping his breath in and groaning it out. His eyes rolled up toward us, like veined white eggs under his bird's-nest eyebrows. He pulled away from the man who was holding him up, got to his feet somehow, took a few tottering steps like a fat enormous infant learning to walk, and went to his knees. He crawled away from us into a forest of furniture, making small noises.

"What's the matter with Broadman?" Wills said.

"See for yourself." The white-hatted man was yellow with compunction, or with panic of his own. "Somebody clobbered him on the head, hard."

"Who hit him, Manuel?" Granada said.

Manuel shrugged, carefully. His neck and face were rigid, as if the big starched hat on his head were a chunk of ice he had to keep balanced there. "How do I know? The walls are thick, I was busy serving tamales. Then I heard him yelling." His eyes dropped. There were blood spots on his apron.

"We'll attend to the poor chap," said one of the lads in white, the taller one.

I gave him a second look, and saw that he was no lad. He was forty, at least, with blue bags under his eyes. Still he had that willowy look—the look of a middle-aging man who can't give up the illusive airs of youth. His sidekick was much younger, bright-eyed and plump like a slightly shop-worn cherub.

"Yeah," Wills said dryly. "You do that, Whitey."

Broadman was trying to crawl under a Hollywood bed. It stood too close to the floor. He rooted at it with his damaged head.

The ambulance men got hold of him with firm and gentle hands. One on each side, they raised him to his feet. He bucked like a wall-eyed bronco in their arms.

"Now, now," the tall old youth kept saying. "You had a hard knock, old chap, but you'll be good as new. We'll get you to a doctor, and he'll fix you up."

Broadman kicked at them. They lifted him clear of the floor, making soothing sounds, with male nurses' almost masochistic patience.

"Is he scared of something?" Granada said.

Broadman answered him, in a high and terrible voice: "I don't want to go! You can't make me go to the hospital."

He renewed his floundering struggles. The ambulance men were tiring. The short one had a livid scratch on his chin. There were tears in Whitey's pale eyes, and his mousy hair was dark with sweat.

"Can't you give us a hand, Sergeant?"

"You said you'd handle him. I didn't want to get in bad with the union." Granada's half-smile was sardonic.

"Get with it, Pike," Wills snapped. "This isn't doing Broadman any good."

Granada was a powerful, bull-shouldered man. With his help Broadman was quickly subdued. They carried him out spread-eagled and head down, and still convulsive. A crowd gathered around the ambulance, buzzing like flies at the sight of blood, while the attendants strapped him to a stretcher.

Granada took the head of the stretcher, and Whitey and his partner took the foot. They hoisted Broadman into the back of the ambulance.

The hurt man cried out once more: "I won't go! Gotta keep store. They rob me behind my back. Robbers and killers!"

"Take it easy now," I heard Granada say in a voice that was surprisingly gentle. "Nobody's going to hurt you."

Broadman had lapsed into silence. Granada's voice went on in a calming rhythm. "You don't have to worry about a thing. We"ll look after your store for you, Hector, that's what we're for."

Granada climbed out and said to Whitey: "I think I got him quieted down. Better get him to emergency in a hurry. His injuries may be worse than they look."

Whitey climbed in. The ambulance roared away, scattering spectators. One of them, a dark woman in a shawl, spoke up in a sepulchral whisper. "Whoever done it, Broadman had it coming to him."

The crowd began to disperse, perhaps to avoid association with these sentiments.

Granada raised his voice. "You people from the neighborhood, come into the store, please, all of you. Mr. Broadman has been assaulted, maybe robbed. Any information you can give us will be appreciated."

Reluctantly, in twos and threes, the people who had gathered moved into the front of the store. There were nearly twenty of them, the desk clerk from the hotel next door, the tamale man and several other Spanish-Americans, women in shabby dresses with frightened eyes, a pensioner leaning on a cane, and the dark Cassandra in the shawl.

They took up awkward positions on Broadman's collection of old furniture. Granada asked them questions while Wills prowled the store. I sat on a worn leather hassock to one side and listened to the answers, hoping for something that would help my client.

Nothing helpful was said. The inhabitants of Pelly Street seemed to lose their power of speech in the presence of the law. When Granada asked the woman in the shawl what she'd meant by her remark, she said she had heard at fourth or fifth hand that Broadman lent money at twenty per cent per week. He had a lot of enemies, but nobody that she knew.

The old man with the cane acted as if he might know something more: nobody could be as deaf and senile as he pretended to be. But he wasn't telling. I made a note of his name: it was Jerry Winkler, and he said he lived in the hotel next door.

Granada saved Manuel for the last, and bore down hard on him. But the blood spots on his apron were easily explained. He had found Broadman half-conscious on the floor and helped him onto the couch. Then he phoned the police. Otherwise he had done nothing, seen nothing, heard nothing.

"Didn't Broadman say anything to you?"

"He said they tried to rob him."

"Who tried to rob him?"

"He didn't say. He said that he was going to fix them himself. He didn't want me to call the—call you, even."

"Why?"

"He didn't say."

Granada dismissed him with an angry gesture, then called him back from the door.

"You want something else, Mr. Granada?"

Granada said with a flashing grin which the rest of his heavy face failed to support: "I just wanted to be remembered to your brother."

"Gus remembers you already. My sister-in-law Secundina is reminding him all the time."

Without obvious alteration, Granada's grin become a scowl. "That's nice. Where is Gus right now?"

"Gone fishing. I gave him the day off."

"He's working for you now, eh?"

"You know that, Mr. Granada."

"But he used to work for Broadman, isn't that right?"

"You know that, too. He quit. I needed help."

"That's not the way I heard it. I heard Broadman fired him the other day."

"People say a lot of things that are not true, Mr. Granada." Manuel put ironic emphasis on the "Mister."

"Just don't you be one of them. And tell Gus I want to see him when he comes back from fishing."

Manuel went out balancing his heavy hat.

"Pelly Street," Granada said to himself. He stood up and said briskly to me: "This could be a grudge case, Mr. Gunnarson. Twenty per cent a week is pretty good motivation for somebody that hasn't got it. I've heard before now that Broadman grinds the faces. He's probably one of these unknown millionaires. You know, like the bums they vag with bankbooks sewn into their rags."

"I wish somebody would sew a nice fat bankbook into one of my suits."

"I thought all lawyers were wealthy."

We walked toward the rear of the store where Wills had disappeared. A rectangular area had been partitioned off and fenced and roofed with steel netting. The reinforced wire door was standing open, with its heavy padlock gaping, and we went into Broadman's unusual office.

An old-fashioned black iron safe squatted in one corner of the wire enclosure. An unmade cot, pillow end against the safe, was partly hidden by a huge old desk. A telephone with the receiver off lay on the desk among a drift of papers. Reaching to replace the receiver, I almost fell through a hole in the floor. Granada grasped my arm with fingers like steel hooks. "Watch it, Mr. Gunnarson."

I stepped back from an open trap door through which a flight of wooden steps descended into watery yellow gloom. Granada put the telephone together. It rang immediately. Wills came up the steps three at a time and lifted the receiver out of Granada's hand. "I'll take it, Pike."

Wills's face was streaked with sweat. It grew pale as he listened to what was said, throwing the grimy streaks into relief.

"Too bad. You better send over the identification squad. Got that?" Wills hung up and said to Granada: "Broadman died."

"Did those blows on the head kill him?"

"We'll go on that assumption unless the autopsy shows different. All we know for certain right now, he was D.O.A. See what you can turn up in the basement, Pike. There's a lot of old rugs and mattresses down there, looks like somebody's been heaving them around. I didn't find anything significant, but maybe you'll have better luck."

"What am I looking for?"

"A blunt instrument, with blood on it." As Granada went down the steps, Wills turned to me. "I'm glad you stuck around, Counselor, I want to talk to you. This changes things for your client."

"For better or worse?"

"That's largely up to her, wouldn't you say? And up to you. She's been in jail the past twenty-four hours, which makes her the one member of the gang who has clean hands, as far as this killing is concerned. There's no sensible reason why she shouldn't talk to us, and maybe save herself a long trip."

"How could she know anything about this murder?"

"I don't claim she knows anything about it specifically. But she must be able to identify the other members of the gang. If she comes clean—" Wills raised his hands in a gesture which didn't go with his personality: the freeing of an imaginary bird. "Understand me, I'm not suggesting a deal. But where would we be if the people of the world didn't co-operate?"

Just where we were, I thought, because they didn't. Still, I was impressed by Wills's attempt to talk my language.

"You blame this murder on the burglary gang?"

He nodded. "We've suspected for some time that Broadman was fencing for them—acting as one of their outlets, anyway. We got our first tangible evidence last week. An ormolu clock turned up in one of the L.A. auction rooms. A member of their robbery detail happened to spot it because it was unique, and checked with our circular. The clock was taken in the Hampshire burglary, out in the Foothill district, and it was part of a shipment from Broadman's store.

"Broadman had a story ready, of course. He bought the ormolu clock from a little old lady in reduced circumstances that he'd never seen before. How did he know it was stolen? He had our pawn-shop list, sure, but his eyes were bad. If he spent all his time reading police lists, what would happen to business?"

Wills leaned on the desk and looked out thoughtfully through the wire netting. The jumbled contents of the store were evidence piled on evidence that you couldn't take it with you.

"Broadman would have been better off in jail," he said, "but the clock wasn't enough to arrest him for. We couldn't prove he had guilty knowledge. He knew we were on to him, though. And he wanted out. When Ella Barker sold him that hot diamond yesterday, he was on the phone practically before she was out of the store."

"You think he knew that diamond ring was stolen?"

"I'm sure of it. He also knew who she was."

"Can you prove that, Lieutenant?"

"I can. I'm telling you this to give you a chance to climb in off that limb. Broadman was a patient in the hospital five-six months ago. Ella was one of his nurses. They got to be quite good friends. Ask her, when you ask her about the watch. And make sure you get an answer, you'll be doing her a favor. Honest to God, I'd hate to see that little client of yours get herself run over by a steam roller."

"You think of yourself as a steam roller, do you?"

"The law," Wills said.

More law arrived, with cameras and fingerprint kits. I went out into the street. The sunlight hurt my eyes. It was reflected like glancing knives from the chrome of the two police cars at the curb.

They drew attention on the poor street, a kind of reverse attention. Passers-by averted their heads from the cars, as if they hoped to escape their black influence. I guessed that the rumor of Broadman's death had spread across town like a prophecy of disaster to Pelly Street.

Jerry Winkler leaned on his cane in front of the hotel, an

unstable tripod supporting a heavy gray head. Carefully re-distributing his weight, he raised his cane and flourished it. I went over to him.

"I heard that Broadman died, son."

"Yes, he died."

He clucked, red tongue vibrating between his bearded lips. "That makes it murder, don't it?"

"It would seem to."

"And you're a lawyer, ain't you?" He touched my arm with a veined, knobbed hand. "I'm Jerry Winkler, everybody knows me. I never been a witness in a trial. Friend of mine was once. He told me they pay the witnesses."

"It doesn't amount to more than a few dollars. The court simply pays you for lost time."

"I got lots of time to lose." He rubbed his furred chin and peered up at my face like a hungry old dog hoping for a bone. "And mighty few dollars."

"Do you have information about Broadman's death?"

"Maybe I do, if it's worth my while. You want to come up to my room and chin a little?"

"I have a little time to lose, Mr. Winkler. My name is Gunnarson."

He led me through the musty lobby, up narrow, foot-worn steps, along a narrow hallway to his cubbyhole at the rear. It contained an iron bed, a washstand, a bureau with a clouded mirror, an old-fashioned rocking chair, and the atmosphere of lonely waiting time.

He made me sit in the rocker beside the single window, which looked out on an alley. Slowly and painfully, he lowered himself onto the bed and sat hunched forward, still leaning on his cane.

"I want to do what's right. On the other hand, I don't want to end up worse than I was before."

"How would you do that?"

"Ramifications. Everything has its ramifications. Try living on a sixty-dollar pension if you think it's so easy. I get my clothes at the Starvation Army, but I still run out before the end of the month. Sometimes Manuel give me free dinners along at the end of the month."

"Did Manuel kill Broadman?"

"I didn't say that. I didn't say nothing yet. I want to do my duty, sure, but there's no harm trying to get a little money out of it, is there?"

"You're obliged to give information to the authorities, Mr. Winkler. You're in hot water now for holding out on them."

"I didn't hold out. I just remembered, is all. My memory ain't so good."

"What did you remember?"

"What I seen." He hesitated. "I thought it would be worth something."

The little room and the sly, sad old man cramped me and oppressed me. I made a gesture I couldn't afford, took a five-dollar bill out of my rather flat wallet, and held it out to him. "This will buy a few dinners, anyway."

He took it with a beaming smile. "Sure will. You're a good boy, and Jerry Winkler will remember you in his prayers." Without any change in tone, he said: "It was Gus Donato that smashed up Broadman. Manuel's young brother Gus."

"Did you see it happen, Mr. Winkler?"

"No, but I seen him go in, and I seen him come out. I was sitting here at the window, thinking about the old days, when Gus drives this pickup into the alley. He gets this tire iron out of the back of the pickup and shoves it down his pant leg and sneaks in the back entrance of Broadman's store. A few minutes later he comes out carrying a burlap bag on his back. He chucks it into the pickup and goes back for more."

"Could you tell what was in the bag?"

"No. It was all chunky with stuff, though. So were the others. He made four or five trips, bringing out those bags, put them all in the pickup and drove away."

I gazed into his washed-out eyes. "Are you certain of your identification?"

"Dead certain." He thumped the bare board floor with his cane. "I see Gus Donato all the time. And this time I paid him special mind because he ain't allowed to drive a car."

"Is he too young?"

"Naw, he's plenty old enough. But they don't let them drive when they're on parole. He had a lot of trouble with cars, that's how he got arrested in the first place."

"Is Gus a friend of yours?"

"I wouldn't say that. His brother Manuel is a good friend."

"You mentioned that you see Gus all the time."

"Sure, in Manuel's place. He's been washing dishes for Manuel since Broadman fired him last week."

"Why did Broadman fire him?"

"I never did get it straight. It was something about a clock, a little gold clock. Gus shipped it off someplace that he wasn't supposed to. I heard Manuel and Broadman arguing about it in the alley."

I opened the window. Two men in plain clothes were conferring at the back door of Broadman's establishment. They looked up at me suspiciously. I pulled my head in and closed the window.

"You don't miss much, Mr. Winkler."
"Try not to."

**《◆《◆《◆《◆《◆《**
**《◆《◆《◆《◆《◆《** *chapter* **3**
**《◆《◆《◆《◆《◆《**

I LEFT HIM TALKING to Wills in Broadman's office cage, and took a cab back to the courthouse. I was eager to question Ella Barker again. But she wasn't so eager to be questioned.

The girl didn't raise her head when the matron let me into the visitors' room. She sat with her thin arms resting on the edge of the table—a hunched and drooping figure like a bird which despaired of liberation. The afternoon sun fell through the bars behind her and striped her back with shadows.

"Snap out of it, Barker, the first day is always the hardest." The matron touched the girl's shoulder. Perhaps she meant to be kind, but she sounded patronizing, almost threatening. "Here's your Mr. Gunnarson again. You don't want him to see you moping."

Ella pulled her shoulder away from the matron's hand. "If he doesn't like it, he doesn't have to come here, now or ever."

"That doesn't make sense," the matron said. "In the spot you're in, you need a lawyer, whether you know it or not."

"Leave me alone with her, will you, Mrs. Clement?"

"Whatever you say." The matron went out, shaking her keys like melancholy castanets.

I sat down across the table from Ella Barker. "Hector Broadman is dead. Murdered."

Her dark lashes curtained her eyes, and she wouldn't look up. I thought I could smell her fear, like a faint sour fermentation in the air. Perhaps it was the odor of the jail.

"You knew Broadman, didn't you?"

"I had him for a patient. I've looked after lots of patients in my life."

"What was the matter with him?"

"He had a growth removed—a benign growth. That was way last summer."

"But you've seen him since?"

"I went out with him, once," she said in her steady monotone. "He took a liking to me, I guess, and I wasn't exactly swamped with invitations."

"What did you and Broadman talk about?"

"Him, mostly. He was an older man, a widower. He did a lot of talking about the Depression. He had some kind of business in the East. Him and his first wife lost it in the Depression. They lost everything they had."

"He had more than one wife?"

"I didn't say that." She looked up for the first time. Her eyes were startled. "If you think I'd marry a fat old bald-headed man like Mr. Broadman, you've got another think coming. Not that I couldn't have."

"You mean he proposed? The first night?"

She hesitated. "I saw him a couple of times after that. You might say I took pity on him."

"Where did he propose to you?"

"In his car. He'd had a couple of drinks, over at—" Her lips froze in an opened position for an instant, then came together tightly.

"Over where?"

"All over," she said. "He took me for a drive. Around town. Up in the hills."

"To meet his friends?"

"He didn't have any friends," she answered, too quickly.

"Where did he have those drinks the night he proposed? At his house?"

"He didn't have a house. He ate in restaurants and slept in his store. I told him he couldn't expect a girl to share that kind of a life with him. So he offered to move into my flat, furnish it for me."

"That was generous of him."

"Yeah, wasn't it?" A smile pinched her mouth. "He had it all figured out. I guess I wasn't very nice to him, that last night. He took it hard." Her smile had turned slightly cruel.

"Where did you say he had those drinks?"

"I didn't say. As a matter of fact, I gave him the drinks myself. I don't drink, but I keep a bottle on hand for my friends."

"Who are your friends, besides Broadman?"

"Nobody special. The girls at the hospital. I didn't say *he* was a friend of mine."

"He must have been a very good friend. He gave you a platinum watch."

She sat up straight, neck taut, as if I'd tied a noose there and sprung a trap. "He certainly did not."

"Who did?"

"Nobody did. If you think I accept expensive gifts from men—"

"The watch was found in your apartment today."

She bit her lower lip. Beyond her head, I could see the courthouse tower. The sun had slipped down behind it. The shadow of the tower leaned on the window like a tangible bulk of darkness. Somewhere in the iron bowels of the building, pots and pans were clashing. It was half past five by the tower clock.

"It wasn't Hector Broadman gave me the watch," she said. "I didn't know it was stolen. When a fellow gives a girl a watch or a ring, she doesn't think of it being stolen."

"It was a dirty trick to play on you," I said. "I'd think you'd be eager to get back at the man who played it."

She nodded, watching me over her fingers.

"Do you want to tell me all about it, Ella? It's nearly suppertime, and they'll be inviting me out of here pretty soon. If you wait until tomorrow or the next day, it may be too late."

"Too late?" she said behind her hand.

"Too late for you. You have a chance to help the police put their hands on Broadman's killer. I strongly advise you to take it. If you don't, and he's caught without your help, it won't be good for our side."

"What did he do to Hector Broadman?"

"Bashed in his head. You don't want to sit here and let him get away."

She fingered her own dark head. She was so preoccupied with the image in her mind that she rumpled her hair and failed to smooth it down.

"You don't want it to happen to you, I know. Doesn't that go for other people, too? You are a nurse, after all, and I'll bet a darn good one."

"You don't have to flatter me, Mr. Gunnarson. I'm ready to tell you who gave me the watch and the ring."

"Gus Donato?"

She didn't react to the name. "No. His name is Larry Gaines."

"And he's the man from San Francisco?"

"He's a lifeguard at the Foothill Club. There isn't any man from San Francisco."

This admission cost her more effort than any of the others. She was so drained that she couldn't speak for a minute. I was content to wait, light a cigarette, and collect my thoughts. Cross-questioning is hard work at the best of times. The worst kind goes on outside of court, in private, when you have to ram your clients' lies down their throats until they choke on them.

Ella had had enough of her lies. She told me the short and not so simple story of her affair with Larry Gaines.

She had met him through Hector Broadman. Broadman had taken her to Larry's place the second time they were out together. Apparently he didn't feel up to entertaining her all by himself. Larry was different—so different that she couldn't understand how he and Broadman happened to be friends. He was good-looking, and polite, and only a few years older than she was herself. He lived in a house in a canyon outside the city limits.

It was an exciting evening, sitting between two men in Larry's little house, drinking the Turkish coffee which Larry made, and listening to good records on his hi-fi. Comparing the two, she made up her mind that Hector Broadman was not for her.

The second evening the trio spent together, she began to dream that possibly Larry might be. He let her know that he liked her, in so many ways. They had a serious talk about life, for example, and he was very interested in her opinions. Broadman nursed a bottle in a corner.

That night she broke with Broadman. She hated men who drank, anyway. Larry waited for four days—the longest four days of Ella's life—and then he phoned her. She was so grateful that she let him seduce her. She was a virgin, but he was so gentle and kind.

He didn't turn on her, either, the way fellows are supposed to. He went right on being kind, and calling her just about every night of the week. He wanted to marry her, he said, but he had so little to offer her. They both knew in the long run a man with his brains and personality was bound to make his mark. But that took time, or a lucky break. While he was waiting for one, his salary at the club was barely enough to support him, even with tips added in. Those wealthy people at the Foothill Club were so tight, he said, you had to use a chisel to pry a thin dime off their palms.

What made it especially hard for him, he told her, was the fact that he came from a wealthy family himself: they lost all their money in the crash before he was born. It drove him crazy, scrounging for nickels and dimes while the members sat on their fat behinds and the money grew on trees for them.

He wanted a silver-dollar tree of his own, he said, and he had a plan for getting it. If it worked, they could marry before the year was out and live in comfort for the rest of their lives. But he was going to need her help in carrying out the plan. He needed someone in the hospital to supply him with the names of new patients, especially well-heeled ones in private suites.

"Did you help him, Ella?"

She shook her head emphatically. "I certainly did not."

"Then how did you get the diamond ring and the watch?"

"He gave them to me before I broke off with him. I guess he thought it would change my mind. But after I found out about him, I didn't want any part of him or his plans. A nurse who would take advantage of her patients like that should have her uniform torn right off her back."

"But you didn't tell the police about his plans."

"I just couldn't." She hung her head. "I was stuck on him, I guess, for a long time after I broke with him. Larry was my first real crush. It made me do crazy things. Like last week —" She interrupted herself again.

"What happened last week?"

"I kept reading about these houses and stores being broken into in town. I couldn't believe Larry was doing it. At the same time I knew he was mixed up in it. I had to do something, settle my mind one way or the other. I borrowed a car from a girl-friend and went out to Larry's place. I intended to ask him outright if he was the burglar. He wouldn't tell me the truth, probably, but I wanted to see the look on his face when I asked him. Then I'd know what to do.

"There was a light in the house. I left the car down the road and sneaked up on it, kind of. I could hear voices inside. He had a woman with him. I knocked on the door—I didn't care what happened. I saw her when he opened the door. She was sitting on the studio couch, a blonde in a Japanese kimono—the same one I used to wear. It sort of set me off, and I called him a name.

"Larry stepped outside and closed the door on her. I never saw him mad before. He was so mad it made his teeth chatter. He said if I ever came there again, or bothered him in any way, that he would tell a friend of his to put a knife in my heart. I was scared. My knees were shaking so that I could hardly get back to the car."

"Did he mention the friend's name?"

"No."

"It wasn't Gus Donato?"

"I never heard of any Donato. All he said was a friend. Some friends he must have."

"You should have gone to the police, Ella."

"I know I should. You think I should talk to them now, don't you?"

"Decidedly."

"You honestly think they'll let me go if I talk?"

"It won't be quite as simple as that, I'm afraid. If you satisfy the District Attorney, he should consent to a lowering of your bail at least. It was set very high."

"Yeah, five thousand dollars. I can't raise that kind of money, and I haven't got the five hundred to pay a bail bondsman. How low do you think you can get it down?"

"I won't make any promises. It depends."

"Depends on what?" she said impatiently.

"On whether or not you've told me the whole truth, and tell the same to the police and the prosecutor."

"Don't you believe this is the truth?"

"I'll be frank with you, Miss Barker. One or two things about your story bother me. Why did you sell Broadman the ring that Larry gave you?"

"I wanted Larry to know what I thought of him and his lousy ring. Broadman was a friend of his, and I thought he'd probably tell him."

"How would Broadman know where you got the ring?"

"I told him."

"You told Broadman?"

"Yes."

"He knew that Larry gave you the ring?"

"After I told him, he must have."

We sat and looked at each other.

"You think Larry killed Broadman, don't you?" the girl said.

"Or had him killed."

## chapter 4

I GOT IN TOUCH with Wills and a Deputy District Attorney named Joe Reach. We convened with Ella Barker in the interrogation room on the first floor of the courthouse. Ella went through her story again. It was recorded on stenotype and wire by an elderly court reporter named Ed Gellhorn.

There are some quite honest people who make poor witnesses because they can't tell the same story twice with any degree of conviction. Ella's story hadn't been too plausible in the first place. The second time around, told in surges of hysterical assurance with stretches of dismal self-doubt in between, it sounded like something she was making up as she went along. Wills and Reach didn't believe her. To make matters worse, they assumed that I didn't, either.

Wills kept bringing up the name Donato, trying to make her admit that she knew the wanted man. Reach kept insisting that she had been fully aware of Gaines's activities, and probably accessory to them. You didn't shack up with a guy—

I stopped him there. "That's enough, Joe. Miss Barker has made a full and voluntary statement. You're trying to twist it around into a confession."

"Any twisting that's being done, I think I know who's doing it."

"What's this about a blonde woman?" Wills put in. "This one you said you saw at Gaines's place in the canyon."

"I saw her, all right," Ella said.

"Can you describe her?"

She looked around the circle of male faces, half despairing.

"I said, can you describe her?"

"Give her a chance to collect her thoughts, Lieutenant."

Wills turned on me. "You don't have to *think* to describe a subject, not if you're telling the truth."

"Why would I lie about her?" Ella said.

"Just in case she never existed, for instance. If she existed, describe her to us."

"I'm trying to. She was very good-looking. Not so fresh, if you know what I mean, and not a natural blonde, I don't think, but very good-looking. You ever go to the movies?"

"What's that got to do with it?"

"You ever see this new actress they have, name of Holly May? The woman that Larry was smooching with looked like Holly May."

Wills and Reach exchanged incredulous glances. Reach said: "What would a movie actress be doing with riffraff like him?"

"I didn't say it was her. I said it looked like her."

"You're certain she existed?"

I got angry at this point, told Ella to say no more, and left the room. Wills and Reach followed me into the anteroom.

"You're making a mistake," the Lieutenant said. "This is a murder case now. That little client of yours is dipping her tootsies into very hot water. You better lay out all your cards on the table."

Joe Reach nodded agreement. "You owe it to your client to instruct her to tell the whole truth. I know what it means when a witness starts picking faces off of movie screens. I've had a lot more experience—"

"It hasn't done you much good. You don't know the truth when you hear it."

"Don't I? Let her bring that story into court, we'll punch it full of holes like wet tissue."

"The hell you will!"

Wills laid a restraining hand on my shoulder. "Come on, now, don't blow your top. Don't be a hothead all your life. Learn something."

"She's conning you," Reach said. "You just haven't got the humility to admit it."

I was blind mad by this time, loaded with hot and cold running adrenalin. I turned on my heel and walked out. Neither of them followed me this time.

The public telephone booth in the corridor stopped me like a sentry box. I stepped inside and phoned home.

"I knew it was you," Sally said, "as soon as I heard the phone ring. *Now* do you believe in ESP?"

"If you're so strong on extra-sensory perception, what am I calling about?"

"Don't tell me you're not coming home for dinner?"

I sidestepped that question. "You go to a lot of movies. Did you ever hear of an actress named Holly May?"

"Naturally I have. Everybody has."

"I haven't."

"That's because you're fixated on your work. If you took me to the movies more often, you'd know what's going on in the world. Not that she's in the movies any more. She decided to get out of the rat-race before it wrecked her emotional health. That's a direct quote."

"Have you been reading movie magazines again?"

"No. She told me herself."

"You know Holly May?"

"I met her."

"Why didn't you tell me?"

"I tried to last night, but you weren't listening. I ran into her in the clinic Monday afternoon. She wanted to know what time it was, and I told her. Then I asked her if she wasn't Holly May. She admitted that she was, but she said she didn't want it spread around. She's trying to stay as incognito as possible."

"What's she doing in town?"

"I gather she's living quietly here with her husband. I only talked to her for a couple of minutes, and then Dr. Trench took me. Dr. Trench said I was in wonderful shape for a woman in her ninth month."

"Good. Did she mention her husband's name?"

"No, but I read it in the columns last summer when she got married. I think she married a Canadian oilman. Let's see, it was some Scotch name—something like Ballantine. Anyway, she seems to have done all right for herself. She was dripping with mink and things."

"What kind of a woman is she?"

"She seemed nice and down-to-earth for a movie actress. She asked me how long I had to go and such. She's a stunning creature, but it doesn't seem to have gone to her head. Why?"

"Nothing special. Her name came up. I had no idea that she was living in town."

"A lot of people live here that you never hear about." Sally's voice changed gears, with a faint ominous clash. "There is, for instance, the unknown housewife whose specialty is leg of lamb. She sits in her modest home awaiting recognition—"

"Are you fixing a leg of lamb?"

"It's already fixed. With mint jelly. I know it's an extravagance, Bill, but I wanted to make you something special for a change. I spend so much time dreaming lately, I haven't been doing my duty by you. You will be home for dinner, won't you?"

"As soon as I can make it. Keep it warm."

"But you can't keep a leg of lamb warm. It dries *out.*"

"I enjoy it that way. Like pemmican."

Sally hung up on me, and there I was again with the adrenalin singing in my veins. I decided to walk it off. Something that was not ESP pushed me down the long slope of Main Street to the lower town.

*chapter* 5

THERE WAS A POLICE SEAL on the front door of Broadman's store. I peered through the dusty pane. The evening light fell slanting across the furniture and bric-à-brac which Broadman had laid up against hard times, before time stopped for him.

I became aware of voices next door, a woman's voice raised high, and a man's growling under it. I strolled over and looked in through the window of the tamale shop. The man in the white hat was arguing across the counter with a black-haired woman. Her hands gripped the edge of the counter as if it was a high ledge from which she would fall to her death if she let go.

"But they will kill him," she cried.

"Let them. He asked for it."

"What will I do if they kill him?"

"You'll be better off."

His eyes were brown liquid slits under his white hat. They widened when they saw me through the glass door. I tried it. It was locked.

He shook his head curtly, and waved me away. The movement of his arm was jerky, like a semaphore's. I pointed at a sign in the window which said: OPEN 7 A.M. TO MIDNIGHT. He came around the counter, opened the door about a foot, and thrust his nose out. His nose was longer and sharper than it had appeared in the afternoon.

"I'm closed, I'm sorry. There's a good place around the corner on Main Street." Then he gave me a second look. "Are you a policeman? I saw you with Mr. Granada this afternoon."

"I'm a lawyer, William Gunnarson. Could I talk to you a little, Mr. Donato?"

"I have already talked about my brother, to the police."

The woman had crowded up behind him. She was a young pretty woman, but her face was puffed and dissolute with trouble. She said with one hand in her tangled licorice hair:

"Tell him nothing!"

"Be quiet, Secundina. You are a fool." He turned back to me, trying to control his feelings. Their pressure forced the flesh of his face into stark shapes, like cracked clay. "I see, you have heard that my brother is wanted by the police. You want to offer your services?"

"That wasn't my idea. I want to talk about your neighbor Broadman. Your ex-neighbor."

Donato didn't seem to hear me. "I have no need for a lawyer. I have no money to pay a lawyer." I guessed he was using me to continue his argument with the woman. "If I had money I would go and buy a nice new rope and hang myself."

"Liar," she said. "You have a savings account. And he is your only brother."

"I am his only brother, too. What has he done for me?"

"He worked for you."

"He broke dishes. He mopped the floor and left it dirty. But I paid him, I kept you eating."

"Big shot!" Her mouth curled.

"Gus is the big shot. He throws his weight, and I pick up the pieces. This time there's one big piece, a dead man. I can't pick it up."

"But he is innocent."

"Like the Devil himself, innocent."

Her teeth flashed. "Dirty liar, you must not say that."

"And Gus is the one who tells the truth? I tell you, I am finished with Gus. He's not my brother. He can live or die, I don't want to know about it." He turned to me. "Go away, Mister, eh?"

"Where is your brother?"

"Out in the tules someplace. How do I know? If I knew, I'd go out and bring him in. He took my pickup."

"He borrowed it," Mrs. Donato said. "He wants to bring it back. He wants to talk to you."

"Have you seen him, Mrs. Donato?"

Her face closed up. "I didn't say that."

"I must have misunderstood you. Can we go someplace and talk? I have some questions I'd very much like to ask you."

"What about?"

"People you may have heard of. There's a man named Larry Gaines, for instance, who works as a lifeguard at the Foothill Club."

Her eyes became hard and dim and dusty, like the glass eyes you see in deer heads. "I never been there in my life. I don't know nobody out there."

"You know Tony Padilla," her brother-in-law said. He looked at her significantly.

"Who's he, Mr. Donato?"

"Fellow tends bar at the Foothill Club."

"What's he got to do with this?"

"Nothing," he said impassively. "We don't, neither. Excuse us now, Mister, how about it? You see what family trouble I got. This is a bad time to visit."

Gently and firmly, he shut the door in my face.

I took a taxi to the Foothill Club and told the driver not to wait. There was a police Mercury with undercover plates among the Cadillacs and sports cars in the tree-shaded parking lot. I was in no mood to talk to policemen. I leaned against the trunk of one of the trees, as far as possible from the Mercury, and waited for Wills's detectives to come out.

The mere idea of detectives at the Foothill Club was incongruous. It was one of those monumentally unpretentious places where you could still imagine that the sun had never set on the international set. It cost five thousand dollars to join, and membership was limited to three hundred. Even if you had the five thousand, you had to wait for one of the members to die. And then take a blood test, for blueness.

The members straggling out in twos and threes from the nineteenth hole all looked as if they intended to live forever. Men with hand-polished leather faces who followed the sun from Acapulco to Juan-les-Pins, elderly striding women in sensible shoes complaining in anglicized accents about the price of drinks or the fact that the club was cutting costs on the heating system of the swimming pool.

One of them wondered audibly what had happened to that nice young pool attendant. A silver-haired man in a white scarf said, with some satisfaction, that the fellow had been fired. He'd made one pass too many at you-know-who, but in his opinion, which his voice caressed, the woman was just as much to blame as the lifeguard, what was his name? Too many new faces, slipping standards.

The trees that lined the parking lot were silver-dollar eucalyptus, appropriately enough. Their metallic leaves gleamed in the dying sunset. Twilight gathered in the folds of the foothills and rolled like blue fog down the valley, catching in the branches of scattered oaks. The slopes of the golf course dissolved away into darkness. Venus lit her candle in the western part of the sky. I thought of Sally and her leg of lamb. Some kind of cooked-meat smell was emanating from the clubhouse. Prime ribs of unicorn, perhaps, or breast of phoenix under glass.

The clubhouse was a rambling building with about an acre of red tile roof and many wings and entrances. Like the hills and trees around it, it had the air of having been there for a long time. I was beginning to feel indigenous myself. Not a member: nothing like that: a wild thing who lived in the neighborhood.

A car came up the road from town. Its headlights wavered like antennae before it entered the parking lot. It stopped just inside the stone gateposts.

A man got out and strode toward me busily. "Park it, bud."

He was very short and wide, broad-faced, and pigeon-breasted, as if a pile driver had fallen on him in his formative years. He wore a light suit, a sunburst tie, and a light hat with a band that matched the tie. He had a voice like a fog-horn and a breath, when he came up close, like the back room of a bar. "You deaf or something?"

I was feeling declassed and surly, but I answered mildly enough: "I'm not a parking attendant. Park it yourself."

He didn't move. "You must be the manager, eh?" Without waiting for an answer, he went on: "Nice place you got here. I'd like to pick up a club like this myself—high class, wealthy clientele, quiet surroundings. I could turn a place like this into a gold mine. How much do you make a week?"

"I have nothing to do with the management of the club."

"I see." For some obscure reason, he decided that I was a member and was snubbing him. He jerked a thumb at his car. "Don't judge me by that Ford, it's just a rental. Back home I keep a four-car garage, nothing in it but Caddies. I don't wanna brag, but I could buy this place outright, cash on the line."

"Bully for you," I said. "Are you in the real-estate business?"

"I guess you could say I am, at that. Salaman's the name."

He offered me his hand. I didn't take it. It hung in the air like a dead haddock. His eyes became bright and moist under his hat brim.

"So you won't take the hand of friendship." His voice was a blend of menace and sentimentality, like asphalt mixed with molasses. "Okay, no hard feelings. I never been in the State of Cal before, but it certainly isn't the friendly place they said it was. It's strickly from chillyville, if you want my opinion."

He took off his hat and looked ready to weep into it. His hair was a frizzy black mass which sprang up vivaciously, adding inches to his height and altering his appearance. In spite of his illicit air, the man was queerly pathetic.

"Where do you come from, Mr. Salaman?"

He said as if he'd been waiting to be asked: "Miami, Florida. I'm in business there, various kinds of business. I flew out here for combined business and pleasure, you might say. Deductible expense. You got a member with you, name of Holly May?"

"Holly May?"

"You may know her as Mrs. Ferguson. I understand she married a man name of Ferguson since her and me were—friends." He smacked his lips over the word or its connotations. "Just between us girls, big blondes were always my weakness."

"I see."

My noncommittal act was wearing thin. So was my patience.

"Do you know her?" Salaman said.

"As a matter of fact I don't."

"Isn't she a member here? It said in the paper she was. It said that she was playing around with the lifeguard."

He was standing almost on my toes, talking breathily up into my face. I pushed him away, not violently, but away. He went through a quivering transformation scene and came out of it haggard and yelping. "Keep your hooks off me, I blow your head off."

His hand went under his jacket and tugged at a tumorous swelling in his armpit. Then he froze. His frozen snarl was a devil mask carved out of white and blue stone.

I croaked from a suddenly dry throat: "Go away. Back to the reservation."

Oddly enough he went.

*chapter* 6

My ILLUSION OF irresistible moral force evaporated when I looked around. Three men were coming up from the clubhouse to the parking area. Two of them were the plain-clothes men I had seen in the alley below Jerry Winkler's hotel window. Salaman, I thought, must have built-in radar for police.

The third man wore a dinner coat with a professional air. He accompanied the policemen to their car and offered his regrets that he hadn't been able to help them as much as he would have liked to. They drove away. He turned back toward the clubhouse, where I caught him at the door:

"I'm William Gunnarson, a local attorney. One of my clients is involved with an employee of the club. Would you be the manager?"

His bright and sorrowful eyes examined me. He had the nervous calm which comes from running other people's parties, and a humorous mouth which took the curse off it. "I am tonight. Tomorrow I'll probably be looking for a job. We who are about to die salute thee. Is it Gaines again? Ill-gotten Gaines?"

"I'm afraid it is."

"Gaines is an ex-employee of ours. I fired him last week. I was just beginning to indulge in the hope that he was out of my hair for good. Now this." He flipped his hand in the direction the police had taken.

"What was the trouble?"

"You undoubtedly know more about that than I do. Is he a burglary suspect, or something of the sort? I've just been talking to a couple of detectives, but they were terribly noncommittal."

"We could trade information, perhaps."

"Why not? My name is Bidwell. Gunnarson, did you say?"

"Bill Gunnarson."

His office was oak-paneled, thickly carpeted, furnished with heavy, dark pieces. An uneaten steak congealed on a tray on the corner of his desk. We faced each other across it. I told him as much as I thought I needed to, and then asked him some questions. "Do you know if Gaines has left town?"

"I gather he has. The police implied as much. Under the circumstances, it's hardly surprising."

"The fact that he's wanted for questioning, you mean?"

"That, and other circumstances," he said vaguely.

"Why did you fire him?"

"I'd sooner not divulge that information. There are other people involved. Let's say it was done at the instance of one of the members, and leave it at that."

I didn't want to leave it at that. "Is there anything to the rumor that he made a rough pass at one of the ladies?"

Bidwell stiffened in his swivel chair. "Good Lord, is that around town?"

"I heard it."

He stroked his mouth with his fingertips. His desk lamp lit only the lower part of his face. I couldn't see his eyes.

"It's not as bad as it sounds. He simply showed too much interest in one of the members' wives. He was very attentive to her, and perhaps she took a little too much advantage of it. Her husband heard about it, and objected. So I fired him." He added: "Thank God I did fire him, before this police investigation came up."

"Did Gaines give any indications that he was using his position here for criminal purposes? To pick out prospects for burglary, for instance?"

"The police asked me that. I had to answer no. But they pointed out that one or two of our members have been victims of burglary in the past six months. Most recently, the Hampshires."

Bidwell's voice was rigidly controlled, but he was under great strain. A drop of sweat formed at the tip of his nose, grew heavy and filled with light, and fell off onto his blotter. It made a dark red stain, like blood, on the red blotter.

"How did you happen to hire Gaines in the first place?"

"I was taken in. I pride myself on my judgment of people, but I was taken in by Larry Gaines. He talked well, you know, and then there was the fact that the college sent him. We nearly always get our lifeguards from Buenavista College. In fact, that may be why Gaines registered there."

"He actually registered at the local college?"

"So they tell me. Apparently he dropped out after a few

days or weeks. But we went on assuming that he was a college student. He was a little old for the role, but you see a lot of that these days."

"I know," I said. "I went through college and law school after Korea."

"Did you, now? I never did make it to college myself. I suppose that's why I feel a certain sympathy for young people trying to educate themselves. Gaines traded on my sympathy, and not only on mine. Quite a few of the members were touched by his scholarly aspirations. He has a certain charm, I suppose—rather greasy, but potent."

"Can you describe him?"

"I can do better than that. The police asked me to rake up some pictures of him. Gaines was always getting himself photographed. He did a lot of picture-taking himself."

Bidwell brought five or six glossy prints out of a drawer and handed them to me. Most of them showed Gaines in bathing trunks. He was slim-hipped and wide-shouldered. He held himself with that actorish air, self-consciousness pretending to be self-assurance, which always made me suspicious of a man. His crew-cut head was handsome, but there was a spoiled expression on his mouth, something obtuse in his dark eyes. In spite of the costume, the tan, the molded muscles, he had the look of a man who hated the sun. I placed his age at twenty-five or six.

Keeping one of the pictures, I gave the rest back to Bidwell. "May I have a look at your membership list?"

It was lying on top of his desk, and he pushed it across to me: several sheets of foolscap covered with names in a fine Spencerian hand. The names were alphabetically grouped, and each was preceded by a number. Patrick Hampshire was number 345. Colonel Ian Ferguson was number 459.

"How many members do you have?"

"Our by-laws limit us to three hundred. The original membership were numbered from one to three hundred. When a member—ah—passes on, we retire his number, and issue a new one. The roster runs up to 461 now, which means that we've lost 161 members since the club was founded, and gained a corresponding number of new members."

He recited these facts as if they constituted a soothing liturgy. I wondered if he was talking to me simply to keep from talking to himself.

"Did Gaines have much to do with the Hampshires, do you know?"

"I'm afraid he did. He gave the Hampshire youngsters some swimming lessons in their private pool."

"The Fergusons?"

He thought about his answer, pushing out his lower lip, and quickly retracting it. "I hadn't heard that they were burglarized."

"Neither had I. Their number is 459. That means they're recent members, does it?"

"Yes, it does," he said with vehemence. "The committee's responsible, of course, but I have power of veto. I should have used it."

"Why?"

"I believe you know why." He rose, and walked to the wall, then turned from it abruptly as if he'd seen handwriting on it. He came back to the desk and leaned above me on his fingertips. "Let's not beat around the bush, shall we?"

"I haven't been."

"All right. I admit I have. I make no apologies. The situation is explosive."

"You mean the situation between Colonel Ferguson and his wife?"

"That's part of it. I see you do know something about it, and I'm going to be candid with you. This club is on the brink of a major scandal. I'm doing all I can to avert it." His tone was portentous; he might have been telling me that war had just been declared. "Look at this."

Bidwell opened a drawer in his desk and brought out a folded newspaper clipping. He unfolded it with shaking hands, spreading it out on the blotter for me to read:

> *Rumor hath it that ex-movie-tidbit Holly May, who was too sweet-smelling for movietown, is trying to prove the old saw about the Colonel's lady. Her partner in the Great Experiment is a gorgeous hunk of muscle (she seems to think) who works as a marine menial in her millionaire hubby's millionaire clubby. We ordinary mortals wish that we could eat our fake and have it, too. But gather ye sub-rosas while ye may, Mrs. Ferguson.*

Bidwell read it over my shoulder, groaning audibly. "That came out last weekend in a syndicated column which went all over the country."

"It doesn't prove anything."

"Perhaps not, but it's ghastly publicity for us. Can I depend on you, Mr. Gunnarson?"

"To do what?"

"Not to repeat to others what you've just said to me?"

I hadn't really said anything, but he imagined I had. "I won't, unless my client's interests are affected. You have my word."

"How would your client's interests be affected?"

"She's suspected of being in complicity with Gaines. She was involved with Gaines, but innocently. She was in love with him."

"Another one in love with him? How does he do it? I admit he's a handsome brute, but that's as far as it goes. He's raw."

"Some like them raw. I take it Mrs. Ferguson is one of those who do."

"She and her husband aren't too delightful themselves. I've made two big mistakes in the past year, hiring Gaines, and admitting the Fergusons to membership. Those two mistakes have combined into the biggest mistake of my life."

"It can't be that bad."

"Can't it? My life may be in danger."

"From Gaines?"

"Hardly. He's long gone. They may be in Acapulco by now, or Hawaii."

"They?"

"I thought you knew. The Holly May creature went with him. And Colonel Ferguson blames me for the whole thing. He's out in the club bar now, lapping up rye whisky. I think he's building up his courage to kill me."

"Are you serious, Bidwell?"

He leaned forward into the light. His eyes were intensely serious. "The man's a maniac. He's been drinking ever since she took off, and he's taken it into his head to blame me for the elopement."

"When did she leave?"

"Last night, from here. She and her husband were having dinner in the dining room. There was a telephone call for her. She took it, and then walked right out of the club. Gaines was waiting in the parking lot."

"How do you know?"

"One of the members saw him there, and mentioned it to me later."

"Did you tell the police about this?"

"I should certainly say I didn't. This is a delicate situation, Mr. Gunnarson. An insane situation, but a delicate one." He managed a small pale smile. "Ours is the most respected club west of the Mississippi—"

"It won't be if one of the members shoots the manager for conspiring with a lifeguard against Holly May's chastity."

"Please don't spell it out." He closed his eyes, and shuddered. "At least, if he did shoot me, it would be the end of my worries."

"You almost mean that, don't you?"

He opened his eyes, wide. "I almost do."

"Does Ferguson have a gun?"

"He has an entire arsenal. Really. He's a big-game hunter, among other things. He actually *enjoys* killing."

"Maybe you better go home."

"He knows where I live. He was there early this morning, shouting at the front door."

"I think you should have him picked up. He may be dangerous."

"He is. He is dangerous. But I cannot and will not bring the police into this. There is simply too much at stake."

"What, exactly?"

"The reputation of the club. There hasn't been a major scandal here since the Abernathy suicide pact, and that was before my tenure. All I can do now is hold on and hope that something will happen to save us at the eleventh hour."

"Let's hope so, Mr. Bidwell."

"Call me Arthur, if you like. Here, let me pour you a drink."

"No, thanks."

He was trying to prolong the conversation. I looked at my watch. It wasn't the eleventh hour, but it was nearly the ninth. The Ella Barker case had led me far afield, and threatened to lead me further. It was time to go home to Sally. The thought of her was like a stretching elastic which never quite snapped.

But sometimes it went on stretching.

The phone on Bidwell's desk rang. He lifted the receiver with an effort, as if it were a heavy iron dumbbell. He listened to a scratchy voice, and said: "For God's sake, Padilla, I told you to head him off. . . . No! Don't call them, that's an order."

Bidwell sprang to the door, slammed it shut, and locked it. He leaned against it with his arms spread out, like someone getting ready to be crucified. "Padilla says he's coming here now."

"Then you better get away from the door. Who's Padilla?"

"The bartender. Ferguson told him he's waited long enough." Droplets were forming on his face as they do on a cold glass. "Talk to him, won't you? Explain that I'm utterly blameless. Utterly. I had nothing to do with his blessed wife's departure." He stepped sideways, tanglefooted, and leaned in the corner.

"Why does he think you had?"

"Because he's insane. He makes mountains out of mole-hills. I merely called her into my office to take a telephone call."

"From Gaines?"

"If so, he must have disguised his voice. I thought myself it was a woman's voice—not one I recognized. But Ferguson seems to think I'm in cahoots with Gaines, simply because I called his wife out of the dining room."

"I hear you, Bidwell," a voice said through the door.

Bidwell jumped as if he'd felt an electric shock, then slumped against the wall as if the shock had killed him.

"If I didn't hear you, Bidwell, I could smell you. I could tell that you were in there by the smell." The doorknob rattled. The voice outside rose an octave. "Let me in, you lily-livered swine. I want to talk to you, you Bidwell swine. And you know what about, Bidwell."

Bidwell shuddered each time he heard his name. He looked at me pleadingly. "Talk to him, will you? It only makes him angrier when I try to talk to him. You're a lawyer, you know how to talk to people."

"What you need is a bodyguard."

Ferguson punctuated this remark with a heavy thud on the bottom of the door. "Open up, Bidwell, or I'll kick the bloody well door down."

He kicked it again. One of the panels cracked, and sprinkled varnish on the rug.

Bidwell said urgently: "Go out and talk to him. You have nothing to fear. He doesn't hate you. I'm the one he hates."

Under Ferguson's third kick, the cracked panel started to give. Standing to one side of it, I unlocked and opened the door.

Ferguson kicked air and lurched in past me. He was a big man in his fifties, shaggy in Harris tweeds. His face was long and equine. Small eyes were closely and deeply set under his overhanging gray eyebrows. They scowled around the room. "Where is he? Where is the pandering little swine?"

Bidwell was behind the door. He stayed there.

"That's pretty rough language, isn't it?" I said.

Ferguson swung his head to look at me. The movement tipped him off balance. He fell back against the side of the doorway. Something metallic in his jacket pocket rapped the door frame.

"You better give me your gun, Colonel. It might go off and shoot you in the hip. Those hip wounds can be painful."

"I know how to handle firearms."

"Still, I think you better give me your gun, just for the present. You wouldn't want to hurt anybody—"

"Wouldn't I, though! I'm going to hurt Bidwell. I'm going to put a hole in that hide of his. And then I'm going to skin him and nail his coyote hide on his own front door to tan."

He sounded like a blustering drunk, but blustering drunks could be dangerous. "No, you're not. I happen to be an attorney, and I'm arresting you. Now hand over your gun."

"To hell with you. You look to me like another one of Bidwell's wife-stealing pretty boys."

He lunged toward me, lost his balance again, and hung onto the edge of the door. It closed enough to reveal Bidwell pasted to the wall behind it. Ferguson emitted a skirling cry, like bagpipes, and reached for his pocket.

I inserted my left hand between his prominent adam's-apple and the collar of his shirt, jerked him toward me, and hit him with my right hand on the jut of the jaw. I had always wanted to hit a Colonel.

This one drew himself erect, marched stiffly to Bidwell's desk, made a teetering half-turn on his heels, and sat down ponderously in Bidwell's chair. He opened his mouth to speak, like an executive about to lay down company policy, then smiled at the foolishness of it all, and passed out. The swivel chair spilled him backward onto the floor.

"Now look what you've done," Bidwell said. "He'll sue us."

"We'll sue him first."

"Impossible. You can't bring suit against twenty million dollars. He's capable of hiring the best lawyers in the country."

"You're talking to one of them." I was feeling slightly elated, after hitting a Colonel. "That's the kind of suit I've always dreamed of bringing."

"But he didn't do anything to me," Bidwell said.

"You sound disappointed."

Bidwell looked at me glumly. "No doubt I should thank you for saving my life. But, frankly, I don't feel thankful."

I squatted by the recumbent man and got the gun out of his pocket. It was a cute little snub-nosed medium-caliber automatic, heavy with clip. I held it up for Bidwell to see.

He refused to look at it. "Put it away. Please."

"So you got his gun," somebody said from the doorway. "I talked him into handing over one gun, couple hours ago. But I guess he had another one in the car."

"Go away, Padilla," Bidwell said. "Don't come in here."

"Yessir."

Padilla smiled and came in. He was a curly-headed young man with a twisted ear, wearing a white bartender's jacket. He looked over Ferguson with a professional eye.

"There's a cut on his chin. You have to hit him?"

"It seemed like a good idea at the time. Mr. Bidwell would rather have been shot. But this is a nice rug. I didn't want them to get blood all over it."

"It isn't funny," Bidwell said. "What are we going to do with him?"

"Let him sleep it off," Padilla answered cheerfully.

"Not here. Not in my office."

"Naw, we'll take him home. You tell Frankie to take over the bar, we'll take him home, put him to bed. He won't even remember in the morning. He'll think he cut himself shaving."

"How do you know he won't remember?"

"Because I been making his drinks. He killed a fifth of Seagram's since six o'clock. I kept pouring it into him, hoping that he'd pass out any minute. But he's got a stomach like a charred oak barrel bound with brass."

He stooped and touched Ferguson's stomach with his finger. Ferguson smiled in his sleep.

## chapter 7

PADILLA KNEW WHERE Ferguson lived. He said that he had driven his blue Imperial home before. I went along for the ride, and the answers to some questions.

"Were you acquainted with Larry Gaines?"

"Used-to-be lifeguard? Sure. I figured him for a no-good, but it was not my business. I had a call-down with him first week he was here, back in September. He tried to buy a drink for a sixteen-year-old girl. I told him, get out of my bar and stay out."

Padilla pressed a button which opened the left front window of the car. He spat into the night air and closed the window again, glancing over his shoulder at Ferguson. "Don't want to give him wind in his face. Might bring him to. That man's got a capacity on him, I tell you."

I looked back at Ferguson. He was sleeping peacefully.

"I suppose you know Mrs. Ferguson."

"Sure thing. She's a damn fine woman. Always nice to the help, can hold her liquor, a real lady in my book. I've seen a lot of these Hollywood people when I was at the Oasis Club in Palm Springs. Most of them, they get their front feet in the trough, and bingo, they think they're the kings of the world. But not Holly—Mrs. Ferguson."

"You call her Holly?"

"Sure. She called me Tony, I called her Holly, in the bar, you know. You can't make anything out of that. She's democratic. Her parents were working people, she told me so herself."

"Was she democratic with Larry Gaines?"

"So I hear." He sounded disappointed, in Holly, perhaps in me. "I never saw them together. He stayed out of my territory. Something was going on there, but I'll lay you odds it ain't what people think. I saw a lot of her in the last six months, over the bar, and that's when you see people plain. I've seen her handle a lot of heavy passes, some of them from experts. But she wasn't having any. She isn't that type at all."

"I heard different."

Padilla said aggressively: "I know there's people don't like her. So what? I didn't say she was perfect. I said she isn't the type to play around. If you ask me, I'd say she loved her husband. He isn't much to look at, but the old boy must have his points. She always lit up like a candle when he came into the room."

"Then why did she walk out on him?"

"I don't think she did, Mr. Gunnarson. I think something

happened to her. There she was, the life of the party one minute, and the next minute she was gone."

"Where did she go?"

"I dunno. I had my hands full at the bar. I didn't see her leave. All I know is, she left and didn't come back. And her husband's damned worried about her. If you ask me, that's what's driving him crazy."

"What could have happened to her?"

Padilla sighed. "You don't know this town like I do, Mr. Gunnarson. I was born and brought up here, right down at the end of Pelly Street. There's people who will knock you off for the change in your pockets. And Holly—Mrs. Ferguson— was wearing fifty grand in diamonds last night."

"How do you know what her jewels were worth?"

"Don't get suspicious of me now. I wouldn't hurt a hair of that lady's head. Show me the bum that would, and I'll beat him within an inch of his life."

"You didn't answer my question."

"About the diamond brooch? Hell, she told me. Her husband gave it to her, and she was kind of bragging. I warned her to shut up about it. Even at the Foothill Club, you don't want to broadcast— Hey!" The car swerved under the pressure of his hands. "You think that Gaines was after her jewels?"

"It's possible." Two versions of Holly May were forming in my mind, but they refused to combine into a single understandable woman. "Have you spoken to anybody about your suspicions?"

"Just to Frankie, he's my helper. I tried to talk to Mr. Bidwell, but he didn't want to hear it. And the Colonel had enough on his mind already."

"Does he believe his wife has met with foul play?"

"I think he does, in a way. Only he won't admit it to himself. He keeps pretending she ran off with a guy, so he can be mad about it, instead of—scared."

"You're quite a psychologist, Tony."

"Yeah. That will be twenty-five dollars, please." But there was no laughter in his voice. He'd succeeded in frightening himself, as well as me.

We had crossed the ridge that walled off the valley from the coastal shelf. I could smell the sea, and sense its dark immensity opening below us. The rotating beam of a lighthouse scanned the night. It flashed along a line of trees standing on a bluff, on the flat roof of a solitary house, then seaward on a bank of fog which absorbed it like cotton batting.

Padilla turned down a hedged lane, a green trench carved out of darkness. We emerged in a turnaround at the rear of the flat-roofed house on the bluff. Parking as close to the door as possible, Padilla plucked Ferguson's key ring from the ignition, opened the house, and turned on inside and outside lights.

We wrestled Ferguson out of the car and carried him through the house into a bedroom. He was as limp as a rag doll, but as heavy as though his bones were made of iron. I was beginning to be worried about him. I switched on the bed lamp and looked at his closed face. It was propped on the pillow like a dead man's in a coffin.

"He's okay," Padilla said reassuringly. "He's just sleeping now."

"You don't think he needs a doctor? I hit him pretty hard."

"It's easy enough to find out."

He went into the adjoining bathroom and came back with a plastic tumbler full of water. He poured a little of it on Ferguson. The water splashed on his forehead and ran down into his hollow temples, wetting his thin hair. His eyes snapped open. He sat up on the bed and said distinctly: "What's the trouble, boys? Is the dugout leaking again?"

"Yeah. It's raining whisky," Padilla said. "How you feeling, Colonel?"

Ferguson sat leaning on his arms, his high shoulders up around his ears, and permitted himself to realize how he was feeling. "I'm drunk. Drunk as a skunk. My God, but I'm drunk." He thrust a hairy fist in one eye and focused the other eye on Padilla's face. "Why didn't you cut me off, Padilla?"

"You're a hard man to say no to, Colonel. The hardest."

"No matter, cut me off."

Ferguson swung his heavy legs over the edge of the bed, got up on them like a man mounting rubber stilts, and staggered across the room to the bathroom door. "Got to take a cold shower, clear the old brain. Mustn't let Holly see me like this."

He walked into the stall shower fully clothed and turned on the water. He was in there for what seemed a long time, snorting and swearing. Padilla kept a protective eye on him.

I looked around the room. It was a woman's bedroom, the kind that used to be called a boudoir, luxuriously furnished in silk and padded satin. A pink clock and a pink telephone shared the top of the bedside table. It was five minutes to ten. The thought of Sally went through me like a pang.

I reached for the telephone. It rang in my hand, as if I had closed a connection. I picked up the receiver and said: "This is the Ferguson residence."

"Colonel Ferguson, please."

"Sorry, the Colonel is busy."

"Who is that speaking, please?" It was a man's voice, quiet and careful and rather impersonal.

"A friend."

"Is the Colonel there?"

"Yes. As a matter of fact, he's taking a bath."

"Get him on the line," the voice said less impersonally. "In a hurry, friend."

I was tempted to argue, but I sensed an urgency here which tied my tongue. I went to the door of the bathroom. Padilla was helping Ferguson to take off his soggy tweeds. Ferguson was shivering so hard that I could feel the vibrations through my feet.

He looked at me without recognition. "What do you want? Padilla, what does he want?"

"You're wanted on the telephone, Colonel. Can you make it all right?"

Padilla helped him across the room.

Ferguson sat on the bed and lifted the receiver to his ear. He was naked to the waist, goose-pimpled and white except for the iron-gray hair matted on his chest. He listened with his eyes half shut and his face growing longer and slacker. I would have supposed he was passing out again if he hadn't said, several times, "Yes," and finally: "Yes, I will. You can depend on that. I'm sorry we didn't make contact until now."

He replaced the receiver, fumblingly, and stood up. He looked at Padilla, then at me, from under heavy eyelids. "Make me some coffee, will you, Padilla?"

"Sure." Padilla trotted cheerfully out of the room.

Ferguson turned to me. "Are you an FBI man?"

"Nothing like that. I'm an attorney. William Gunnarson is my name."

"You answered the telephone?"

"Yes."

"What was said to you?"

"The man who called said he wanted to speak to you. In a hurry."

"Did he say why?"

"No."

"Are you certain?"

"I'm certain."

His tone was insulting, but I went on humoring him. I didn't know how sober he was, or how rational.

"And you're not an officer of the law?"

"In a sense, I am. I'm an officer of the court, but enforcement is not my business. What's this all about, Colonel?"

"It's a personal matter," he said shortly. "May I ask what you're doing in my wife's room?"

"I helped Padilla to bring you home from the Foothill Club. You were out."

"I see. Thank you. Now do you mind leaving?"

"When Tony Padilla is ready. We used your car."

"I see. Thank you again, Mr. Gunnarson."

He'd lost interest in me. His eyes moved restlessly around the walls. He uttered one word in a tearing voice: "Holly." Then he said: "A fine time to get stinking drunk."

He walked across the room to a dressing table, and leaned to examine his face in the mirror above it. The sight of his face must have displeased him. He smashed the mirror with one blow of his fist.

"Knock it off," I said in my sergeant voice.

He turned, and answered meekly enough. "You're right. This is no time for childishness."

Padilla looked through the doorway. "More trouble?"

"No trouble," Ferguson said. "I merely shattered a mirror. I'll buy my wife another in the morning. How about that coffee, Tony?"

"Coming right up. You better put on something dry, Colonel. You don't want to catch pneumonia."

Padilla seemed to be fond of the man. I could hardly share his feeling, and yet I stayed around. The phone call, and Ferguson's reaction to it, puzzled me. It had left the atmosphere heavy and charged.

Padilla served coffee in the living room. It was a huge room with windows on two sides, and teak paneling in a faintly nautical style. The lap of the surf below, the intermittent sweep of the lighthouse beam, contributed to the illusion that we were in the glassed-in deckhouse of a ship.

Ferguson drank about a quart of coffee. As the effects of alcohol wore off, he seemed to grow constantly more tense. Wrapped in a terrycloth robe, he bore a queer resemblance to a Himalayan holy man on the verge of having a mystical experience.

He finally rose and went into another room. I could see through the archway, when he switched on the light, that it contained a white concert grand piano and a draped harp. A photograph of a woman, framed in silver, stood on the piano.

Ferguson picked it up and studied it. He clasped it to his chest. A paroxysm went through him, making his ugly face uglier. He looked as if he was weeping, dry-eyed, in silence.

"Poor guy," Padilla said.

He went as far as the archway, and paused there, deterred by the privacy of grief. I wasn't so sensitive. I went in past him. "Ferguson, was that phone call about your wife?"

He nodded.

"Is she dead?"

"They claim not. I don't know."

" 'They'?"

"Her abductors. Holly has been abducted."

"Kidnapped?"

"Yes. They demand two hundred thousand dollars for her return."

Padilla whistled softly behind me.

"Have they called you before?"

"Yes, but I wasn't home. I haven't been here much in the past day."

"This phone call was your first communication from them?"

"Yes."

"Why didn't you say so at the time? We might have had some chance of tracing the call."

"I don't want anything done along those lines. I didn't even intend to tell you and Padilla. I'm sorry now that I did."

"You can't handle a thing like this all by yourself."

"Why not? I have the cash. They're welcome to it if they give Holly back to me."

"You have two hundred thousand dollars in cash?"

"I have more than that. I had it transferred to the local Bank of America because I've been intending to buy some property here. I can draw it out when the bank opens in the morning."

"When and where are you supposed to pay them?"

"He said I was to wait for further instructions."

"Did you recognize his voice on the telephone?"

"No."

"Then it wasn't Larry Gaines?"

"It wasn't Gaines, no. It wouldn't make any difference to me if it was. They have her. I'm willing to pay for her."

"It may not be quite that simple. I hate to say this, Colonel, but this could be a shakedown. Some petty crook may have heard that your wife is missing, and is trying to cash in on the fact."

"I hadn't thought of that." The thought sat heavy on him for a moment. Then he shook it off. "But it can't be the case. Even if it were, I'd have to go ahead with it."

He was still holding the photograph against his chest. He polished its glass with his sleeve and held it up to the light, gazing at it almost reverently. The pictured woman was a blonde in her middle twenties.

Ferguson set the picture on the piano, very carefully, as if it were an icon whose exact position might somehow affect his wife's fate. I took a closer look at it, and remembered seeing the same face on movie marquees and in the newspapers.

It had the standard perfections of her trade, but it had an individual cast as well. It was a face which had known trouble, and smiled back at it. The smile was a little too bold for comfort. The knowledge in the eyes was a little too definite. Holly May would be interesting to know, but perhaps not easy to live with.

"It's a good picture of her," Padilla said at my shoulder. "You ever see her?"

"Not in the flesh."

"Christ, I hope she's all right. I was afraid that something happened to her, I told you that. But I didn't think it could be a snatch."

Ferguson moved between us and the picture. Perhaps he was jealous of our stares. I could understand why jealousy of Gaines had been eating him. He was at least twice his wife's age, and not nearly so pretty. An unlikely match, in spite of all the money he had, or was supposed to have.

"I want you men to keep this affair to yourselves," Ferguson said. "It's of the utmost importance that you do. If the authorities get wind of it, it will put her life in danger."

"The dirty crumbs," Padilla growled. "Is that what they said on the telephone?"

"Yes. He said that they are in a position to know every move the police make. If I call in the police, they will kill my wife."

I said: "This may not be the way to save her, Colonel. You've had a hard day, and you may not be thinking as straight as usual. In a situation like this, you need all the help you can get. You should take the local police into your confidence. The chief detective, Wills, is a friend of mine. He can advise you about contacting the FBI—"

Ferguson cut me short. "It's absolutely out of the question. I want your solemn word that you won't go to the police, or anyone else!"

"You should listen to the man," Padilla said. "Like he was saying, you've had a lot to drink. Maybe you could use a little advice."

"I know what I have to do. No amount of advice will change the facts. I'm bound and determined to do my part."

"Let's hope that they do theirs, Ferguson. I think you're handling it wrong. But it's your wife."

"I'll trust you to remember that. I don't want either of you to endanger Holly by going to the police. The criminals have a friend on the force, apparently—"

"That I doubt."

"I know something about American police. If the RCMP was available, I'd gladly go to them."

The man's naïveté would have been funny under other circumstances. I made one last attempt. "Listen to me, Ferguson. I urge you to discuss this matter with someone. Do you have a lawyer you trust?"

"I have in Calgary, Alberta. If you think I'm going to hire you to give me advice I don't want and won't take—"

"I'm not trying to get myself hired."

"That's good, because I know you American lawyers. I had dealings with some of your breed when Holly was trying to get free from that wretched studio." He paused, and gave me a canny look. "Of course, if a small retainer will keep you quiet—you can have a couple of hundred."

"Keep it."

He smiled grimly, as if an angry atmosphere suited him. "We're mutually agreed then. Can I trust you to respect my confidence?"

"Naturally." I realized, a second too late, that I had been manipulated—maneuvered into a dubious position.

"What about you, Padilla?"

"You can trust me, Colonel."

chapter 8

"THE OLD BOY HAS GUTS," Padilla said in the car.

"Yes, where his brains should be. I've got a good mind to go to the police, in spite of what he said."

"You can't do that."

"Why not? You surely don't believe the police are collaborating with the kidnappers?"

"Naw, but it wouldn't be fair. You got to give him a chance to handle it his own way. He's no dope, you know. He may talk like a dope, and act like one, but he's got a head on his shoulders. You don't make his kind of money without a head on your shoulders."

"I don't make his kind of money, period. Where did he get his money?"

"Out of the ground, he told me. He started out on a ranch in Alberta where they discovered oil. He used his royalties to buy more oil rights, and the thing just went on mounting up. I guess he ran out of things to buy in Canada, so he moved in on California."

"And bought Holly May?"

"I don't think it was like that. If you ask me, the lady was never for sale."

"She is now."

"Yeah. I only wish I could do something."

We emerged from the hedge-lined private lane. With a sudden, angry twist of the wheel, Padilla swung the big car into the road. "Where do you want me to drop you off?"

"Downtown, if you have the time."

"I have the time. I'm not going back to the Club tonight, let Frankie wash the glasses. Maybe I'll cut over after and see how the Colonel's doing. He shouldn't ought to be alone all night. Where downtown?"

"Pelly Street."

"What you want to go down there for? You could get yourself rolled."

"That's not what I had in mind. You know that street pretty well, don't you?"

"Like the back of my hand." In the glow of the dash lights, he glanced at the back of his hand. "I just moved my mother off it within the last four years, when the old man died. Four years ago next November twenty-three."

"Do you know Gus Donato?"

"I know him. Frankie told me he heard on the radio that Gus is wanted for murder. Old man Broadman. Is that what you heard?"

"It's no rumor. How well do you know him, Tony?"

"About as well as I want to. I see him on the street. I know his brother better, Manuel. He's the worker in the family. Manuel and me was in the same class at Sacred Heart school one year, before he quit to go to work. Gus has always been a cross on his back. They sent him up to Preston when he was sixteen years old."

"What for?"

"Stealing cars and stuff. He was stealing cars when he was so little he couldn't see over the top of the steering wheel. I guess they taught him some fancier tricks at Preston. He's been in and out of jail most of his life. Now he's really fixed himself good."

Padilla's tone was carefully indifferent. He performed his ritual of rolling down the window and spitting.

"I talked to his brother and his wife tonight. The wife claims he's innocent."

"Gus's wife?"

"Secundina, her brother-in-law called her. You know her, don't you?"

"I know her. Working in different kinds of bars, you see a lot of people. I watch them the way you watch the flies on the wall. But let's get this straight, Mr. Gunnarson, they're not my kind of people." His tone was formal. The discussion had put an obscure strain on our relationship.

"I realize that, Tony."

"Why ask me questions about them, then?"

"Because you know Holly May, and want to do something for her. There seems to be some connection between what happened to her and the Broadman killing. Gus Donato may be the key to it. And I got an impression talking to his relatives that he may be ready to give himself up. If he's approached carefully, through his brother, or through his wife—"

"I don't like to step on cops' toes."

"Neither do I. But I'm within my rights as a lawyer in trying to reach Donato and talk him into surrendering."

"Sure, we could get knocked off, too. That's within anybody's rights." But Padilla was with me. "I know where Manuel lives."

The shoreline road crossed the highway on an overpass and curved around to the left to join the northbound lane. Neon-lighted clouds hung low over the city, changing like red smoke as we moved under them.

The freeway slanted up across a wilderness of railroad sidings, packing plants, and warehouses, and then the residences of the lower town. Its swarming courts and overflowing cottages were squeezed like living sponge between the freeway and the railroad. Padilla turned off on a ramp and circled under the freeway between concrete pillars that seemed as ancient and deserted as Coliseum arches. Somewhere ahead, the sound of a siren rose in jungle howling and fell away into animal sobbing.

"Jeeze, I hate that noise," Padilla said. "Practically every night of my life for twenty years I heard that noise. It's the main reason I had to get out to the other side of the tracks."

Manuel Donato lived on this side of the tracks, in a white

clapboard bungalow which stood out among its neighbors. The rectangle of lawn behind its picket fence was green and smooth, hedged by white-blossoming oleanders. The porch light was on. Padilla knocked on the door.

In the yard next door, shadowed by the oleanders, some boys and girls were playing late giggling games. One of the boys raised his voice. "Donato ain't home."

"Is he still downtown?" Padilla said.

"I guess so." The boy came up to the fence. His fluorescent shirt made him look like a torso miraculously suspended, until I saw his eyeballs reflecting the light. "You cops?"

"We're friends of Manuel Donato's," Padilla said.

"He may be down at the police station. A cop came a few minutes ago, and Manuel went away with him. Is he in trouble?"

"I hope not," Padilla said.

"Reason I asked, it looked like he was crying."

"Yeah," one of the girls said from the shadows. "He was crying. I felt sorry for him."

The desk sergeant at the police station told us the reason for Manuel Donato's grief. His brother Gus was in the morgue. Pike Granada had shot him.

"Just like that, eh?" Padilla said.

The desk sergeant looked at him thoughtfully, then at me. "You representing the family, Mr. Gunnarson?"

I pretended not to hear him. "When did all this happen?"

"Within the last hour or so. It wasn't channeled through me," he said with disappointment. "Pike was off duty. He got a tip where Donato was hiding out. He's young and eager."

"Who tipped him?"

"Ask him yourself. He's back in the squad room making up his preliminary report. He probably won't tell you, but go ahead and ask him."

The squad room was dim except for the circle of light from the lamp on Granada's desk. His two-fingered typewriter stuttered and gave up when we walked in. He lifted his head, heavily, as if it had been cast in the bronze it resembled.

"I understand you shot Augustine Donato."

"Yeah. He went for his gun."

"Too bad you had to silence him. He might have told us some useful things."

"You sound like Wills. He just got off my back. Don't you climb on, Mr. Gunnarson." He peered through the dimness at Padilla. "Who's your friend?"

"You remember me," Padilla said. "I used to tend bar in the Rosarita Room."

"Oh, yeah. Tony. Still working around town?"

"At the Foothill Club," Padilla said in his formal voice. There was tension between the two men.

"Where did you catch up with Donato?" I said.

"In the old ice plant out by the railroad tracks. It's a good place to hide, truck and all, and I figured he was out there."

"That's pretty close figuring."

"I had some help. A little bird told me they seen a truck. I live on that side of town, so I mosied over. I caught him unloading the stuff."

"What stuff was it?"

"Loot from the burglaries, cameras and furs and dresses. Apparently Broadman had it stashed in his basement. Donato killed him to get at it."

"Then you killed Donato."

"It was my neck or his." In the light from the green-shaded lamp, Granada's face was greenish, his eyes gold. "You sound as if you wished it was my neck. I'm not asking for the rubber medal, but I did go out on my own time and take a killer."

"His wife claims he's not a killer."

"Naturally. She's been claiming he's innocent through four or five arrests. He's been innocent of everything from pushing dope on the high-school grounds to armed robbery. So now he's innocent of murder."

"Innocent and dead."

Granada looked up quickly, his eyes glinting like coins. "You don't take her seriously, for Christ sake? She's been lying her head off for years."

"You ought to know," Padilla said.

Granada rose slowly, about three feet wide in his linen suit, and well over six feet tall. He leaned with both hands gripping the edges of the desk. He appeared to be getting ready to pick up the desk and throw it. "What is that supposed to mean? I used to run with lots of dames before I got wise to myself and settled down."

"Her husband is the only one you shot," Padilla said. "Was she the little bird?"

Granada said in a very gentle tone: "Mother told me there would be nights like this. I go out of my way to take a killer, and what happens? The Lieutenant eats me out. People come in off the street to tell me off."

Padilla said: "I'll bring you a crying towel."

Granada called him a bad name and lifted his hand. A woman scurried and moaned in the hallway. Then she shrieked in the doorway. Granada looked at the lockers along the wall as though he was considering hiding in one.

"Who let her in, for Christ sake?"

Secundina Donato ran at him, stumbling and sobbing. One of her stockings was down around her ankles.

"Murderer! I knew you would kill him. I warned him. I warn you now. Look out for me."

Granada was. He kept the desk between them.

"Calm down, now, Sexy. You threaten an officer, I got to lock you up."

"Lock me up! Kill me! Put me in the morgue with Gus!"

She went on in Spanish, pouring a torrent of words at Granada. She tore her dress at the neck and scratched her breast with chipped carmine fingernails.

"Don't do that," Granada said helplessly. "You'll hurt yourself. You don't want to hurt yourself."

He moved around the desk and caught her by the wrists. She sank her teeth in his hand. Granada shook her loose. She backed up to the row of lockers and sat down against them with a crash.

Granada looked at his bitten hand. It was his gun hand, and the trigger finger was dripping blood. Nursing it in his other hand, he went into the washroom.

Padilla stood over the woman. "Get up, Secundina. I'll take you home before you get into worse trouble."

She covered her head with her skirt.

"At least she isn't Granada's little bird."

"I'm not so sure, Mr. Gunnarson. Women can do one thing and mean something else."

"Not this time. Don't let that psychology kick get the best of you, Tony. What did she say to Granada in Spanish?"

He regarded me coldly. "I don't remember my Spanish so good. We always talk American at home. Besides, she was talking *bracero*. Her old man was a wetback."

"Come on, Tony, don't play dumb."

He was embarrassed by her presence. He waved me to the far side of the room and said with the air of a schoolboy reciting a lesson: "She said that Gus was very good-looking, better-looking than Granada even when—even now that he's dead. She said she would rather have Gus dead than Granada alive. She said that Gus didn't kill Broadman, and he didn't steal from him, either. The stuff he took from Broadman belonged to Gus, and the Holy Mother would see to it Gus got his rights in Heaven. She said she was looking forward to the day when Gus and her would be looking down from Heaven and see Granada burning in Hell, so they could take turns spitting."

Padilla's embarrassment had become acute. "That's the way they talk when they get roused up."

Granada came out of the washroom. He groaned when he saw the woman sitting on the floor with head hidden and thighs glaring. He pointed his band-aided forefinger at her. "Get her out of here before I book her."

She wouldn't move for me. I was a lawyer, subtler than policemen, as treacherous as doctors. Padilla brushed me aside politely. He lifted and wheedled her up to her feet, coaxed and propelled her into the corridor and along its gauntlet of official doors.

"What happened?" the desk sergeant asked me.

"She bit Granada."

"Did she, now?"

chapter 9

THE DOOR OF OUR APARTMENT opened directly into the living room. Sally was curled up asleep in the corner of the chesterfield. She had on the quilted bathrobe which I had given her for her twenty-third birthday. Her brushed hair shone like gold in the dim light of the turned-down lamp.

I stood and looked at her. She stirred in her sleep, and made a small quiet noise. It reminded me of an infant's gurgle. Except for the pearlike curve of her body, and the swelling breasts that threatened to burst her robe, she looked about twelve. I was kind of glad she wasn't.

I tiptoed into the kitchen, turned on the fluorescent light over the stove, and peered into the oven. It was still warm, though the gas had been turned off. My dinner was there, in a pyrex dish with a cover. I ate it off the sinkboard, standing up. The china clock looked down at me from the wall, pointing its hands accusingly at twelve midnight.

I heard Sally's slippered feet cross the living room.

"So you finally decided to come home," she said from the doorway.

"Wait. The condemned man has the right to a last meal. It's not precisely a legal right, perhaps, but it's recognized by long tradition." I put another piece of lamb in my mouth and smiled at her, munching.

She didn't smile back. "I hope it chokes you."

"On the contrary, it's delicious."

"You are a liar, Bill Gunnarson. It's dry as a bone. I can actually hear it crunching. And after all the trouble I went to with that dinner. Honestly, if I wasn't so mad, I could cry."

"I'm sorry. It really is delicious, though. Have a slice."

"I couldn't possibly eat anything," she said distantly. "Don't worry. I've had my dinner. I waited until after nine o'clock, and then I broke down and ate by myself. While you were out rampaging."

"Rampaging isn't exactly the word."

"Give me a better one."

"Moiling and toiling. Chasing the buck. Seeking the bubble reputation."

"Please don't try to be amusing. You're about as funny as a crutch."

This stung me to retort that she could carry on for both of us in the wit department, what with her brilliant similes like the one about the crutch. I requested her permission to quote it to friends.

She gave me a glazed and shiny look which reminded me of the china clock on the wall. "Maybe I can't compete with movie actresses. I'm getting big and fat and physically repugnant. It's no wonder you go off rampaging and leave me in the lurch."

"You're not fat and repugnant. I wasn't rampaging. I've never met a movie actress in my life. I didn't leave you in the lurch."

"It felt like the lurch to me. You didn't even telephone."

"I know. I tried, but things kept getting in the way."

"What sort of things?"

"Things and people," I said vaguely.

"What people? Who were you with?"

"Wait a minute, Sally. We don't ask that question, remember?"

"I always tell you where I go, and who with, and everything."

"If I told you, I'd be a lousy lawyer."

"You can't use your profession to cover up every time."

"Cover up what?"

"Your failure as a husband," she said shinily. "When a man deliberately avoids his own home the way you do, it's easy enough to understand what it means. You're essentially unmarried—a perennial bachelor. You don't want the responsibility of a wife and family. No wonder you get fixated on your clients. It's a safe relationship, an ego-feeding activity, which makes no demands on your essential self."

"That's quite a mouthful," I said. "What have you been reading?"

"I am perfectly capable of observing the state of my own marriage and drawing the necessary conclusions. This marriage is in grave danger, Bill."

"Are you serious?"

"I have never been more serious in my life. Do you know what you are, Bill Gunnarson? You're nothing but a profession that walks like a man. When I tried to tell you on the phone about my good report from Dr. Trench, you weren't even interested. You don't even care about Bill Gunnarson, Jr."

"I care about him very much."

"You may think you do, but you don't. You spend days and weeks of your good time trying to save criminals from going to jail where they belong. But when I tell you that Bill Gunnarson, Jr., is going to have to have a room of his own, you fob me off with empty promises."

"My promises are not empty. I told you we're going to find a bigger place, and we're going to."

"When? After all the burglars and murderers are taken care of? When Bill Gunnarson, Jr., is an old man with a long gray beard?"

"For God's sake, Sally, he isn't even born yet."

"How dare you swear at me?"

She looked around her kitchen as if for the last time. Her glance went over my head, parting my hair like a stainless steel comb. She turned grandly and went out. Her hip bumped the door frame.

I didn't know whether to laugh or cry. I wolfed the rest of my dinner, masticating it thoroughly. It was a good excuse for grinding my teeth.

Ten minutes later, after a hot shower not followed by a cold one, I climbed into bed behind her. Sally lay with her face to the wall. I put my hand in the soft fold of her waist. She pretended to be dead.

I pushed my hand farther around her. Her skin was as smooth as milk. "I'm sorry, I should have phoned you. I got carried away by the case."

"It must be some case," she answered after a while. "I was worried about you. The murder was in the paper. So I thought I'd calm myself down by reading that book on Successful Marriage—the one that Mother sent me. There's a chapter in it that was very upsetting."

"About perennial bachelors?"

She snorted slightly. "You're not a perennial bachelor, are you, Bill? You want to be married to me and everything?"

"And everything."

She turned toward me, but not all the way around. "I know, there hasn't been much everything lately."

"I can wait for everything."

"And you don't mind? The book says this is a bad time for men, because they're so passionate. Is it a bad time for you?"

"It's a wonderful time." I slid my hand down her belly. She was radiant even in darkness.

"Ouch," she said.

"Ouch what?"

"Feel."

She moved my hand, and I could feel him kicking. He might turn out to be a her, of course, but the kicks felt like masculine kicks to me.

Sally's breathing slowed down into sleep. I turned over to go to sleep myself. The telephone rang like an alarm set off by my movement. I levitated, dropped to the floor running on tiptoe, and got to the damn thing before it could ring again.

A muffled voice said: "Is that Gunnarson? William Gunnarson the lawyer?"

"This is Gunnarson, and I'm an attorney."

"You want to go on being one?"

"I don't understand you."

But I understood. There was a threat in the words, underlined by soft menace in the voice. I thought it was the same man who had called Ferguson, but I couldn't be sure. The voice was blurred, as though the man at the other end of the line was talking through a mask. "You want to go on living, don't you, Gunnarson?"

"Who is this?"

"Just a well-wisher." He snickered. "If you do want to go on living, you better drop the case you're on, and I mean any part of it."

"Go to hell."

"You better give that some thought. You have a wife, I hear, and I hear she's pregnant. You wouldn't want her to take a bad fall or anything. So forget about Holly May and her little friends. You got that, Mr. Gunnarson?"

I didn't answer. The anger in my head was like scalding ice. I slammed the receiver down. The fraction of a second later I regretted the action, and picked it up again. There was nothing to be heard but the dial tone, the voice of idiot space. I laid the receiver down for the second time, more gently.

But the bedroom light was on, and Sally was standing at the bedroom door.

"What on earth was that, Bill?"

I tried to recall the exact words I had spoken. I'd said too much to pretend that it was a wrong number.

"Some drunk. He seems to have a grudge against someone."

"Against you?"

"No. Not against me. Against everybody."

"You told him to go to hell."

"You would have, too, if you'd heard him."

"He upset you, didn't he, William?"

"I don't like my sleep to be interrupted by maniacs."

"What did he say?"

"Nothing repeatable. Gibberish."

She accepted my explanation, at least for the present. We went back to bed, and she dropped off again like a lamb. I lay awake for a long time beside her quiet breathing.

We had been married for nearly three years; tonight for the first time I was fully aware of her preciousness to me. But

I was more determined than ever to stick with the case and do my duty in it. The problem was to know where my duty lay.

Blue dawn was at the window before I went to sleep. The Perrys' radio woke me at seven o'clock. It nearly always did. They were a couple of schoolteachers who lived on schedule for the purpose of improving themselves. Their morning schedule began with setting-up exercises.

I flopped around on my side of the bed for a while, trying to shut out the announcer's voice blaring through the wallboard. Finally I got up with that stiff gray insomniac feeling on my face. Sally went on sleeping like one of the seven sleepers.

Since she was sleeping for two, I dressed quietly and went downtown for breakfast. I bought a morning paper on the way. The front page carried a picture of Donato, a huddled figure with a shock of black Indian hair sticking out from under the sheet that covered him.

While I was waiting for my bacon and eggs, I read the accompanying news story. Granada was praised for his courage and marksmanship, and given credit for solving the series of burglaries. The story implied that the gang had other members besides Donato, but none of them was named, not even Gaines. I assumed that Wills was holding back, and had persuaded the local paper to go along.

The waitress brought my breakfast. The eggs stared up from the plate like wide yellow eyes. The toast had a gunpowder flavor. I caught myself sitting tensely in the booth like a condemned criminal waiting for the executioner to throw the switch.

It wasn't purely empathy with Donato: I doubt that there's such a feeling as pure empathy. For no clear reason, I'd put myself in the position of withholding information about a major crime. And the man whose request I was honoring wasn't even a client.

I sat there trying to convince myself that Ferguson had been having alcoholic delusions about his wife. Or that the whole thing was a publicity hoax. Movie actresses didn't get themselves kidnapped in Buenavista. Most of our crimes were done in the lower town, cheap fraud or senseless violence. But my mind couldn't evade the connection between the Broadman killing and the Ferguson case. And I knew in my bowels that the threatening call at midnight had been no hoax.

I left the ugly eggs on my plate and went to the police station. Wills wasn't in yet, but the sergeant on duty at the desk assured me that he would have the men in the patrol cars keep an eye on my home. By the time I had walked the several blocks to the office, past the familiar faces of the downtown buildings, I felt better. Nothing could happen to Sally in Buenavista.

My office was one of a suite of two, with an anteroom between, on the second floor of an old mustard-colored stucco court behind the post office. In the middle of the imitation flagstone courtyard there was a fountain, a dry concrete concavity inhabited by a lead dolphin which had long since emitted its last watery gasp.

I shared the suite and Mrs. Weinstein with another attorney, a middle-aged man named Barney Millrace who specialized in tax and probate work. We were not partners. I was on my way up, I hoped; Barney Millrace was on his way down, I feared. He was a quiet drinker, so quiet that I sometimes forgot about him for days.

Bella Weinstein never let me forget her. She was a widow, fortyish, dark, and intense, who had appointed herself my personal goad. She looked up from her desk when I walked into the anteroom. Fixing me with her eye, she said in a congratulatory way: "You're early this morning, Mr. Gunnarson."

"That's because I've been up all night. Rampaging and carousing."

"I bet. You have an appointment at nine-fifteen with Mrs. Al Stabile. I think she wants a divorce again."

"I'll head her off. Did she say why?"

"She didn't go into the gory details. But I gather Stabile's been rampaging and carousing again. You see where it leads. Also, a man named Padilla tried to reach you."

"How long ago?"

"Just a few minutes. He left a number. Shall I call him back?"

"Right away, yes. I'll take it inside."

I closed the door of my office and sat down at the ancient golden-oak roll-top desk which I had imported at great expense from the Pennsylvania town where I was born. My father had willed it to me, along with the small law library which took up most of the shelves along one wall.

It's oddly pleasing to sit at your father's desk. Diminishing, too. It's a long time before you begin to feel that you're up to it. I was beginning.

Padilla was on the line when I lifted the receiver. "Mr. Gunnarson? I'm out at Colonel Ferguson's. He says I got to make this fast."

"What is it, Tony?"

"I don't want to go into it over the phone. Can you come out here?"

"Why don't you come to my office?"

"I would, but I hate to leave the Colonel. He needs somebody to hold his hand."

"The hell I do," I heard Ferguson say. Then his voice roared in my ear: "Get off the line!"

I got off the line, and started out through the anteroom. Mrs. Weinstein detained me with one of her complex looks; it combined satire, pathos, and despair.

"Are you going out, Mr. Gunnarson?" she said in her polite, furious monotone.

"Yes. Out."

"But Mrs. Stabile will be here in a few minutes. What can I say to her?"

"Tell her I'll see her later."

"She'll go to another lawyer."

"No, she won't. Stabile won't let her."

## chapter 10

FERGUSON'S HOUSE WAS IMPRESSIVE by daylight, a green and gray modern structure of stone and wood and glass, distributed in unobtrusive low shapes which blended with the landscape and the seascape.

The door opened as my car entered the turnaround. Colonel Ferguson came out, trailed by Padilla. Padilla looked a little soiled and sallow, but he managed a smile. Ferguson was grimly unsmiling. The lines in his face were deep and inflexible. Heavy beard, jet black and pure white mixed, sprouted around the scab on his chin.

He came up to my car. "What in hell do you want?"

"I'm naturally worried about your wife—"

"It's my affair. I'm handling it."

I got out. "It's my affair, too, whether I like it or not. You can't expect me simply to sit by."

"It's what I have to do."

"You haven't had any further messages?"

"No. I'll tell you this, though it's none of your business. I've been in touch with the manager of the bank. They'll have the money ready for me."

"Since you've gone that far, don't you think you should take the further step of going to the authorities?"

He bristled. "And get Holly killed?"

"You can go to them on the quiet, without any fanfare."

"What good will that do, if her abductors have a pipeline to the police?"

"I don't believe they have. They're trying to scare you, paralyze you so you won't act. I know the local police, as I told you last night. They're a decent bunch."

Padilla looked uneasy. I shared his feeling, to some extent, but suppressed it. Ferguson was listening to me, his long jaw calipered between thumb and fingers. I noticed that the nail of his thumb was bitten down to the raw.

"I'm taking no chances," he said.

"You may be taking the worst possible chance."

"I don't understand you."

"Your wife may be dead now."

I'd meant to shock him, but he was appalled by the thought. His jaw gaped, showing his lower teeth. He ran the tip of his tongue over his lips. "She's dead, is she? They found her dead?"

"No. But it could happen, that they should find her dead."

"Why? I intend to pay them the money. All they want is the money. Why should they harm her? The money means nothing to me—"

I cut him short. "There's a good chance that you'll pay your money and still not see her again. Do you understand that, Ferguson? Once they've got the money, there's no advantage to them in returning her to you. No advantage, and a great deal of risk."

"They wouldn't take the money and kill her anyway."

"They're killers, some of them at least. She's in danger every hour she's with them."

"You don't have to tell him, he knows it." Padilla shook his dark head. "Lay off, eh?"

Ferguson spoke gruffly. "I'm perfectly all right. Don't concern yourself about me."

"I'm more concerned about your wife. She may be killed while we stand here talking, and you'll end up financing the killer's getaway."

"I know she's in danger. I've been sitting with it staring me in the face all night. You don't have to grind it in."

"Then go to the police."

"I will not. Stop badgering me."

He ran his fingers through his thin hair. It stuck up and fluttered like gray feathers in the wind from the sea. He walked away to the edge of the cliff and stood there looking down. I could hear the surf pouring and lapsing, a continual sound of grief running under the morning.

"Let him alone now," Padilla said. "You want to drive him over the edge?"

"I'm not doing it for fun. This is a bad situation all round."

"You're not making it any better, Mr. Gunnarson."

"Somebody has to do something."

"Maybe. Maybe not. We don't want to do the wrong thing, that's for sure. The Colonel could be right. He's had a lot of experience in his life. He didn't get where he is by letting other people carry the ball."

"Nobody's carrying it, that's the trouble."

"Sometimes you just have to wait. You press too hard, and everything goes to pieces."

"Don't give me the *mañana* treatment."

Padilla was hurt. He turned away from me in silence.

"Listen to me," I said to Ferguson's back. "You're not the only person involved in this. Your wife is deeply involved, more deeply than you are by a long shot. You're taking a heavy responsibility for her."

"I know that," he said without turning.

"Then spread it around. Give other people a chance to help you."

"You can help me by getting off my back." He turned, his small eyes hot and dry. "I have to work this out for myself, and for Holly. Alone."

"Don't you have any friends in California?"

"None that I trust. Those people at the Club care nothing for me. The people we know in Hollywood are worse. They have a grudge against me, and for good reason. I found that my wife's so-called friends were living off her like leeches. I got rid of them for her."

"So you're completely alone here?"

"I choose to be. I hope I make that clear."

"No servants?"

"I won't have servants under my feet, prying into my affairs. Holly was glad to be alone with me, and look after my needs. I don't like anyone prying, do you understand me?"

He stalked into the house, stiff-necked and high-shouldered, mimicked by his dwarf shadow. I was beginning to understand something about him. He was a pigheaded Scots-Canadian, made arrogant and lonely by his money. But he was a man, and had a depth of feeling I hadn't suspected. It's hard to begin to understand a man without beginning to like him.

Padilla lingered outside. "Could I talk to you, Mr. Gunnarson? Person to person? I'm no great brain, and I never studied law—"

I didn't like his guarded, apologetic tone. "We can sit in my car."

I climbed in behind the wheel. He got in the other side, closing the door very gently as if it might shatter under his hand. I offered him a cigarette and meant to light it for him. But before I could move, he was lighting mine, in a quick, smooth bartender's gesture.

"Thanks, Tony. I got a little wordy, there. It's the occupational hazard of my profession."

"Yeah, I've noticed that about lawyers. I thought maybe you were pressing a little hard about him going to the cops. I got nothing against cops. They're human like everybody else, though. I see them fumble a lot of balls, so do you. Most of the time they make a good try for it, but sometimes they just turn their back and let the ball bounce."

"Get down to cases, eh?"

"I drove Secundina Donato home last night. She did some

talking. Some of it made sense, some of it didn't. But I thought I better pass the word to somebody who'd know what to do. I can't take it to the cops."

"Why?"

He hesitated, and then said rapidly: "She thinks Pike Granada is mixed up with the robbery gang. Don't quote me, and don't quote her." He peered through the windshield as if searching for hovering helicopters. "She's in bad enough trouble now, with her husband dead, and kids to feed. I don't want to get them orphaned completely."

"You take her seriously, do you?"

"I dunno." Padilla drew in half an inch of his cigarette and blew it out in a long, sighing puff, brown-gray on the blue sky. "She may be making it up, but I didn't think she was that smart. She's known Granada for a long time. He used to be one of her boy-friends. Her and Gus and Granada ran with the same gang. It was a pretty wild gang, smoking weed, stealing cars, beating people up. They used to have parties out in the old ice plant—the same place where Pike shot Gus."

"How long ago was this?"

"Not as long as you'd think. Ten years at the outside. These people aren't old. Sexy—they used to call her Sexy— Secundina says that Gus and Granada fought for her one night. Granada was a football player, and Gus couldn't take him with his bare hands. He took him with a knife. He put a little hole in Granada's chest, and Granada ran away. Next thing they knew, the place was raided, and Gus was in the reformatory for stealing a car."

"There's no necessary connection."

"I know that, but Secundina thinks there is. Once Gus was out of the way, Granada moved in on her. She claims that's the way it's been ever since. Granada keeps making trouble for Gus, so he can get at her."

"She's not that much of an attraction, is she?"

"You didn't see her ten years ago, even five. She used to melt the asphalt. And I know for a fact Granada chased her for years, and had a down on Gus. According to Secundina, he never forgave Gus for making him run, and that's why he shot Gus last night."

"It sounds like a one-sided story to me. She's trying to get back at Granada."

"I hope that's all there is in it. She said other things, too. Granada was always dropping in Broadman's store. Manuel and Gus saw him there every week, oftener. They used to go in the back and talk."

"That's interesting."

"Yeah, it is. Because Broadman was fencing for the gang, that's definite. Gus was one of the break-in boys, and naturally he knew who handled the stuff. He also told Secundina that they had police information, somebody on the force tipping them off on when and where to strike. She thinks it was Granada."

"I don't believe it."

"That's your privilege." Padilla's tone made it clear that he did believe it. "Then I won't bother going into the rest of it."

"Is there more?"

"Yeah. I'll give it to you if you want. It may be a lot of crazy talk. Like I said, I hope it is. There must be some truth in it, though, because it checks out. This business about the kidnapping, for instance. Secundina got wind of it long ago. She didn't know what the job was going to be, neither did Gus. But it was going to be big—a lot of money

for everybody, enough to solve all their problems." Padilla
grinned ironically.

"Who all are involved?"

"She doesn't know that. Gus was one, of course. And this
character Gaines. Gus knew him from way back, met him in
Preston years ago under another name."

"What name?"

"Secundina doesn't know. Gus didn't tell her everything.
Most of what she learned, she had to pick up for herself.
She did find out that Gaines was the leader, anyway after
Broadman broke with the gang. Broadman goofed some way,
and the cops threw a scare into him. He decided to pull in
his horns. He didn't want any part of the big deal. Sexy
says that's why they killed him. He was ready to turn State's
evidence against them."

I was losing my scepticism of Padilla's story. It tied in
with some of the things I knew. A split between Gaines and
Broadman would account for Broadman's handling of Ella
Barker's diamond ring.

"Does Secundina admit that Gus killed Broadman?"

"No. She claims that Gus was sent to take care of Broadman. Gaines told him to gather up the loot in Broadman's
basement and knock the old boy off. But Gus couldn't go
through with it. He'd never killed a man. He hit Broadman
a couple of times and beat it. She saw Gus right after, that
same afternoon, and he was ashamed of himself for chicken-
ing out. You get that? He was *ashamed*. She didn't make
that up."

"But maybe he did."

"Gus? He's—he was no better than a moron."

"Then he could have been mistaken about what happened. He may have struck Broadman a fatal blow with-

out knowing it."

Padilla said: "You're sure Broadman wasn't choked to death?"

"I'm not sure, no. Why do you ask?"

"Secundina thinks he was."

"By Granada?"

"No names mentioned," Tony said. He wasn't a timid man, but he looked frightened. "I don't know what to do about all this, Mr. Gunnarson. I been carrying it around ever since she spilled it in my lap. It's too big for me to handle."

"I'll talk to her. Where does she live?"

"In a court in lower town." He gave me the address, and I wrote it down.

Tony got out and looked up at the sky. A high jet was cutting white double tracks across it, towing along them at a distance rattling loads of sound. Ferguson's telephone rang, like a tiny protest.

I started for the service entrance. Padilla was there ahead of me, blocking my way.

"What's the matter with you?"

He answered me quietly. "It's his baby, Mr. Gunnarson. Let him handle it."

"You think he's qualified?"

"As much as anybody is, I guess."

Padilla flicked his twisted ear with a fingertip and held his hand outspread beside his face. Ferguson's voice was a murmur far inside the house; then almost a shout: "Holly! Is that you, Holly?"

"My gosh, he's talking to her," Padilla said.

He'd forgotten his intention of keeping me out. We went in together. Ferguson met us in the central hallway. His weathered face was broken with joy. "I talked to her. She's alive and well, and she'll be home today."

"Not kidnapped, after all?" I said.

"Oh, they're holding her, all right." He seemed to consider this a minor detail. "But they haven't mistreated her. She told me so herself."

"You're sure it was your wife you talked to?"

"Absolutely certain. I couldn't be mistaken about her voice."

"Was it a local call?"

"So far as I could tell."

"Who else did you talk to?" Padilla said.

"A man—one of her captors. I didn't recognize his voice. But it doesn't matter. They're releasing her."

"Without ransom?"

He looked at me with displeasure. In the relief of hearing from his wife, he didn't want to be reminded of obstacles to her return. Relief like that, I thought, was very close to despair.

"I'm paying the ransom," he said in a flat voice. "I'm glad to do it."

"When and where?"

"With your permission, I'll keep my instructions to myself. I have a schedule to meet."

He turned with awkward haste and walked a rather erratic course to his bedroom. It was large, with an open blue fall to the sea from one window; and so austerely furnished that it seemed empty. There were photographs of his wife on the walls and the bare surfaces of the furniture, and several of the Colonel himself. He lounged with raw-boned rakishness in battle dress, under a hat like a pancake. He stood on his hands on a pair of parallel bars. One photograph showed him standing straight and alone against a flat prairie landscape under an empty sky.

"What are you doing in here, Gunnarson?"

"Are you sure that phone call wasn't phony?"

"How could it be? I spoke directly to Holly."

"It wasn't a tape you heard?"

"No." He considered this. "What she said was responsive to what I said."

"Why would she co-operate with them?"

"Because she wants to come home, of course," he said with a large, stark smile. "Why shouldn't she co-operate? She knows that I don't care about the money. She knows how much I love her."

"Sure she does," Padilla said from the doorway, and beckoned me with his head.

There were feelings in the air, like a complex electricity, which I didn't understand. Moving jerkily, galvanically, Ferguson went to a wall mirror and started to take off his shirt. His fingers fumbled at the buttons. In a rage of impatience, he tore it off with both hands. Buttons struck the glass like tiny bullets.

Ferguson's reflected face was gaunt. He saw me watching him, and met my gaze in the mirror. His eyes were old and stony, his forehead steaming with sweat. "I warn you. If you do anything to interfere with her safe return, I'll kill you. I have killed men."

He said it without turning, to his reflection and me.

*chapter* 11

I DROVE UNDER THE COLISEUM arches of the overpass and through an area of truckyards and lumber-yards. The air smelled of fresh-cut wood and burned diesel oil. Along the high wire fences of the trucking firms, against the blank walls of the building-materials warehouses, dark men leaned in the sun. I turned up Pelly Street.

The court where the Donato family lived was a collection of board-and-batten houses which resembled chickenhouses, built on three sides of a dusty patch of ground at the end of an alley. A single Cotoneaster tree, which can grow any-where, held its bright red berries up to the sun. In the tree's long straggling shade a swarm of children played gravely in the dust.

They were pretending to be Indians. Half of them prob-ably were, if you traced their blood lines. An old woman with a seamed Indian face overlooked them from the door-step of one of the huts.

She pretended not to see me. I was the wrong color and I had on a business suit and business suits cost money and where did the money come from? The sweat of the poor.

I said: "Is Mrs. Donato here? Secundina Donato?"

The old woman didn't raise her eyes or answer me. She was as still as a lizard in my shadow. Behind me the children had fallen silent. Through the open doorway of the hut, I could hear a woman's voice softly singing a lullaby in Spanish.

"Secundina lives here, doesn't she?"

The old woman moved her shoulders. The shrug was almost imperceptible under her rusty black shawl. A young woman holding a baby appeared in the doorway. She had Madonna eyes and a mournful drooping mouth which was beautiful until it spoke. "What are you looking for, Mister?"

"Secundina Donato. Do you know her?"

"Secundina is my sister. She isn't here."

"Where is she?"

"I dunno. Ask her." She looked down at the silent old woman on the doorstep.

"She won't give me an answer. Doesn't she understand English?"

"She understands it, all right, but she ain't talking today. One of her boys got shot last night. I guess you know that, Mister."

"Yes. I want to talk to Secundina about her husband."

"Are you a policeman?"

"I'm a lawyer. Tony Padilla sent me here."

The old woman spoke in husky, rapid Spanish. I caught Padilla's name, and Secundina's, and that was all.

"You a friend of Tony Padilla?" the young woman said.

"Yes. What does she say?"

"Secundina went to the hospital."

"Is she hurt?"

"Her Gus is there in the morgue."

"What did she say about Tony Padilla?"

"Nothing. She says Secundina should have married him."

"Married Tony?"

"That's what she says."

The old woman was still talking, head down, her gaze in the dust between her cracked black shoes.

"What else does she say?"

"Nothing. She says a woman is a fool to go to the hospital. Nobody ain't gonna make *her*. The hospital is where you die, she says. Her sister is a *medica*."

I started for the hospital, but got waylaid by the thought of other things I should do. My first duty was to Ella Barker. She was starting her third day in jail, and I'd promised to try and have her bail reduced. While I didn't have too much hope of accomplishing this, I had to make the attempt.

My timing was good. It was just eleven by the courthouse clock, and when I entered the courtroom, the court was taking a recess. The jury box was half full of prisoners, which meant that the break would be a short one. The prisoners were handcuffed together in pairs. They sat stolid and mute under the guard of an armed bailiff. Most of them looked like the men who leaned on the walls and fences off Pelly Street.

Judge Bennett came in from his chambers, trailing his black robe. I caught his eye, and he nodded. The judge was an impressive man in his sixties. He reminded me of my grandmother's Calvinist God, minus the beard and plus a sense of humor. The judge's sense of humor didn't show in court. Whenever I made the trek across the well of the old high-ceilinged courtroom up to the bench, I had to fight off the feeling that it was judgment day and my sins had found me out.

The judge leaned sideways to speak to me, as if to detach himself from the majesty of the law. "Good morning. How is Sally?"

"Very well. Thank you."

"She must be approaching the end of her term."

"Any day now."

"Good for her. I like to see nice people having children." His wise, experienced gaze rested on my face. "You're showing the tension, William."

"It isn't Sally I'm concerned about at the moment. It's the young Barker woman." I hesitated. "Mr. Sterling ought to hear what I have to say, Your Honor."

Keith Sterling, the D.A., was sitting at the prosecution table on the right, his iron-gray head bent over a stack of papers. The judge called him up to the bench, and resumed his upright posture.

I went on: "It seems unjust to me that Ella Barker should have to remain in jail. I'm strongly convinced that her involvement in these burglaries was innocent. The stolen property she received came to her as a gift. Her only real fault was gullibility, which hardly seems grounds for punishment."

"She isn't being punished," Sterling said. "She's simply being held for due disposition."

"The fact remains that she's in jail."

"I set bail, Mr. Gunnarson," the judge said.

"But isn't five thousand dollars rather high?"

"Not in our opinion," Sterling said. "It's a serious crime she's charged with."

"I mean it's high in the sense that she can't possibly make it. She has no family, no savings, no property—"

The judge cut me short: "I don't have time to hear further argument now." He hitched his black robe up with one shoulder. The clerk, who had been watching for this signal, called court back into session.

Sterling said to me in an undertone: "Take it up with Joe Reach, Bill. I think he wants to talk to you, anyway."

Joe was in his office on the second floor of the courthouse. He sat behind a desk littered with papers and law books with markers in them. He was the D.A.'s wheelhorse, and the Barker case would be one of a score that he was currently concerned with.

He let me wait for a minute, then gave me the up-from-under look that he used on hostile witnesses. "Rough night, Bill? You look hungover."

"Not from drinking, that's for sure. From thinking."

"Sit down. You still all roused up about the Barker girl? She must have a nest egg hidden away."

"I'm glad you brought that up. She's broke. Five thousand dollars is high bail for a girl with no resources. A first offender who isn't even guilty."

"So you keep saying. We differ. Judge Bennett set bail, anyway."

"I believe he'll lower it if you people don't object."

"But we do object." Reach opened a drawer, produced a chocolate and almond bar, unwrapped it, broke it in two pieces, and handed me the smaller piece. "Here. For energy. We can't have her jumping bail with murder in the picture. My advice to you is, leave it lay. Open up the question of bail, and you could get it raised."

"That sounds like persecution to me."

Reach munched at me ferociously. "I'm sorry you said that, Bill. She's wormed her way into your sympathies, hasn't she? Too bad. You've got to learn not to take these things so seriously."

"I take everything seriously. That's why I don't get along with frivolous people like you."

Reach looked pained. He was about as frivolous as the Supreme Court. "It strikes me I'm taking quite a lot from you this morning. Put the needle away, and do some more of your famous thinking. Try to look at the whole picture. Ella Barker's boy-friend was the leading spirit in a burglary gang, and worse than that. But she won't talk about him. She won't co-operate in helping us find him."

"She's co-operated fully, with all she knows. And incidentally, he wasn't her boy-friend once she got a line on him."

"Why didn't she come to us, then?"

"She was afraid to. Nothing in law obliges people to run to you with everything they find out." I heard what I said, and became obscurely aware that I was defending myself as well as Ella Barker.

"She would have saved us all a lot of trouble, not to mention herself."

"So you're punishing her."

"We're not planning to give her a good citizenship award, that's for sure."

"I say it's cruel and unusual punishment—"

"Save that for the courtroom."

"What courtroom? The calendar's so full, she won't be brought to trial for at least two weeks. Meantime she rots in jail."

"Is she willing to take a lie-detector test? That's not just my question. The reporters are asking it."

"Since when are you letting the newspapers do your thinking for you?"

"Don't get warm now, Bill. This is an important case. It affects a lot of people in town, not just your one little client. If she could give us a lead to Gaines—"

"All right. I'll try her again. But I'm sure you're barking up the wrong tree."

"I'm not sure about anything, Bill. You depend too much on preconceptions. Don't. I've spent twenty years in this game, and people are always surprising me. Not only with their deviousness. With their goodness. Give Ella Barker a chance to surprise you, why don't you?"

"I said I'd see her again today. Let's forget her now. There must be other potential leads to Larry Gaines. Didn't he leave any traces in the place he rented?"

"Not a vestige. He's one of these men from Mars, which probably means he has a record, and 'Larry Gaines' is an alias. He took out a driving license last fall, under the name of Gaines, and refused to give the Bureau people his thumbprint."

"What kind of a car does he drive?"

"Late-model Plymouth, green tudor. I'm giving you a lot of information. When do I get some back?"

"Now. Gaines registered at Buenavista College last September. That means they'll have his high-school transcript."

"They don't, though. Wills was there this morning. Gaines registered provisionally, without a transcript. He said it would be along any day, but it never arrived. So they kicked him out."

"What was he going to study?"

"Theater arts," Reach said. "He's an actor, all right."

(C+(C+(C+(C+(C
(C+(C+(C+(C+(C  *chapter*  **12**
(C+(C+(C+(C+(C

"HE TOLD ME HE ALWAYS wanted to be
an actor," Ella said. "Something big, but mainly an actor. I
guess he'd make a good one."

Her tone was sardonic. She was finding her armor, harden-
ing her personality against life in jail. Her eyes were sharp
as the edges of broken dreams.

"Why do you say that?"

"Look how he took me in. The great lover. When he gave
me that diamond ring, that watch, I thought he'd bought
them for me. Honest to God."

"I believe you."

"Nobody else around here does. Even the other girls think
I'm holding out. They keep asking me questions about
Larry, like I was really close to him, and knew all about him.
I been asked so many questions, my head spins. I wake up
in the middle of the night, and hear voices asking me ques-
tions. I'm going to go nuts if I don't get out of here."

"If we can get our hands on Gaines, it's going to help
you."

"Where is he?"

"That's the question. It's why I'm bothering you again."

"You're not bothering me. It's nice to see a friendly face,
somebody I can talk to. I don't mean to be snippy about the
other girls, but they're not my type at all. You ought to hear
the way they talk about *men*."

"It'll all wash out of your mind when you get out of here. You're a nurse. Think of it as a sickness you have to go through."

"I'll try."

I waited a minute, while her face composed itself. Outside the barred window the courthouse tower was stark white in the morning sun. On the balcony that encircled it, below the clock, a pair of tourists were looking out over the city. They leaned on the iron railing, a young man, and a young woman in a light blue dress and hat. It was the kind of dress and hat brides wore on honeymoons.

Ella had followed my look. "Lucky people."

"You'll be free soon. Your luck is all ahead of you."

"Let's hope so. You're nice to me, Mr. Gunnarson. Don't think I don't appreciate it." She gave me a dim smile, her first.

"You should smile more often. Your smile is your best feature."

It was a broad compliment, but not too broad for the occasion. She really smiled this time, and dropped five years. "Thank you, sir."

"Getting back to Gaines, if you can bear to—did he talk much about acting?"

"No, just once or twice. He mentioned that he did some acting."

"Where?"

"I think in high school."

"Did he say where he went to high school? Think hard."

Dutifully, she wrinkled up her forehead. "No," she said after a pause, "he never mentioned that. He never told me anything about his past life."

"Did he talk about his friends?"

"Just Broadman. He thought Broadman was a slob."

"Did he ever say anything about actors or actresses?"

"No. He never even took me to the movies." She added bitterly: "I guess he was saving his money for the blonde."

"What blonde do you mean?"

"The one I caught him with, out in the canyon. I guess he was going with her all the time."

"All what time?"

"When I thought he was my boy-friend, and maybe we'd get married, and everything. It's really her he was interested in, probably."

"What makes you think so?"

"What she said."

"I didn't know you ever talked to her. How often did you see her?"

"Only the once—the time I told you about. When she was sitting there in Larry's kimono. I remember exactly what she said, it made me feel so small. She laughed at me, and she said: 'You little tomcat'—talking to Larry—'have you been playing games behind my back?' She said: 'I'm not flattered by your choice of a—choice of a substitute,' something like that."

A slow blush mounted from Ella's neck to her cheeks. It softened her mouth, and then her eyes. She said in an unsteady voice that ranged up and down the register: "God, I made a fool of myself with that Gaines, didn't I?"

"Everybody's entitled to one big mistake. You could have come out of it worse."

"Yeah, if he really had married me. I see that now. And you know, what you were saying about a sickness, it applies to me and him. He was like a sickness I had—a sickness pretending to be something else. All my dreams coming true in one handsome package. I knew it couldn't be real, I just wanted it to be, so bad."

"Did he ever give you presents, besides the watch and the ring?"

"No. He gave me flowers once. One flower, a gardenia. He said that it would be our flower. That was the night he let me in on the big robbery plan. Thank God I didn't go for that, anyway."

"Do you have anything of his? Clothes, for example, that he may have left with you?"

"What do you think I am? He never took off his clothes in *my* apartment!"

"Sorry, I didn't mean anything wrong, Miss Barker. I thought you might have something personal of his. Some keepsake."

"No, all I had was the ring, and I sold that. I forgot about the watch." She wrinkled up her brow again. "There's something else I forgot. It doesn't have any value, though. It's just an old sharkskin wallet."

"Larry's wallet?"

"Yeah. I noticed one night when I gave him my picture— one of those wallet-sized pictures. I noticed that his wallet was all worn out. So I went downtown next day and bought him a new one, an alligator wallet. It cost me twenty dollars, with the tax. I gave it to him next time I saw him. He liked it. He took all his money and stuff out of the old one, and he was going to throw the old one away. I wouldn't let him."

"Did he leave anything in the wallet?"

"I don't think so. But wait a minute. There was a piece of paper in the back compartment—something cut out of a newspaper."

"What newspaper?"

"It didn't say. It was just a piece cut out of the middle of a page."

"What was the piece about?"

"A show, some kind of a show. I think it was a school play."

"Did you ever ask Larry about it?"

"No. He would have thought I was silly, keeping it."

"You kept the clipping?"

"Yeah, I tucked it back inside and kept it. You'd think it was money or something. How silly can a girl get?"

"Do you still have it?"

She nodded. "I forgot to throw it out. It's in my apartment."

"Where in your apartment?"

"In the bureau, the top drawer of the bureau in the bedroom. I have a little redwood chest I call my treasure chest. I put it in there. Mrs. Cline will let you in." She shook her head. "I hate to think what her opinion of me must be."

"I'm sure it hasn't changed. Do I need a key to get into this treasure chest?"

"Yeah, it's locked. But I don't know where the key is. I must have lost it. It doesn't matter, though. Break it open. I can get another."

She raised her head and looked at me levelly with soft, bright eyes.

Mrs. Cline stood breathing on my shoulder and watched me open the bureau drawer. She was a short, egg-shaped woman wearing an upside-down nest of gray hair. She had snappy, suspicious eyes, a generous mouth, and an air of frustrated decency. Without saying anything about it, she

left me in no doubt that my presence in Ella's bedchamber
was a violation of feminine privacy.

I lifted out the little redwood chest. It had brass corners
and a brass lock.

"Do you have a key for it?" Mrs. Cline said.

"No. Ella lost it. She authorized me to break it open."

"That would be a pity. She's had it ever since high school.
Here, let me see."

She clamped the box between her thick arm and her
thicker chest, plucked an old-fashioned steel hairpin from
her head, and went to work on the lock. It came open.

"You'd make a good burglar, Mrs. Cline."

"That isn't funny, young man, under the circumstances.
But then I know you lawyers get very callous. We knew
lawyers. Cline was an accountant, he worked with lawyers
in Portland, Oregon. Portland, Oregon, was our home. But
after his demise, I couldn't bear to stay on in the old town.
Every building, every street corner, had its memory. So I
said to myself, it's time to start a new chapter."

She stopped, when I was expecting her to go on. But
that was all. She had told me her life story.

The contents of the treasure box told Ella's life story, in
fragments of another language: a Valentine from a boy
named Chris who had written in brackets under his signa-
ture: "Your nice"; a grammar-school report card in which
Ella was praised for obedience and neatness, and gently
chided for lack of leadership; snapshots of girls of high-
school age, including Ella, and one or two boys; an en-
larged photograph of three people: a smiling man in a
boiler-plate blue suit and a straw hat, a wistful woman
who looked like an older version of Ella, and a small girl in
a starchy dress who was her younger self, with the same

hopeful dark eyes. There was a high-school graduation program in which her name was listed, a dance program almost full of young men's names, a black-bordered card announcing the death of Asa Barker, and a gold-bordered card announcing Ella Barker's graduation from nursing school.

Larry Gaines was represented by a brown gardenia and a worn sharkskin wallet.

I opened the back compartment of the wallet and found a tired old clipping, which was beginning to come apart at the folds. As Ella had said, it seemed to be a review of a high-school play. Part of it, including the headline and byline, was missing. The rest of it said:

> *Dorothy Drennan was her usual charming self in the role of ingenue. Claire Zanella and Marguerite Wood were charming as the bride's-maids. Stephen Roche and Hilda Dotery performed excellently as the comic servant couple and had the large audience of friends and parents in stitches, as did Frank Treco and Walter Van Horn with their usual live-wire antics.*
>
> *The surprise of the evening was Harry Haines in the demanding role of Jack Treloar. Harry is a newcomer to local high-school theatrics, and impressed us all with his talent. Also to be commended are Sheila Wood and Mesa McNab, who performed well in supporting roles, as did Jimmie Spence. The play itself left something to be desired in the writing department, but our young Thespians made it an enjoyable evening for all concerned.*

The sentences about Harry Haines had been underlined in pencil. For a boy of that name, I thought, Larry Gaines would be a natural alias. I turned the clipping over. The other side carried a news-service story about Dwight Eisenhower's election to the Presidency, late in the fall of 1952. I folded the clipping carefully, replaced it in the wallet, and dropped the wallet in my jacket pocket.

Mrs. Cline had picked up the Valentine, and was studying it. "Ella *is* a nice girl—one of the best I ever had in my apartment building. It's a pity she had to get into trouble."

"Her only crime was lack of judgment. They don't keep people in jail for showing poor judgment."

"You mean she really isn't guilty?"

"I'm convinced she isn't."

"The police are convinced she is."

"They always are, when they arrest people. It takes more than that to make them guilty."

"But Lieutenant Wills showed me the watch that was stolen."

"Ella didn't know it was stolen."

"I'm glad to hear you say so. Stolen property doesn't fit in with my idea of Ella."

"What's your idea of Ella?"

"I've always considered her a good, sound country girl— no saint, of course, but a girl that you can count on. She nursed me through a bad spell last summer, when my blood pressure was acting up, and she'd never take a cent for it. There aren't many like that any more. I tried to make it up to her when she was sick in the winter, but then I'm not a nurse. I was worried about her the way she lay around, with those big brown eyes of hers."

"When was this?"

"In January. She cried through most of that month. The doctor said there was nothing the matter with her physically, but she couldn't seem to summon up the energy to go to work. That was when she got so far behind. I lent her the money to go up north for a few days, the beginning of February—that seemed to snap her out of it."

"Does she owe you any money?"

"Not a cent. She's always been honest in our financial transactions. When she was behind for a while then, it really bothered her."

"If this case comes to trial—I don't think it will, but if it should—would you be willing to testify to Ella's good character?"

"Yes, I would. And I'm not the only one. Her friends have been phoning her from the hospital—nurses and head nurses and even a doctor. They want to know if they can visit her in —jail." She wrinkled her nose at the word. "I've been wondering the same thing myself."

"Wait a day or two, Mrs. Cline. I'm trying to get her out. The trouble is, it's going to cost money."

Something descended over her face, like a hard transparent glaze. "How much do you plan to charge?"

"It isn't money for me. It's the bail. I haven't been able to get it reduced."

"It's five thousand dollars, isn't it?" She made a clicking noise between tongue and teeth, which had the effect of dissolving the hard glaze. "I don't possess anything like that kind of money."

"Five hundred dollars would do it, if we used a bail bondsman. But you wouldn't get the five hundred back."

She narrowed her eyes and imagined her bank balance with five hundred dollars lopped off. "They charge, don't they?"

"Ten per cent."

"Isn't there any other way?"

"You could put up property, but that doubles the amount. Ten thousand dollars' worth of property covers five thousand dollars cash bail."

"Ten thousand dollars' equity?"

"That's right. I have to warn you, though, if Ella skipped, you'd lose your property."

"I realize that." She narrowed her eyes again and imagined herself without her property. "It's quite a thing to think about, but I'll think about it. Don't tell Ella we discussed this, will you? I wouldn't want her to build up any false hopes."

"I won't say a word on the subject. I take it there's nobody else. No well-heeled friends or relatives?"

She shook her head. "She has no one. That's the lack in her life, somebody to look after her. She's all right at the hospital, taking orders. But when she's out in the world on her own, she needs someone to look after her—a good man. But then who doesn't?"

"Men," I said. "We need a good woman. I have one, incidentally."

"I'm delighted to hear it."

She followed me out of the frothy little bedroom, across the diminutive rattan-furnished sitting room, to the door. "About this other thing, I'll think about it. Do *you* think she'd run out and lose my property for me?"

"Only if she were frightened."

"Of going to prison?"

"Of being killed," I said. "Did you ever see this Larry Gaines—the young man who fouled her up?"

"No, he never came here, to my knowledge. I did meet

Mr. Broadman on one occasion. He seemed harmless enough. But you never can tell about people."

"Sometimes you can, Mrs. Cline."

She got the message, and her smile returned it.

*chapter* **13**

I DROVE THE SHORT two blocks from Mrs. Cline's house to the hospital. It was a five-story brick building which stood in a quiet middle-class neighborhood. The quiet seemed oddly ominous to me. I couldn't help wondering if Larry Gaines had suborned other hospital employees after Ella Barker turned him down. There was something chilling about the idea of criminals infiltrating a hospital.

Perhaps the police had the same idea. There was a police car in the hospital parking lot. On my way to the morgue in the basement, I ran into Wills and Granada, almost literally.

They were coming up the fire stairs with their heads thrust forward in identical attitudes. Granada had always imitated Wills's movements and gestures. Wills stopped below me, with an impatient look, as if I was deliberately blocking his way. "What brings you here?"

"The Broadman killing. Do you have a minute?"

"No. But what can I do for you?"

Granada came up past me without a word. His bitten hand was hidden in his pocket. He stood at the head of the iron stairs, lips and chin thrust out, like a Janizary waiting for orders.

"I'm very much interested in the results of the autopsy on Broadman. Are they in?"

"Yeah, I just got a report from Dr. Simeon. Why are you so interested?"

"You know why I'm interested in Broadman. He seemed in fair shape at first. I can't understand why he died."

"He died of his injuries," Wills said shortly.

"What specific injuries did he have?"

I was watching Granada. If he heard what I said, or cared, he gave no sign. He put a cigarette in his mouth, lit it with a match held in his left hand, and flicked the match down the stairwell.

"Broadman had head injuries," Wills was saying. "You get a delayed reaction with them sometimes."

"I see. Is it all right with you if I talk to the pathologist?"

"Go ahead. Dr. Simeon will tell you the same thing." Wills's voice was coldly polite. "Joe Reach mentioned you were going to take another crack at Barker."

"Miss Barker," I corrected him. "I had another interview with her this morning."

"Any result?"

"I'd prefer to discuss that in private."

Wills glanced down the empty stairs, then up to the landing where Granada was waiting. "This is private, isn't it?"

"Not private enough."

"Granada's my right-hand man."

"He isn't mine."

Wills gave me a dour look, but he called up the stairs to Granada: "I'll meet you outside, Pike." Granada left, and Wills turned to me. "What's all the mystery about?"

"No mystery, Lieutenant, at least as far as I'm concerned. My client tells me Gaines is mixed up with a blonde woman."

"We got that from other sources. She know who the blonde woman is?"

"No." I was hyperconscious of the line of truth that I was trying to straddle. "She doesn't. She only saw her once."

"And that's your special private information?"

"There's this." I produced my lone piece of evidence, the sharkskin wallet, and handed it to Wills.

He looked at it glumly. "What is this supposed to signify?"

"It belonged to Gaines. Ella Barker kept it as a memento."

"How touching." Wills flipped it open, and sniffed at it disparagingly. "It stinks of perfume. Did she give it to you?"

"I found it in her apartment. She told me where it was. The girl is doing her best to co-operate."

"She can do better than this. Did Joe Reach talk to you about a polygraph?"

"He mentioned it."

"Why dillydally around? People are dying."

"One of them died of a policeman's bullets. The other one died in a manner that's not yet established to my satisfaction."

"To *your* satisfaction, for God's sake." Wills seldom swore. "Who do you think you are?"

"An attorney trying to protect a client from harassment."

Wills rounded his mouth and blew out a gust of air. "Words. Big empty words. That's all they are, and they make me sick to my stomach. What the hell is this all about? Are you trying to stick a knife in Granada's back, or what?"

"You reamed him out last night after the Donato shooting. Why?"

"That's between him and I. Not," he added, "that it's any big secret. It would have helped if Donato had lived to talk. He didn't, so that's that. Granada did his duty as he saw it."

"Do you always let him interpret his duties as he sees them?"

Wills said stubbornly: "Pike Granada is a good officer. I'd rather have a hood like Donato dead, ten times over, than him."

"Are you aware of his prior relations with Donato?"

"Yes, I'm aware of it," Wills said on a rising note. "Pike's lived here all his life, he knows everybody in town, it's one of his values to us."

"How well did he know Broadman?"

"Pretty well, he worked the pawnshop detail—"

The sentence dwindled off. Wills's face took on the appearance of pitted silver. Then it darkened like silver tarnishing all in a moment. He said in his chest: "What is this?"

"Granada had his hands on Broadman yesterday. Broadman was in fair shape before that. After that he died, very suddenly."

"Donato killed Broadman, you know that."

"Donato will never be able to deny it."

Wills looked at me in silence. The silence was stitched and woven through by the noises of the hospital, the quiet footsteps of nurses, wisps of voices, the closing of a door.

"I don't like this, Mr. Gunnarson. You're running loose at the mouth, and I don't like it. Granada's one of my best men. What you're saying is libel."

"You're his superior. Who else would I communicate my suspicions to?"

"You better not take 'em anywhere else, that's for sure."

"Is that a threat?"

"I don't mean it that way. You want my opinion, you've gone off the deep end. You ought to be more careful what you say."

"Can't you control Granada?"

I spoke the words in anger, and regretted them as soon as they were out. The pain in my eyes was intense, and jabbing deeper into my head. The worst of it was, I couldn't tell if it was the pain of knowledge or ignorance.

Wills let out an inarticulate sound, and made a reflex motion, striking the wall with the back of his hand. He became aware of the wallet he was holding.

"Here. This is worthless."

Perhaps he meant to hand it to me, but it flew from his hand and slid down the iron stairs. I went down after it, and he went up after Granada. The fire door closed behind him.

Dr. Simeon was a middle-aging man with traces of a dedicated look. His office was a corner room with small windows set high in the wall, and fluorescent lighting which was probably never turned off. Under it, the doctor was as pale as one of his own cadavers.

"The results of a head injury can be surprising," he said. "There's often a delayed reaction, as I've just been telling Lieutenant Wills. It results from hemorrhaging, and the formation of a blood clot."

"Did you find a blood clot?"

"No, I didn't. And there was no actual fracture of the skull." He raised a finicky, nicotine-stained hand and drummed a few dull bars on the front of his own skull. "As a matter of fact, I've been thinking of taking another whack at him."

"You mean you haven't done a complete post-mortem?"

"It was as complete as seemed called for. I found some cerebral hemorrhaging, probably enough to account for death." He was hedging.

"You're not satisfied that he died of his head injuries, are you?"

"Not entirely. I've seen people walking around with equally serious injuries. Not," he added dryly, "that I recommend walking around regardless as therapy for head injuries."

"What killed him if they didn't? Was he strangled?"

"I've seen no indications to that effect. There are nearly always external marks, broken veins under the skin. I've found no such marks outside, and nothing in the internal neck structures."

"Are you sure?"

It was a poor question. The pathologist gave me a quick bright look. I had injured him in his professional pride.

"You can have a look at the body yourself if you like."

It lay open on a table in the next room. I tried, but I couldn't go near it. I'd softened up considerably since Korea. A chill seemed to emanate from the body. I realized that the impression was fantastic: the room was simply cold. But I couldn't go near Broadman.

Simeon regarded me with satisfaction. "I'm going to go into the thoracic cavity. I'll let you know if I discover anything, Mr. Gunnarson."

I hardly heard him. Through an archway half obscured by rubberized curtains, I could see the wall of drawers in the adjoining room. One of the drawers was partly open. An old woman in black sat on a stool beside it, her head bowed and hooded by a shawl.

Simeon passed through the archway and touched her shoulder gently. "You mustn't stay here in this chill, Mrs. Donato. You'll catch cold."

I thought it was Gus Donato's mother. Then she turned up her face, with her eyes like black blisters. It was Donato's widow, Secundina.

"I hope I catch double ammonia and die," she said.

"That doesn't make sense. Go home now and get some rest, and you'll feel better."

"I can't sleep. My head goes round in circles."

"I'll give you a sleeping prescription. You can fill it at the hospital pharmacy."

"No. I wanna stay here. I got a right. I wanna stay here with Gus."

"I can't permit you to. It isn't healthy. Come into my office now," Simeon said firmly. "I'll give you that prescription."

"I got no money."

"I'll make it no charge."

He grasped her upper arm and half lifted her from the stool. She went along with him on dragging feet.

*chapter* 14

I WAS WAITING OUTSIDE the hospital pharmacy when she emerged, blinking her eyes against the noon sun.

"Mrs. Donato?"

She didn't know me immediately, just as I hadn't known her. Close up, in the sunlight, I saw what the night and the morning had done to her. Her generation had changed. The looks and gestures of youth had dropped away. What remained was the heavy stolidity of middle age. Gravity pulled at her flesh, and the sun was cruel.

"I'm Gunnarson the lawyer, Mrs. Donato. I was with Tony Padilla last night. Tony and I had a little talk this morning. He said you had some important information."

She let her face fall inert. Her whole body went stupid. "Tony must of been dreaming. I don't know nothing."

"It had to do with your husband's death," I said. "And other matters. He said Gus didn't kill Broadman."

"Don't you say that."

Her fingers closed like pincers on my arm.

She looked around her at the sunlit street corner. Some student nurses were waiting by the bus stop, twittering like white-breasted birds. Secundina's circling glance seemed to press reality away. It formed a zone of strangeness, empty and cold, a vacuum in the sunlight into which darkness surged from the darkness in her head.

I took her elbow and set her in motion. Her body moved slowly and reluctantly. We crossed the street to the bus stop on the diagonally opposite corner. An unoccupied concrete bench stood under a pepper tree. I persuaded her to sit down. The shadow of the pepper tree fell like cool lace on our faces.

"Tony said that your husband didn't kill Broadman."

"Did he?"

"I gather that you think Granada did."

She stirred in her trance of sorrow. "What does it matter what I think? I can't prove nothing."

"Maybe not, but other people can."

"Who, for instance?"

"Dr. Simeon. The police."

"Don't make me laugh. They like it the way it is. It's all finished and done with."

"Not in my book it isn't."

She regarded me with dull-eyed suspicion. "You're a lawyer, ain't you?"

"That's correct."

"I got no money, no way of getting none. My brother-in-law Manuel has money, but he is not interested. So there's nothing in it for you, not a thing."

"I realize that. I'm simply trying to get at the truth."

"You running for something?"

"I might at that, someday."

"Then go and run on somebody else's time. I'm tired and sick. I wanna go home."

"I'll take you home."

"No, thank you."

But she couldn't maintain her aloofness. She began to speak in Spanish, and in a different voice which buzzed and crackled like fire. It was like the voice of another personality, in which her youth and her sex and her anger survived. Her body came alive, and her face changed its shape.

I couldn't understand a word. "Say it in English, Secundina."

"So you can run down to the courthouse and get me locked up?"

"Why would I do that?"

She was silent for a minute, though her lips continued to move. "I don't know what you want from me."

"Information about the Broadman killing."

"I told it all to Tony. Get it from him."

"Is it true?"

She flared up darkly. "You calling me a liar?"

"No. But would you swear to it in court?"

"I'd never get to court, you know that. He'd do it to me, too."

"Who would?"

"Pike Granada. He always used to be hot for me. And when I wouldn't let him, he got a down on me. He tried to force me one night out at the icehouse. Gus nicked him good with a knife. So he turned Gus in to the cops for stealing a car. They picked me up, too. When I got out of Juvie, Pike took it out on me."

"That was a long time ago, I thought."

"It started a long time ago. He's been taking it out on me and Gus ever since. Last night the bastard had to go and shoot him."

"He was doing his duty, wasn't he?"

"He didn't have to shoot him. Gus never carried no gun. He didn't have the guts to carry a gun. He let Granada shoot him down like a dog."

"Why do you hate Granada so much?"

"He's a crooked cop. A cop is bad enough. A crooked cop is the worst animal there is."

"You still claim he murdered Broadman?"

"Sure he did."

"How do you know?"

"I hear things."

"Voices?"

"I'm not nuts, if that's what you think. I got a friend, a nurse's aide in emergency. She's been working in the hospital twenty years. She knows things the doctors never hear of. She said that Broadman was dead when they brought him in. She said he looked to her like he was strangulated. And Manuel saw Granada crawl into the ambulance with him. Granada was in there talking to Broadman, but Broadman wasn't saying anything." She gave me a sideways glance that was dark and heavy. It was like the knowledge of evil itself peering out between her eyelids. "You were there, weren't you? You saw it happen."

My mind picked its way back through the obstacle course of the night's events, to the previous afternoon. Broadman had cried out in fear and rage. Granada had been in the ambulance alone with him, ostensibly soothing him. He had soothed him very effectively, perhaps.

"I couldn't see what happened," I said. "What is your friend's name—the nurse's aide?"

"I promised her I wouldn't pass it on. That promise I keep."

"Why would Granada kill Broadman?"

"To keep him quiet. Broadman knew Granada is a crook."

"A member of the burglary gang?"

"Maybe."

"But if Granada was in on the burglaries, Gus would know."

"They didn't tell Gus everything."

"So you can't say for sure that Granada was involved?"

"No, but I think he was. When Gus bust into a house or a store he always knew where the cops were, and he didn't do it by X ray. He had a pipeline to them."

"He told you that?"

She nodded emphatically. The shawl slipped down from her head. Her hair was uncombed and matted, like torn black felt. She covered it, with a quick and angry gesture.

"But he didn't say it was Granada?"

"No. He didn't say that. Maybe he didn't know. There wasn't much I couldn't get out of him, if he had it in him."

Her refusal to make a blanket accusation against Granada was the most convincing element in her story so far. After stating my suspicions to Wills, I was having a reaction. I had to be very sure of Granada's guilt before I spoke out again.

"Who else was in the gang, Secundina?"

"Nobody else that I know of."

"No women?"

Her eyes shrank to bright dark points turned on me from the ambush of her shawl. "You got no call to point a finger at me. I did my best to talk Gus out of doing what he was doing."

"I don't mean you. You're not the only woman in the world. Didn't Gaines have any girl-friends?"

Her heavy black lashes came down and veiled her eyes completely. "No. I mean, how would I know?"

"I heard he was running with a blonde."

Her eyelids quivered, but her mouth was stubborn. "Then you heard more than I did."

"Who is she, Secundina?"

"I told you I didn't know about any blonde. I never ever see the guy. Maybe twice in the last two months."

"Under what circumstances?"

"I don't know what you mean."

"I mean where did you see Gaines? What was he doing?"

"I don't remember," she said stolidly.

"Have you known Gaines long?"

"Gus did. He knew him for six-seven years. He met him in Preston, and after they got out, they drove around the country for a while, living off of the country. Then Gus came back and married me, but he used to talk about this Harry. Gaines called himself Harry in those days. He was kind of a hero to Gus, he did such wild things."

"Like what?"

"Like conning people and stealing cars and driving faster than anybody and all like that. Crazy stuff. I warned Gus when he took up with Gaines again, last fall. I warned him that Gaines was trouble. He didn't listen to me. He never had the brains to listen to me."

She gazed across the street at the hospital. A local bus stopped at the opposite corner, and the student nurses got on. Secundina became aware of the bus as it roared away. "Now I missed my bus."

"I'll take you home."

"What's the use of go home?" she cried in a raw voice. "So I can tell my children they got no father? What's the use of anything?"

She sat like a monument to her own grief. Something had broken in her, releasing the bitter forces of her nature. She seemed to be submitting to them, hoping they would destroy her.

There was nothing I could think of to say, except: "Your children need you, Mrs. Donato. You have to think of them."

"To hell with them!"

But she was terrified by her words. She crossed herself, and started to mutter a prayer. In spite of the cool shade of the pepper tree, I was beginning to sweat. I'd never been so conscious of the wall between my side of town and hers.

A dirty black Buick convertible came down the street in front of the hospital. Tony Padilla was driving, slowly, looking for someone. He saw us on the bench and drew in to the red curb.

"Hello, Mr. Gunnarson," he said in a subdued voice. "I was in the hospital looking for you, Mrs. Donato. Your sister said I should bring you home. You want to get in?" He leaned across the front seat and opened the door for her.

I caught a glimpse of her tiny, high-arched foot. Red toenails gleamed through the plastic toe of her shoe. "May I see you for a minute, Tony?"

"You see me," he said across her. He didn't want to talk to me, and was using her as a buffer.

"What happened to Colonel Ferguson? I thought you were holding his hand."

"Until he gave me the brush-off. He went to drop the money off—"

"Where?"

"I dunno. He didn't tell me, didn't want me along. So I went down to Secundina's place. I wanted to talk to her some more. Her sister said she was here at the hospital." He smiled and shrugged automatically, and glanced at the watch on his wrist. "I just got time to take her home before I go to work."

He put his car in gear.

chapter 15

MY PATH TO THE PARKING LOT led past the emergency entrance of the hospital. The ambulances were garaged across the street, and one of them was parked in the driveway facing into the street. The old youth named Whitey lounged at the wheel, listening to the radio. He turned it low when I came up to the window of the cab. "Can I help you, sir?"

"You may be able to. I saw you at Broadman's store yesterday when you took him away. My name is Gunnarson."

"I remember you, Mr. Gunnarson." He tried to smile, without much success. His pale lippy face wasn't made for smiling. "Broadman died on the way here, poor old boy. I hated to see it happen."

"Was he a friend of yours?"

"I never saw him before in my life. But I have an empathy with them. Like we're all fellow mortals together. Dead or alive. You know?"

I knew, though I didn't like the way he put it. He seemed to be one of those sick-bay philosophers—sensitive wounded souls who lived by choice in the odor of sickness, flourished like mushrooms under the shadow of death.

Whitey's eyes were like nerve ends. "It *kills* me to see a man die."

"How did Broadman die?"

"He simply passed away, man. One minute he was yelling and struggling, trying to get up—he was real panicky. The next minute he sighed and was gone." Whitey sighed and went a little himself. "I blame myself."

"Why blame yourself?"

"Because I didn't *dream* he was going to die on me. If I had only known, I could have given him oxygen, or drugs. But I let him slip away between my fingers."

He raised one hand to the window and looked at his fingers. They dangled limply. He rested his chin on his chest, and his long face sloped into sorrow. His pale eyes appeared ready to spurt tears. "I don't know why I stay in this awful business. There are so many disappointments. I might as well be a mortician and get it over with. I *mean* it, man." He was going down for the third time in an ocean of self-pity.

I said: "What did he die of?"

"Search me. I've had a lot of experience, but I'm not a medical man. You'll have to take it up with the doctors." His tone implied obscurely that doctors could be wrong, and often were.

"The doctors don't seem to understand the case. Can't you give me the benefit of your experience?"

He glanced at me sideways, warily. "I don't know what you're getting at."

"I want your opinion of what killed Broadman."

"I'm not entitled to any opinion, I'm just a lackey around here. But it must have been those injuries at the back of his head."

"Did Broadman sustain any other injuries?"

"How do you mean?"

"On the throat, for instance."

"Heavens, no. He certainly wasn't choked to death, if that's what you're getting at."

"I'll be frank with you, Whitey. It's been suggested that Broadman was injured fatally after I found him in the store. Between the time that I found him and you took him away."

"Who by, for goodness' sake?"

"That remains to be seen. It's been suggested that he was roughly handled."

"No!" He was deeply shocked by the suggestion. "I handled him like a baby, with the upmost care. I always handle head injuries with the upmost care."

"You weren't the only one who had your hands on him."

His eyes appeared to turn white. The flesh around them crinkled like blue crepe. He opened and closed his mouth, making noises like a hot-water bottle under stress.

"You wouldn't be pointing a finger at my partner? Ronny wouldn't hurt a fly. We been working together for years, ever since he got out of the Medical Corps. He wouldn't even hurt a *mosquito!* I've seen him take a mosquito by the wings, pluck it right off his arm, and set it free."

"Calm down, Whitey. I'm not pointing a finger at you or your sidekick. I simply want to know if you noticed anything out of the ordinary."

"Listen, Mr. Gunnarson," he complained, "I'm supposed to be monitoring police calls. The manager catches me out here batting the breeze—"

"If you saw anything, it won't take long to tell me."

"Sure, and get my own neck in a sling."

"You can trust me to hold any information you have. It may be very important. It's not just a matter of one man's death, though that's important enough."

He pushed his fingers up into his hair and slowly closed his fist. His hair sprouted out like pale weeds between his fingers. "What do you want me to say? And who does it go to?"

"Just to me."

"I don't know you, Mr. Gunnarson. I do know what happens to me and my job if certain people get a down on me."

"Name them."

"How can I? What protection have *I* got? I'm no muscle man and I don't pretend to be smart."

"You're not acting too smart. You seem to have evidence in a murder case, and you think you can sit on it until it explodes."

He twisted tensely in the seat, turning his head away. His neck was thin and vulnerable-looking, like a plucked chicken's.

"A man name of Donato murdered Broadman. I heard it on the radio. Can't we just leave it like that?"

"Not if it isn't true."

"Donato's dead, isn't he?"

"Yes. Pike Granada shot him. You know Granada, don't you?"

"Sure. I run into him in the course of work." A tremor ran through his long, asthenic body. It was curled in the seat protectively, knees up. "You think I want to get myself shot, too? Leave me alone, why don't you? I'm no hero."

"I'm beginning to get the idea."

All this time the radio had been murmuring in fits and starts. Now the rhythm of the dispatcher's voice quickened. Whitey reached out and turned the radio up. It said that a new blue Imperial had been clocked at sixty proceeding east on Ocean Boulevard east of the pier.

I shouted above it: "Did Granada do something to Broadman?"

Whitey sat and pretended to be deaf. The dispatcher's voice went on like the voice of doom. The Imperial had collided with a truck at the intersection of Ocean Boulevard and Roundtable Street. Traffic Control Car Seven was directed to the scene of the accident. A few seconds later the dispatcher relayed a report that the driver was injured.

"You see?" Whitey cried aggrievedly. "You almost made me miss an accident."

He started his engine, and honked softly. His fat little partner, the mosquito liberator, came running out of the garage. The ambulance rolled into the street and turned toward the foot of the city, singing its siren song.

I followed it. Colonel Ferguson had a blue Imperial.

*chapter* 16

THE LONG BLUE CAR had smashed its nose on the side of an aluminum semitrailer. A policeman was directing traffic around the damaged vehicles. At the curb, another policeman was talking to a tough-looking man in oil-stained coveralls. They were looking down in attitudes of angry sympathy at a third man who was sitting on the curb with his face in his hands. It was Ferguson.

Whitey and his partner got out of the ambulance and trotted toward him. I was close on their heels. Whitey said to the policeman in a tone of whining solicitude: "Is the poor fellow badly hurt, Mahan?"

"Not too serious. But you better take him to Emergency."

Ferguson lifted his head. "Nonsense. I don't need an ambulance. I'm perfectly all right."

It was an overstatement. Worms of blood crawled down from his nostrils to his mouth. His eyes were like starred glass.

"You better go along to the hospital," Mahan said. "Looks to me like you bust your nose."

"It doesn't matter, I've broken it before." Ferguson was a little high with shock. "What I need is a stiff drink, and I'll be right as rain."

Mahan and the ambulance men looked at each other with uneasy smiles. The man in coveralls muttered to no one in particular: "Probably had one too many already. He sure picked a hell of a time to run a red light."

Ferguson heard him and lunged up to his feet. "I assure you I haven't been drinking. I do assume full responsibility for the accident. And I apologize for the inconvenience."

"I hope so. Who's going to pay for the damage to the truck?"

"I am, of course."

Ferguson was doing a fine job of setting himself up for a lawsuit. I couldn't help interjecting: "Don't say any more, Colonel. It may not have been your fault."

Mahan turned on me hotly. "He was doing sixty down the Boulevard. He's due for a pile of citations. Take a look at his skidmarks."

I took a look. The broad black lines which Ferguson's car had laid down on the concrete were nearly two hundred feet long.

"I've said I'm sorry."

"It ain't that simple, Mister. I want to know how it happened. What did you say your name was?"

I answered for him. "Ferguson. Colonel Ferguson is not obliged to answer your questions."

"The hell he isn't. Read the Vehicle Code."

"I have, I'm an attorney. He'll make a report to you later. At the present time he's obviously dazed."

"That's right," Whitey said. "We'll take him along to the hospital, they'll fix him up."

He put his pale thin hand on Ferguson's shoulder, like a butcher testing meat. Ferguson moved impatiently, stumbled on the curb, and almost fell. He glanced around at the growing circle of onlookers with something like panic in his eyes. "Let me out of here. My wife—" His hand went to his face and came away bloody.

"What about your wife?" Mahan said. "Was she in the car?"

"No."

"How did the accident happen? What did you think you were doing?"

I stepped between them. "Colonel Ferguson will be in touch with you later, when he's himself."

I got hold of Ferguson's bony elbow and propelled him through the gathering crowd to my car.

Mahan pursued us, waving citation blanks. "Where do you think you're going?"

"To a doctor. If I were you, officer, I wouldn't push this any further right now."

I opened the door for Ferguson. He got in, disdaining my assistance. Mahan stood and watched us drive away, his pad of blanks crumpled in his hand.

"You're Johnny-on-the-spot, aren't you?" Ferguson said.

"I happened to be listening to the local police calls, and got the first report of your accident. Do you have a doctor in town?"

"I never go to doctors." He emitted a sort of snuffling neigh through his damaged nose. "Look here, I need a drink. Isn't there someplace we can go for a drink?"

"If you say so."

I took him to a bar and grill on the edge of the lower town. The noon-hour crowd had thinned down to a few tables of men drinking their lunches. I hustled Ferguson to the rear of the establishment and suggested he wash his face.

He came out of the men's room looking a little better, and ordered rye on the rocks. I ordered a corned-beef sandwich. When the waiter was out of hearing, he pushed his battered face across the table toward me. His eyes were bleak. "What sort of a man are you? Can I trust you?"

"I think so."

"You haven't simply been hanging around hoping that some of my money will rub off on you?"

It was an insulting question, but I didn't let it insult me. I was willing to put up with a good deal for the sake of candor. "It's a natural human hope, isn't it? Money isn't an overriding motive with me. As you may have noticed."

"Yes. You've talked to me straight from the shoulder. I'd like to feel I can do the same with you." His voice altered. "God knows I have to talk to someone."

"Shoot. In my profession you learn to listen, and you learn to forget."

The waiter brought his drink. Ferguson sucked at it greedily and set the glass down with a rap. "I want to engage your professional services, Mr. Gunnarson. That will insure your forgetting, won't it? Confidential relationship, and all that."

"I take it seriously."

"I don't mean to be offensive. I realize I have been offensive, when this matter came up between us. I apologize." He was trying to be quiet and charming. I preferred him loud and natural.

"No apology needed. You've been under quite a strain. But we're not getting anywhere."

"We have if we've reached an agreement. Will you be my legal adviser in this matter?"

"I'll be glad to. So long as it doesn't interfere with my representing my other client. Other clients."

"How could that be?"

"We don't need to go into detail. I have a client in the county jail who was involved with Larry Gaines. Innocently involved, like your wife."

His eyes winced.

"And like your wife," I added, "she's suffering out the consequences."

Ferguson took a deep, yawning breath. "I saw Gaines today. It's why I lost my head. I threw discretion to the winds and tried to run him down. God knows what will happen now."

"Have you delivered the money?"

"Yes. It's when I saw him. I was instructed to procure a cardboard carton and place the money in it, then leave the carton on the front seat of my car, with the door unlocked. I parked the car where they told me to, on Ocean Boulevard near the foot of the pier, and left it standing there with the carton of money in it. Then I was supposed to walk out to the end of the wharf. It's a distance of a couple of hundred yards."

"I know the place. My wife and I often go there."

"Then you probably remember that there's a public telescope on the pier. I couldn't resist dropping a dime in the slot and training the thing on my car. It's how I happened to see them."

"Them?"

"Him. I meant to say him. Gaines. He pulled up beside my car, got out and retrieved the carton, and away he went. If I had had a deer rifle with me, I could have plugged him. I wish I had."

"What kind of a car was he driving?"

"A fairly new car, green in color. I don't know what make exactly. I'm not familiar with the cheaper makes."

"It was one of the cheaper makes?"

"Yes, a Chevrolet perhaps."

"Or a Plymouth?"

"It may have been a Plymouth. At any rate it was Gaines who got out and picked up the money. And I saw red. I sprinted the length of the pier and chased th—chased him in my car. You know the result."

He gingerly touched his swelling nose with his fingertips.

"You don't lie well, Colonel. Who was with Gaines in the green Plymouth?"

"No one."

But he wouldn't meet my eyes. His gaze roved around the room and fastened on an elk head high on the opposite wall above the bar. The waiter brought my sandwich. Ferguson ordered another double rye.

I ate mechanically. My mind was racing, fitting together

pieces of fact. The picture was far from complete, but its outlines were forming.

"Was your wife in the car with Gaines?"

His head hung as if his neck had been broken. "She was driving."

"Are you certain of the identification?"

"Positive."

His second drink arrived. He drank it down like hemlock. Remembering the previous night at the Foothill Club, I persuaded him not to order a third. "We have some more talking to do, Ferguson. We don't have to do it here."

"I like it here." His gaze repeated its circuit of the room, which was almost deserted now, and returned to the friendly elk.

"Ever hunt elk?"

"Indeed I have. I have several fine heads at home."

"Where is home, exactly?"

"I keep most of my trophies in my lodge at Banff. But that's not exactly what you mean, is it? You mean where I really live, and that's hard to say. I have a house in Calgary, and I keep hotel suites in Montreal and Vancouver. None of them are places I feel at home." Like other lonely men, he seemed glad to be relieved of the burden of loneliness. "Home for me was always the family homestead in Alberta. But it's nothing but an oil field now."

"You haven't mentioned your place here."

"No. I feel decidedly *out* of place in California. I came here because it offered investment opportunities, and because Holly was unwilling to leave California."

"Was there conflict between you on the subject?"

"I wouldn't say so, no. I wanted to please her. We've only

been married six months." He'd been still and quiet for a few minutes, but the thought of his wife was too much for him. He twisted in his seat as though he'd been kicked in the groin. "Why are we beating around the bush, with this talk of homes and places?"

"I'm trying to get some idea of you and your situation. I can't very well advise you in the dark. Would you object to some more personal questions, about your wife and your relationship?"

"I don't object. In fact, it may help to clarify my own thinking." He paused, and said in astonishment, like a man who has made a personal discovery: "I'm an emotional man, you know. I used to think of myself as a cold fish. Holly changed all that. I hardly know whether to be glad or sorry."

"You're pretty ambivalent about her, aren't you? Running hot and cold, I mean."

"I know what you mean, very well. I'm scalding and freezing. The two conditions are just about equally painful." Ferguson kept surprising me. He added: " *'Odi et amo. Excrucior.'* Do you know Latin, Gunnarson?"

"Some legal Latin."

"I'm no Latinist myself, but my mother taught me a little. That was Catullus. 'I hate her and I love her, and I'm on the rack.' " His voice rose out of control, as if he was literally on the rack. Then he said in a deeper voice: "She's the only person I've ever really loved. Except one. And I didn't love her enough."

"Have you been married before?"

"No. I'd reached the point of believing that marriage was not for me. I should have stuck to that. A man can't expect to be lucky more than once."

"I don't follow you."

"I've been lucky enough to make a good deal of money. I knew instinctively that a man like me couldn't be lucky in love. And I've always shied away from women. It's nothing to be vain about, because I know the reason, but plenty of women have thrown themselves at my head."

"Did Holly?"

"No, she didn't. I was the pursuer in her case—very much the pursuer."

"How did you happen to meet her?"

"It didn't *happen*, in the strictest sense. I arranged to meet her. I saw her in a film last spring in London—I was over there for a trade meeting at Canada House—and decided I had to meet her, somehow. A few months later, at the end of July, I happened to be passing through Vancouver. I have interests in British Columbia, and some of my property was threatened by forest fires.

"I picked up a newspaper and saw Holly's picture. Her film was to be shown at the Vancouver film festival, and she was to be a guest at the showing. I decided to stop over in Vancouver, and the forest fires be damned. All I could think about was meeting her in the flesh."

"Do you mean to tell me you fell in love with her picture, at first sight?"

"Does that sound foolish and sentimental?"

"It sounds incredible."

"Not if you realize how I felt. She was what I'd been missing all my life. She stood for the things I'd turned my back on when I was a young man. Love, and marriage, and fatherhood. A lovely girl that I could call my own." He was talking like a man in a dream, a rosy sentimental dream of the sort that burns like celluloid and leaves angry ashes in the eyes.

"You felt all this simply because you'd seen her in a movie?"

"There was more to it than that. I prefer not to go into it."

"I think you should go into it."

"What purpose would it serve? That other girl had nothing to do with Holly, except that Holly reminded me of her."

"Tell me about the other girl."

"There's no point in going into the subject of *her,* not at this late date. She was simply a girl I picked up in Boston twenty-five years ago, when I was at Harvard Business School. For a while I planned to marry her, and then I decided not to. Perhaps I should have." He stared down into his empty glass, twisting and turning it like a crystal ball that revealed the past but kept the future hidden. "Holly seemed like a reincarnation of that girl in Boston."

He fell silent. He seemed to have forgotten that I was sitting across from him.

"So you arranged to meet Holly," I prompted him.

"Yes. It wasn't difficult. I have strong connections in Vancouver, among them some of the backers of the festival. A dinner in her honor was set up, and I had the privilege of sitting beside her. She was charming, and so *young.*" His voice broke, leaving me unmoved. "It was like being given a second chance at youth."

"Obviously, you made the most of your chances."

"Yes. We got along from the start—in a perfectly straightforward, companionable way. And she didn't know who I was. I was simply a fellow she met at a party who had a few business interests. That was the beauty of it. She didn't know I had money until we'd been seeing each other for several days." Ferguson spoke of his money as if it was a communicable disease.

"Are you certain of that?"

"Quite certain." He nodded emphatically, as though he

had to reassure himself. "She didn't know who I really was until it developed that she was going to Banff. I invited her to stay at my lodge there—properly chaperoned, of course. We got together a little party, and rode up in a private railway car that a friend of mine makes available to me.

"It was a wonderful trip. I felt terrifically excited, just to be with her. I don't mean in a sexual way." Ferguson's eyes became faintly anxious whenever he approached the subject of sex. "I've had sex with various women, but the feeling I had for Holly was very much more than that. She was like a golden image sitting there by the train window. I didn't like to stare directly at her, so I looked at her reflection in the window. I watched her reflected face with the mountains moving through it and behind it. I felt as though I was moving with her into the heart of life, a golden time. Do you understand me?"

"Not too well."

"I don't pretend to understand it myself. I only know I'd lived for twenty-five years without that feeling. I'd been going through the motions for twenty-five years, piling up money and acquiring property. Suddenly Holly was the reason for it, the meaning of it all. *She* understood when I told her these things. We went on long walks together in the mountains. I poured out my heart to her, and she understood. She said that she loved me, and would share my life."

Shock and whisky were working in him like truth serum. There was no trace of irony in his voice; only the tragic irony of the circumstances. He had founded his brief marriage on a dream and was trying to convince himself that the dream was real.

"And share your money, too?" I said.

"Holly didn't marry me for money," he insisted doggedly.

"Remember that she was a successful actress, with a future. It's true her studio had her tied up in a low-salaried contract, but she could have done much better if she'd stayed in Hollywood. Her agent told me she was bound to become a great star. But the fact is, she wasn't interested in money, or in stardom. She wanted to improve herself, become a cultivated woman. That was the project we had in mind when we came here. We planned to learn together, read good books, study music and other worthwhile things."

He looked around the shabby restaurant as if he had somehow fallen into a trap. I remembered the hooded harp and the white concert grand.

"Was your wife studying music seriously?"

He nodded. "She has a voice, you know. I engaged a voice teacher for her, also a speech teacher. She wasn't happy about the way she spoke, her use of English. I'm no great grammarian myself, but I was always having to correct her."

"All these lessons she was taking—were they her idea or yours?"

"They were her idea, originally. I'm still in my prime, and at first I wasn't too fond of the notion that we should take a year or two out to develop our minds and all that. I went along with it because I loved her, because I felt grateful to her."

"Grateful for what?"

"For marrying me." He seemed surprised by my lack of understanding. Puzzled surprise was threatening to become his permanent expression. "I'm not a handsome man, and I'm not young. I suppose I can hardly blame her for running out on me."

"It's possible she hasn't. Gaines may have been pointing a gun at her today."

"No. I saw him get out of the car. She sat behind the wheel and waited for him."

"Then he may have some other hold on her. How long has she known him?"

"Just since we've come here."

"You're sure?"

He shook his head. "I can't be sure, no. She might have known him before, and pulled the wool over my eyes."

"Do you know much about her background? Where she came from, what sort of girlhood she had?"

"She had a difficult girlhood, I don't know where or how. Holly preferred not to talk about herself. She said when she married me, she intended to start a fresh page in her life, with no crying over spilt milk."

"Have you met her parents?"

"No. I'm not even aware that they exist. It may be that she's ashamed of them. She's never told me her real name. She married me under her stage name."

"Did she tell you that?"

"Her agent did, Michael Speare. I met him last fall, when I was breaking her studio contract. His agency has her under a long-term contract which I couldn't break."

"Would you object if I talked to Speare?"

"You mustn't tell him what's happened." Ferguson's voice was almost plaintive. The past had opened like a wound, bleeding away his force. "Whether or not she deserves it, we have to protect Holly. If I could just get her out of this frightful mess she's landed herself in—"

"I don't see much hope of that. There is one thing you could do which we haven't discussed. I know of some good private detectives in Los Angeles."

"No! I'm not going in for that sort of thing."

Ferguson struck the table with his fist. His glass jumped and rattled against my plate. Fresh blood began to run from his nose. I stood up and got him out of there.

"I'm taking you to a doctor," I said in the car. "You must know some local doctor. If not, you can get one in the emergency ward of the hospital."

"It isn't necessary," he said. "I'm perfectly all right."

"We won't argue, Colonel. Haven't you ever been to a local doctor?"

"I don't go to doctors. The blasted doctors killed my mother." His voice was strained and high. Perhaps he heard himself, because he added in a calmer tone: "Holly visited the Buenavista Clinic once or twice."

"It's a good place. Who was her doctor?"

"Chap by the name of Trench."

"Are you sure?"

"Quite certain, yes." He gave me a questioning look. "Is this Trench a quack of some sort?"

"Hardly. He's my wife's doctor. He's the best obstetrician in town."

"Is your wife going to—" Then he caught the rest of the implications, and didn't finish the sentence.

"Yes," I said, "she is. Is yours?"

"I don't know. We never spoke of the matter."

There seemed to be a number of things they hadn't spoken of.

((◄((◄((◄((◄((◄((◄((◄((◄
((◄((◄((◄((◄((◄((◄((◄((◄ *chapter* **17**
((◄((◄((◄((◄((◄((◄

I WALKED AND TALKED Ferguson into the clinic and made an emergency appointment for him with their bone man, Dr. Root. It was one of those highly specialized medical partnerships where practically every organ of the human body was represented by a separate doctor. I left Ferguson in the waiting room and told him I'd be back in half an hour. He sat on the edge of a leather chair, bolt upright, like one of the stone figures you see on old tombs.

Mrs. Weinstein glanced at the clock when I walked into my office.

"It's nearly two, Mr. Gunnarson. I hope you enjoyed your lunch."

"Thanks for reminding me. Would you call my wife and tell her I won't be home for lunch?"

"I presume she knows by this time."

"Call her anyway, will you? Then I want you to place a call for me, to a man in Beverly Hills named Michael Speare." I recited the address which Ferguson had given me. "You can probably get the number from Information. I'll take the call in my office."

I sat at my desk with the door closed. I spread out the clipping from Larry Gaines's old wallet, and made an alphabetical list of the names mentioned in it: Dotery, Drennan, Haines, McNab, Roche, Spence, Treco, Van Horn, Wood, Zanella. I had an idea.

My telephone rang.

"Mr. Speare is on the line," Mrs. Weinstein said. Over her, a man's voice was saying: "Mike Speare here."

"This is William Gunnarson. I'm an attorney out in Buena-vista. Can you give me a few minutes of your time?"

"Not right now. I'm at Television City. My secretary transferred the call. What's it all about?"

"A client of yours. Holly May."

"What does Holly want?"

"It's too confidential for the telephone," I said, trying to sound tantalizing. "Can I talk to you in person, Mr. Speare?"

"Why not? I'll be back in my office by three or so. You know where it is—just off Santa Monica Boulevard?"

"I'll be there. Thanks."

I hung up and went out and presented my list of names to Mrs. Weinstein. "I have a little job for you. It may only take a few minutes, if we're lucky. It may take today and tomorrow. I want you to stay with it until it's finished."

"But I have a pile of tax forms to type up for Mr. Mill-race."

"They can wait. This is an emergency."

"What kind of an emergency?"

"I'll tell you when it's over. Maybe. It could be a matter of life or death."

"Really?"

"Here's your problem. In 1952 the people listed here lived in a certain town. I hope in California. I don't know the name of the town, and that's what I'm trying to find out, the name of the town."

"You don't have to repeat yourself." Mrs. Weinstein was getting interested. "So what do I do?"

"Take these names over to the telephone company and

check them against their out-of-town directories—especially the smaller ones. See if you can find a directory that contains most of these names. Start with the towns near here."

She peered at the list. "What about the first names?"

"First names are not important. When you find the right grouping of last names, or anything approximating it, I want you to make a note of the addresses."

"It may not be so easy. 1952 is a long time ago, the way people move around nowadays."

"I know that. But give it a good try. It really is important."

"You can count on me."

Ferguson was waiting outside the clinic, standing in the shadow of the cornice. His eyes still held their unseeing expression; he seemed oblivious to the life of the town around him. Though we spoke the same language, more or less, I realized how much of a foreigner he was in southern California. He was doubly alienated by what had been happening to him.

I leaned across to open the car door. "How's your nose?"

"My nose is the least of my worries," he said as he got in. "I spoke to that Dr. Trench of yours."

"What did he say?"

"My wife is over two months pregnant. It's probably Gaines's child she's carrying."

"Did Trench say that?"

"Naturally I didn't ask him. But it's obvious. No wonder she decided to run away with him. No wonder they needed money. Now they have it." He grinned fiercely at nothing in particular. "Why didn't she simply ask me for the money? I'd have given it to her."

"Would you?"

He opened his hands and looked down into them. "I might have killed her. When I went after them today, I intended to kill them both. Then I saw that truck ahead coming into the intersection. I had the idea, for a split second, that I would kill myself. My reflexes wouldn't let me." His right foot thumped the floor of the car. "That's a shameful admission for a man to have to make." He didn't explain whether he meant his suicidal intent or his failure to carry it out.

I said: "I have an appointment with Michael Speare at three o'clock. Do you want me to drop you at home? It's more or less on the way. You can make your accident report later."

"Yes. I'd better get home, in case they try to get in touch."

I set the car in motion and turned down Main Street toward the highway. "Do you have any idea where they've gone?"

"No, and I don't want you getting ideas. I have no desire to see them tracked down. Is that understood? I want nothing done to either of them."

"That may be hard to manage."

He didn't seem to hear me. He was back in conflict with himself, wrestling with the obscure guilt he felt. "I blame myself, you see, almost as much as I blame her. I should never have talked her into marrying me. She belonged to another generation, she needed younger blood. I was a dreaming fool even to imagine I had anything to offer to a young, beautiful woman."

"Your attitude is very unselfish, Ferguson. I'm not so sure it's wise."

"That's a private matter, between me and my—me and my conscience."

"It isn't wholly private. Gaines is a known criminal,

wanted by the police." I said in response to his hot and wounded look: "No, I haven't broken your confidence and gone to the police. Gaines is wanted on other charges, burglary for one. If your wife is taken with him, there'll be hell to pay all round. And what you want isn't going to affect the outcome much."

"I know I can't assume responsibility for what happens to her." His generosity had limits after all, which made me believe in it more. "I simply refuse to have anything to do with hunting them down myself."

"That needs more thought, perhaps. Your wife may be more innocent than you assume. Gaines seems to be a con artist—one of those people who can talk birds out of trees. He may have sold her some fantastic story—"

"Holly is not a fool."

"Any woman can be, when she's infatuated. I take it you're morally certain they're lovers?"

"I'm afraid so. He's been sniffing after her for months. I let it go on right under my nose."

"Did you ever catch them *in flagrante delicto?*"

"Nothing like that. I was gone a lot of the time, though. They had no end of opportunities. He danced attendance on her like a gigolo. They spent whole evenings together, in my house, pretending to read plays."

"How do you know?"

"I was there myself more than once. On other occasions Holly told me about it. No doubt she was afraid I'd find out anyway."

"What sort of explanation did she give you?"

"The theory was that she was developing the fellow's acting talent, and her own as well. She claimed she had to have someone to work out with." He grunted. "I shouldn't have been taken in by such a thin story. But she managed to convince me that she cared nothing for him personally. I actually thought she considered him a bit of an outsider, that she was simply using him for her own professional purposes."

I made a left turn onto the highway, and climbed the ramp which rose across lower town. "Did they have professional plans together?"

"Not to my knowledge. Holly was thinking of trying the legitimate stage eventually."

"With your backing?"

"That was the idea, I suppose."

"Did she ever try to persuade you to back Gaines?"

"No. She knew what I thought of the fellow—a cheap gigolo."

"Did she pay him for his company?"

"That would hardly be necessary. I fail to see what you're getting at."

"I'm trying to find out if they had business dealings of any kind, before today's transaction. Was he supplying her with drugs, by any chance?"

He snorted at me: "The notion is ridiculous!"

"It's not as strange as what we know she's done. Leave the personal part out of it and consider. Your wife walked out on an assured fortune, and a man who would give her anything she wanted, in order to share the chances of a wanted criminal. Does it make any sense to you?"

"Yes. I'm afraid it does." He sounded querulous. The dressing in his nose had lightened and thinned his voice. "I'm the reason. I'm physically disgusting to her."

"Did she ever say so?"

"I'm saying so. It's the only possible inference. She married me for my money, but even that couldn't hold her."

I looked sideways at him. Pain leered like skull bones through the flesh of his face. "I was simply a dirty old man pawing at her. I had no right to her."

"You're not exactly an octogenarian. How old are you?"

"We won't discuss it."

"Fifty?"

"Older than that."

"How much money are you worth?"

His eyes veiled themselves like a bird's. "I'd have to ask my accountants."

"Give me a bracket, anyway, to help fill in the picture. Let me assure you, I'm not trying to figure out the size of my retainer. We'll set it at five hundred now, if that's all right with you."

"Very well." He actually smiled, at least on my side. God knew what he was doing with the other side of his face. "I suppose I could realize ten or twelve million if I had to. Why do you think it's important?"

"If your wife had been out for the money, she could have taken you for a lot more than two hundred thousand. Without sharing it with Gaines."

"How?"

"By divorcing you. It happens every day, or don't you read the papers?"

"I've given her no grounds."

"Never an unkind word?"

"Practically never. I was very much in love with my wife. The fact is, I still am."

"Would you take her back if you had the chance?"

"I don't know. I think so." His voice had changed, as his

eyes had changed when I mentioned money. We had left the highway and were approaching the green lane that led to his house. "It's hard to imagine her ever coming back."

But he had leaned forward, urging the car along in wild unconscious hopefulness.

His shoulders slumped as he got out of the car. The house on the cliff had an abandoned air.

Far out over the sea, a flight of birds blew in a changing line like a fragmentary sentence whose meaning was never quite intelligible. All the way in to Beverly Hills I kept thinking about those birds. They'd been too far out for me to identify, but it was the season when certain kinds of sea birds migrated, I didn't know exactly where or why.

*chapter* 18

THE BUILDING WAS long and low, almost hidden from the street by discreet plantings. It had pastel pink walls and lavender doors which opened directly onto a kind of veranda. Michael Speare's name was tastefully printed on one of the doors in lower-case letters, like a line from a modern poem.

It was one of those so-called studio offices, meant to suggest that doing business with the occupants was an aesthetic experience. The girl at the front desk underlined the suggestion. She had Matisse lines, and a voice like violins at a nuptial feast. She used it to tell me that Mr. Speare wasn't back from his afternoon calls. Did I have an appointment?

I said I had, at three. She glanced at the clock imbedded in the blonde mahogany wall. It had no numbers on its face, but it seemed to indicate that it was ten minutes after three.

"Mr. Speare must have been delayed. I expect him at any moment. Will you sit down, sir? And what was your name?"

"William Gunnarson. It still is."

She looked at me like a startled doe, but "Thank you, sir," was all she said. I sat down on an arrangement of molded plywood and glass tubing which turned out to be comfortable enough. The girl returned to her electric typewriter, and began to play kitten on the keys.

I sat and watched her. She had reddish-brown hair, but in other respects her resemblance to Holly May was striking. It was a phenomenon I'd noticed before: whole generations of girls looked like the movie actresses of their period. Perhaps they made themselves over to resemble the actresses. Perhaps the actresses made themselves up to embody some common ideal. Or perhaps they became actresses by virtue of the fact that they already resembled the common ideal.

My eyes were still on the girl, without quite taking her in. She became restless under my stare. Everything about her, varnished hair, shadowed lids, gleaming red lips, breasts that thrust themselves on the attention, was meant to attract stares and hold them. But the girl behind the attractions was uneasy when they worked.

The advertisements didn't tell you what to do next.

She looked up at me, her green eyes defensively hard. A different voice, her own, said: "Well?"

"Sorry, I didn't mean to be obnoxious. I was struck by your resemblance to someone."

"I know. Holly May. People keep telling me that. A lot of good it does me."

"Are you interested in acting?"

"I wouldn't be here if I wasn't. I'd be home in Indiana, to coin a phrase. Raising brats." The nuptial violins in her voice had gone badly out of tune. "Would you be in pictures?"

"I played a starring role in the family album. That was as far as it went."

"The Family Album? I never heard of it. Has it been released?"

"I keep it at home in a trunk," I said. "The family album. Photographs."

"Is that supposed to be funny?"

"It was one of my feebler efforts. Forgive me."

"That's all right," she said magnanimously. "Mr. Speare says I got—I have no sense of humor, anyway." She frowned at the clock. "I wonder what's keeping him."

"I can wait. Do you know Holly May?"

"I wouldn't say I *knew* her. She left town a few months after I got this job. But I used to see her come in and out."

"What sort of person was she?"

"It's hard for me to tell. Some of the girls in the studios thought she was real cool—real down-to-earth, no airs about her and all. At least that was what they said. With me she was always standoffish. I don't think she liked me." After a pause, she said: "Maybe she didn't like me because I look like her. She did a double take the first time she ever saw me."

And after another pause: "Some people think I'm better-looking than her, even. But a fat lot of good it does me. I tried to get Mr. Speare to get me a job standing in for her. He said I didn't know how to handle myself. So I took this course in standing, walking and standing. It cost me a hundred and sixty dollars, and just when I was getting real good at it, she had to go and give up the movie business."

"That was a tough break for you," I said. "I wonder why she left."

"She wanted to get married. But it's still a good question if you ever saw *him*. Why a girl would give up a career to marry *him*. Of course they say he owns half the oil in Canada, but he's just an ugly old man. I wouldn't marry him for all the money in the world."

Her voice and her look were faintly doubtful. She sat with her green gaze resting unconsciously on me, balancing Ferguson's money against his personal charms.

"You know Colonel Ferguson, do you?"

"I saw him once. He marched in here one day last summer. Mr. Speare was in conference with some very important clients, but that made no difference to him. He walked into Mr. Speare's private office and started an argument, right in front of a producing *star*."

"What was the argument about?"

"Her studio didn't want her to get married. Neither did Mr. Speare. You can hardly blame him. She had a chance to be a real big name. But that wasn't good enough for her." She went into meditation again. "Imagine getting the breaks she got, and not even wanting them."

A man in a blue Italian suit and a confidential tie came in breathing dramatically. When I stood up, I was tall enough to look down at the bald spot on top of his sleek dark head.

"Mr. Speare?"

"Yeah. You must be Gunnarson. I'm twenty minutes late. They were taping a new show and a lady who shall be nameless got hysterical when they wouldn't let her use her idiot cards. So I had to hold her hand, in case you wonder where I got the talon wounds. Come in, will you?"

I followed him along a skylit corridor to a room which contained, in addition to office equipment, a couch and a portable bar. He went to the latter like a homing pigeon. "I need a drink. Will you join me?"

"A short bourbon will be fine."

He poured me a long one, and himself another. "Sit down. How do you like the furniture? The drapes? I chose everything myself, I wanted a place where a man can relax as he creates."

"You're an artist, are you?"

"More than that," he said between gulps of bourbon. "I create artists. I make names and reputations."

He flung his empty hand toward the wall beside his desk. It was covered with photographs of faces, the bold, shy, wistful, arrogant, hungry faces of actors. I recognized some of the faces, but didn't see Holly May's among them. Most of them were actors who hadn't been heard of for years.

"How is Holly?" he said, reading my mind. "I took her picture down, in a moment of childish pique. But I still keep it in my desk drawer. Tell her that."

"I will if I see her."

"I thought you were her lawyer."

"I'm her husband's lawyer."

A kind of gray sickness touched his face for an instant. He covered his bald spot with his left hand, as if he feared scalping or had already been scalped; and gulped the remainder of his drink. This gave him strength to clown it. "What does he want? The rest of my blood? Tell him I'm all out of blood, he can go to a blood bank."

"Did he treat you so badly?"

"Did he? He fixed me good. Three years of work, building her up, talking her into parts, keeping her out of trouble, all gone to bloody hell. Just when she was really getting hot, she had to marry *him*. He's a rough man. As you doubtless know if you work for him."

"I don't work for him. I give him legal advice."

"I see." He poured himself another drink. "Does he take it?"

"I'm hoping he will."

"Then advise him to take a running jump in the Pacific Ocean. I know a nice deep place, complete with sharks." He fortified himself with half of his second drink, and said: "Well, let's have it. What does he want from me, and what is it going to cost me?"

"Nothing. I'll be frank with you." But not so very frank. "I came to you more or less on my own, for information."

"What about?"

"Mrs. Ferguson."

He considered this, and drew the conclusion I wanted him to. "How is the marriage working out?"

"It isn't. You'll keep this to yourself, of course."

"Of course," he said, struggling to suppress his glee. "I knew it couldn't last. A doll like Holly, a girl with her future, tying herself to a dodo. Who's divorcing who?"

"It's too early to talk in those terms. Put it this way. Colonel Ferguson married a woman he knew nothing about. Six or seven months later he's decided that perhaps he ought to look into her background. I thought perhaps you could help."

"Let down her back hair, eh? I wouldn't want to do that to

a client, not even an ex-client. Besides," he said with a lop-sided smile and a pass at the top of his head, "what do I get out of it?"

He had a fishy look. I felt no compunction in playing him like a fish. "She's under contract to you, isn't she? If she works?"

"Why should she go back to work, with the kind of settle-ment he can make on her?"

"There won't be any settlement, if he divorces her. Or gets an annulment."

His secret glee flared up again. He thought that we were having a meeting of minds. "I see. What did you say your name was? Bill?"

"Bill."

"Call me Mike, Bill." He went around his desk and slumped in the swivel chair behind it. "What kind of dope do you need?"

"Everything you have. Her background, her conversa-tions, character, personal habits, men in her life."

"Hell," he said. "I can't do that to her. I'm loyal to my cli-ents. On the other hand, she'd be better off working. It isn't *healthy* for a kid like her to retire. Hell, I'd be doing her a favor, doing the industry a favor. Only what if she finds out?"

"She won't. Not even Ferguson will hear what you tell me. It's strictly for background use."

"I hope so, Bill. I *like* the little doll. I wouldn't want any-thing to come between us. You understand that?"

"Very well. Very well, Mike."

"Okay. We understand each other. Anything I say, you quote me, I'll deny it." But the things he wanted to say were bubbling on his lips. "For divorce purposes, I guess you're mainly interested in how much she slept around."

"It isn't the only consideration. It does enter the picture. How much did she?"

"Not a sensational amount. She did like men. Most of her friends were older men."

"Can you mention any names?"

"For filling in the background, that hardly seems necessary."

"You said you had to keep her out of trouble."

"Yeah, sure, it's one of my services to my clients. I try to be like a father to them, Bill. Holly had no father to advise her."

"What kind of trouble did you keep her out of?"

"She wasn't good at handling money. And she only drew four-oh-oh per week. Big ideas on a small salary can play hell with your credit. She had a lot of credit trouble."

"You mean debts?"

He nodded.

"What did she spend her money on?"

"Clothes and gewgaws, mostly."

"How about narcotics?"

He peered at me through narrowed eyelids. "You don't fool around, do you, Bill?"

"I try not to, Mike. Was she on any form of drugs?"

"That I doubt. I couldn't say for sure she wasn't. Some of the damnedest people are. Have you got reason to suspect narcotics?"

"Nothing definite. The idea did occur to me."

"Why, if you don't mind my asking?"

"It's grounds for annulment, for one thing. I don't mean we'd ever take it into court. All we want is something to use for leverage."

"Yeah, sure." We were having another meeting of minds.

"I don't think there's anything in the narcotics angle, though. It's something I watch for, too. I won't represent a hophead, that's my professional ethics. Unless he or she is—" He searched for the right word.

"Successful?"

"Yeah, already established. Then it's not my responsibility."

"Was Holly established when you took her on?"

"Hell, no. She was nowhere, from nothing. That's what grinds me. She'd never had a decent part. She owned the clothes on her back, and that was all. But I saw something there. I got an X-ray eye for talent. I recognized something unique there, I nurtured it like a flower." His voice took on a lilting lyricism. "I got her fixed up with a wardrobe, I taught her to talk. Christ, I *Pygmalionized* her."

"You what?"

"Pygmalionized her. It's a literary illusion, from a play. Like playing God, you know? I even gave her a name and a biography."

"Didn't she have one of her own?"

"We all do, but about hers she wasn't talking. She wouldn't say a word about her family, or where she was from. If she had a family, she was ashamed of them. Or maybe she thought they'd get in her way. When I tried to press her on the point, she flipped her little lid." He paused, idly fingering a copy of *Hollywood Variety* on his desk. "It could be she was scared of her family. She acted scared."

"Do you know anything about them at all?"

"Not a thing, Bill. Far as I know, she never heard from a relative, and didn't want to. She used the Holly May name for all transactions."

"What was her original name?"

"Let me think." He screwed up his face in a chimpanzee

expression. "It was an unusual name, completely impossible for any serious purposes. I dreamed up the Holly May name to suit the personality I tailored for her. Holly May—Holly Day—Holiday. Get the connection? Holiday. A girl you could have fun with." He fell silent.

"Dotty," he said then. "Dotery. Dee-oh-tee-ee-are-wy." He saw the change in my face. "Is there something there?"

"Could be," I said suavely. "Dotery" was one of the names on Mrs. Weinstein's list. "You said that most of Holly's friends, her male friends, were older men?"

"That's right. She liked to be fatherized. A lot of actresses are like that, I don't know why."

"Didn't she have any young men in her life?"

"Oh, sure, she wasn't strictly from Electra. I'd see her with younger escorts on the Strip from time to time. One boy she was very much interested in, for a while. She didn't confide in me, but I notice things."

"When was this?"

"I used to see them last year, last spring and summer, in the clubs. Rubbing knees under the table, stuff like that. I don't know how long it went on."

"What was his name?"

"I don't remember. She introduced us once, when I ran into them in Vegas. But I didn't pay him much attention. To me he was just another bum—the parking-lot attendant with a pan."

"Does the name Larry Gaines mean anything? Or Harry Haines?"

"Maybe. I can't say for sure." He was being careful.

I brought out my picture of Larry Gaines, got up, and laid it on top of the *Variety*. "Do you recognize this man?"

Speare studied the picture. "It's him."

"What were they doing in Las Vegas?"

"Making music."

"You know that for a fact?"

"It stands to reason. I was having a drink with Holly in her hotel room. Dreamface walked in on us—he had his own key. He was going to throw a punch in my direction, till Holly explained who I was." He grinned. "Her personal eunuch."

"All this is very interesting."

"Why? Is it still going on? Are they still making music?"

"I'd better not answer that."

"It's perfectly all right, Bill. I admire a man of discretion. *I'm* depending on you to be discreet. If anything comes out of this, you never talked to me. We don't even know each other."

That suited me.

**《◇《◇《◇《◇《◇《**
**《◇《◇《◇《◇《◇《** *chapter* **19**
**《◇《◇《◇《◇《**

THE TRAFFIC ON Wilshire and San Vicente alternately raced and crawled. It was past five when I got back to my office. Belle Weinstein was waiting at her desk.

She smiled rather thinly at me. "I'm sorry, Mr. Gunnarson, I had no luck with your list. I didn't have a chance to go through all the books. The telephone company tossed me out at five."

I hated to give up on my idea. At bottom, I suppose, I was trying to justify my withholding of evidence from Wills.

Mrs. Weinstein saw the look on my face, and screwed up her own in commiseration. "If it really is so important, I think I know where I can get hold of some more directories. Velma Copley at the answering service has a fairly complete file."

"Try her, will you? It really is important. Just between you and me, it's the only important case I've had to date."

"I'll get over there right away." She rose and took up her purse from the top of the desk. "I nearly forgot, a Dr. Simeon called. He said that he was going home for dinner, but he'll be back at the hospital after dinner, if you want to talk to him."

"Did he say what his findings were?"

"No. Is he the doctor who is looking after Mrs. Gunnarson?"

"God, no." The very suggestion shook me. "Her doctor is Trench."

"I thought so."

"Dr. Simeon is the pathologist who does the official postmortems. I'll meet you here after I have dinner and talk to him."

Sally was sitting under the lamp in the living room with blue knitting in her lap. She was counting stitches, and she didn't glance up. In the light falling softly on her, she looked like a pre-Raphaelite painting of herself. I stood and watched her while she finished counting.

"I'll never learn to knit properly," she said. *"Nimmer und nimmermehr.* And you're no help, looming over me smirking like that."

"I don't loom. I'm not smirking." I bent over and kissed her. "I was just thinking how lucky I am to have you to come home to. How did I ever trick you into marriage?"

"Ha," she said with her wonderful slow smile. "I was the one with the wiles and the stratagems. You'll never know. But what a perfectly lovely thing to say to me. You must have had a good day."

"As a matter of fact it was a lousy day. The craziest mixed-up day of my life. What makes me feel so good now is the contrast."

"We're full of ornate compliments." She gave me a long, encompassing look. "Are you all right, William?"

"I'm all right."

"I mean really. You seem sort of peaked and fixed."

"I'm fixed on you."

But it didn't sound right. I tried for her mouth again. She held me off and studied me. It was good to be looked at by such grave, bright eyes, but it made me nervous. I think I was afraid she'd see too much reflected in my eyes. The thought of Speare intruded like an odor.

"What happened today, Bill?"

"A lot of things. It would take all night to tell you."

"We have all night." Her tone was faintly questioning.

"I'm afraid we don't, love. I have to go out again as soon as we eat."

She caught her reaction and held it stiff on her face. "Oh. Well. Dinner's in the oven. We can eat any time."

"I don't mean to rush things." But I couldn't help looking at my watch.

"Where do you have to go?"

"It would be better if I didn't say."

"What are you mixed up in, Bill?"

"Nothing. It's just another case."

"I don't believe it. Something's happened to you, personally."

"Not directly. I ran into a couple of unusual situations, and people. They bothered me at the time. They don't any more."

"Are you sure?"

"Don't mother me."

I'd meant it to sound light. It sounded sharp. There was a contagion in the air, seeping in like invisible smog which hurt the eyes. I didn't want Sally to be touched by it. I didn't want her even to have to imagine it.

But she blinked as though her eyes had felt its sting. "Heaven forbid that I should mother you. You're a big boy. And I'm a big girl, aren't I? Big, big, big."

She pushed her knitting aside with an abrupt gesture that disturbed me. I was beginning to catch on to the fact that I was in a chancy mood. We both were.

"Here," she said, "give me a hand, will you? Mother Gunnarson is about to get up. It isn't an earthquake, friends and neighbors. It's only Earth-Mother Gunnarson levitating out of her chair. Alley-oop."

She took my hand and rose smiling, but neither of us felt funny. As she walked toward the kitchen, her movements were heavy. My luck flipped like a coin in my mind, and I saw with breathtaking clarity what was on the other side: Sally carried in herself and in her body everything that I cared about in the world. My world hung by a membrane.

I went into the bathroom to wash my hands and face. Tonight it had the quality of a special ritual. I didn't look at my face in the mirror over the sink.

Sally called from the kitchen. "Soup's on! That is, it will be by the time you get to the table, slowpoke."

I went to the kitchen door. "Sit down. Let me serve you for a change. It's time you took it easier."

She grinned over her shoulder. "Don't father me. Dr. Trench says I should move around and do as much as I feel like. Well, I feel like. I enjoy serving you."

She moved past me with two steaming bowls of soup.

"I made the noodles myself," she said when we were seated at the table. "They've been drying on top of the re- frigerator all afternoon. I admit they're a little thick. It takes enormous strength to roll them out thin, I find. Do they taste all right?"

"Fine. I like them thick."

"At least they're not out of a can," she said earnestly. "Eat them up, and then there's a Spanish casserole."

"You're becoming very creative in the kitchen."

"Yes. It's funny, isn't it? I used to abhor cooking. Now I keep getting all sorts of ideas. Even if I can't knit."

"Wait until you've had five or six. You'll be able to knit."

"I have no intention of having five or six. Three's my limit. Three's a horde. Anyway, that would be an awfully roundabout way to learn to knit. Like in Charles Lamb."

"Who?"

"Charles Lamb, on the invention of roast pork. They thought they had to burn the barn down whenever they wanted roast pork. It would be cheaper and simpler to take knitting lessons. Think of the doctor bills it would save, not to mention the wear and tear on my frame."

"Eat your soup," I said. "Your frame needs sustenance. I've finished mine, and you haven't touched yours."

She looked down into her dish, guiltily. "I'm sorry, I

can't eat them, Bill. I spent so long making those noodles, I have a sort of maternal feeling towards them. Like pupae. Maybe I can be more objective about the Spanish casserole. I've never thought much of Spain since I read *For Whom the Bell Tolls.*" She started to get up, and sat down again. "Would you get the casserole out of the oven? I am a little pooped."

"I know. You always go on a talking jag when you're pooped." I looked into her eyes again, and noticed how very large and dark they were, staining even the flesh around them with blueness. "Did anything happen today, Sally?"

She bit her soft lower lip. "I didn't mean to tell you. You have enough on your mind."

"What happened?"

"Nothing, really. Somebody telephoned this afternoon. It gave me a little bit of a jolt."

"What did he say?"

"I don't even know if it was a he. Whoever it was simply *breathed* at me. I could hear that heavy breathing on the line, but not a word. It sounded like an animal."

"What did you do?"

"Nothing. I hung up. Should I have done something?"

"Not necessarily. But if there's more of the same, or if anybody comes to the door—anybody you don't know well—I want you to call the police. Ask for Lieutenant Wills. If he's not available, ask them to send any detective who is, except—"

I hesitated. I'd meant to say "except Sergeant Granada." But I couldn't say it, or ask Sally to say it. There was a certain solidarity among men which couldn't be broken, even under the circumstances—a certain faith which couldn't be violated. The rule of law that a man was innocent until proved guilty had become as much a part of my thinking as my love for Sally.

"Except who?" she said.

"No exceptions. Call the police if anyone bothers you in any way. And you better keep the door locked."

"Is somebody after us?"

"I'm working on a criminal case. Certain threats have been made—"

"Against you?"

"Against several people."

"Was that telephone call last night one of the threats?"

"Yes."

"You should have told me."

"I didn't want to scare you."

"I'm not scared. Honestly. You go ahead and do your job and I'll look after myself. You don't have to worry about me."

"You're a great woman."

"I'm an extremely ordinary woman. You just don't know too much about women yet, Bill. I'm not a Victorian female given to fainting spells at the slightest provocation. I have your service revolver in the bedroom, and if anybody tries anything on Bill G., Jr., I'll fight like a lady tiger."

She spoke calmly enough, but her eyes were blazing, and her cheeks were flushed.

"Don't get het up, Sally. Nothing is going to happen."

I went around the table and held her head against me. It was precious, like golden fleece in my hands. Death had peered at her through the membrane like a thug in a rubber mask. But I realized obscurely that I couldn't have and hold her by sitting at home. In order to keep what you had, you had to risk it.

"You know," she said between my hands, "I am getting hungry. Never send to ask for whom the casserole cooks. It cooks for me."

**《◆《◆《◆《◆《**
**《◆《◆《◆《◆《** *chapter* **20**
**《◆《◆《◆《◆《**

I FOUND DR. SIMEON in the cold room. He was laying out cutting tools on a stainless-steel table. Light from a ceiling lamp splashed on his clean white smock like luminous paint. The chrome instruments, knives and saws, gleamed under his rubber-gloved fingers. Almost hidden by his shadow, a body lay under a sheet on a second table against the back wall.

"Come in," he said hospitably. "I'm afraid I gave you a rough moment this morning. We all contain the same organs, the same old blood and guts, but we don't like to be reminded of it. We like to imagine that we're simply inflated skins, full of helium or some other ethereal substance."

"I was taken by surprise."

"I know. The shock of mortality. Don't feel too badly about it. I had a horrible week in medical school, when we started dissecting cadavers."

My gaze strayed, against my will, to the body on the table behind him. One of the feet protruded from under the sheet. There was blood on the toenails.

"I promised to get in touch with you," Simeon was saying, "after I'd done a thorough job on Broadman. I finished him up this afternoon, but you're a hard man to reach."

"I had to go into Beverly Hills. I appreciate your going to all this trouble."

"No trouble. In fact, I owe you something. You saved me from making a mistake. I don't say I wouldn't have caught it in the normal course. In fact, I would have, when I got around to making a chemical analysis of the blood. But I wouldn't have caught it so soon."

"What did Broadman die of?"

"Asphyxia."

"He was strangled?"

Simeon shook his head. "I've found no evidence of strangulation. The neck structures are intact. There's no sign of external violence at all, apart from the injuries to the back of the head. But the internal evidence points conclusively to asphyxia: edema of the lungs, some dilation of the right side of the heart, some petechial hemorrhaging of the pleura. There's no doubt at all that Broadman died from lack of oxygen."

"How did it happen?"

"That's a difficult question. There's a possibility that it was an accident, if Broadman lapsed into unconsciousness and swallowed his tongue, as they say. The possibility of accident is remote. The tongue was in a normal position when I examined him. I'd say that he was smothered in some way."

"In what way?"

"I wish I knew, Mr. Gunnarson. Since he was in a weakened state, it's possible that someone simply placed a hand over his mouth and nostrils, and cut off his air. I've seen infants that were smothered in that way. Never a grown man."

"Wouldn't the marks show on his face?"

"They usually do, yes. But as I said, he was in a weakened

condition, perhaps unconscious. Not too much pressure would be required."

"Have you passed on your findings to the police?"

"Naturally. Lieutenant Wills was very much interested. So was Sergeant Granada." His eyes were bland. "Granada was in here just before dinner."

"Inquiring about Broadman?"

"Incidentally he was inquiring about Broadman. But his main interest was in the other cadaver."

"Donato?"

"Donato's wife. I can understand Granada's interest. He was the one who found her."

I did a moral double-take that rocked me on my heels. "Donato's wife?"

"That's correct. She took an overdose of sleeping pills. At least that's what Granada thinks."

"What do you think, Doctor?"

"I'll let the condition of the organs tell me what to think. I do know this. I didn't give her enough sleeping pills to make a fatal dose. It's possible she had some already, though, or got hold of some more."

He uncovered the body. It glistened like a fish thrown up on an iron shore. The red on the tips of the feet was toe-nail polish. Secundina's face was very deep in sleep.

"And now I give you fair warning." Simeon picked up a curved knife with a sharp point. "You'd better get out of here, unless you want to see me make a butterfly incision. To an untrained eye, it ain't pretty."

I turned away as he raised the knife. Tony Padilla was standing in the doorway.

"My God, is he going to cut her?" His voice was incredulous. His eyes had a fixed stare.

"It won't hurt her, Tony. She's dead."

"I know that. Frankie heard it on the radio."

He brushed past me and looked down at the dead woman. Through half-closed eyelids she regarded him without fear or favor.

He touched her naked shoulder. "You don't want to cut her, Doc."

"It's necessary, I'm afraid. In cases of violent death, or death from unknown causes, an autopsy is normal procedure. Under the present circumstances, it's absolutely imperative."

"How did she get herself killed?"

"If we knew that, I wouldn't *have* to cut her. Sergeant Granada believes she took an overdose of sleeping pills."

"What has Granada got to do with it?"

"He found her. He went to her house to ask her some questions—"

"What about?"

The abruptness of the question made Simeon raise his eyebrows, but he answered it civilly. "About her husband's activities, I believe. He found her on the bed, with her children crying around her. Apparently she was dead, but he couldn't be sure, so he rushed her here in an ambulance. Unfortunately she was dead."

"Just like Broadman, eh?"

Simeon shrugged and looked up impatiently. "I'm sorry, I don't have time to canvass all these issues with you. Lieutenant Wills and Sergeant Granada are in a hurry for my results."

"Why? Don't they know the answers already?" Padilla spoke from his whole jerking body, as a dog does when it barks.

"I don't know what that's supposed to mean." Simeon turned to me. "I gather this chap is a friend of yours. Explain to him that I'm a pathologist, will you—a scientist? I can't discuss police matters—"

"You think I'm stupid?" Padilla cried.

"You're acting stupidly," I said. "If you have no respect for the living, show some for the dead."

Padilla became silent. With an apologetic glance at the dead woman, he turned and trudged out of the room. I followed him out into the corridor. "I didn't know you cared so much for her, Tony."

"Me, either. I used to think I hated her for a long time. I used to see her on the streets, in the bars, with her husband, with Granada. I always got mad when I saw her. And then last night when Gus was knocked off, I thought, I can marry her now. It came to me all of a sudden: that I could marry her now. I would of, too."

"Have you ever married?"

"No, and I never will."

The metal door had closed behind us. He looked at it as if life was on the other side, and the automatic door had cut him off from life.

"This is a bad time to make decisions," I said. "Why don't you go back to work now? Forget about death and destruction."

"Sure, and let Granada get away with it."

"You sound pretty sure he's guilty."

"Aren't you, Mr. Gunnarson?"

It wasn't an easy question to answer. I was less sure than I had been. I knew that Granada had shot Donato. I could imagine him killing Broadman. The thought of him killing Secundina, a woman he was said to have loved, seemed impossible to me. And Tony's very insistence on his guilt aroused my occupational reaction, which was doubt.

"I'm not at all sure of his guilt. I certainly don't think you should go around making accusations."

"I see." His voice was wooden. He'd asked a question of a man and been answered by a profession. Which was the way I wanted it for the time being.

I offered Padilla a cigarette. He refused it. I sat down on a bench against the wall. Padilla remained standing. An uneasy silence set in, and continued for quite a long time.

"You could be right, Mr. Gunnarson," he said at last. "It's been a bad day for me. I go along calm and cool for months at a time, and then something happens, and I lose my head. You think I'm punchy, maybe? I took a lot of blows in the head when I was a kid fighting."

"No. I think you're human."

After another long silence, he said: "I can use a cigarette, since you were so kind to offer. I left mine out at the club behind the bar."

I gave him a cigarette and lit it for him. Before it had burned up, Dr. Simeon opened the metal door and glanced out. "There you are. I didn't know whether or not you were waiting. I have some preliminary findings. I'd say it's practically certain she died in the same way Broadman did, of asphyxia."

Padilla spoke up. "Does that mean she was gassed?"

"That's one form of asphyxia. There are several. In the present case, as in Broadman's, indications are that death resulted from simple lack of oxygen. There's a similar edema—a waterlogged condition—in the pleural cavity. And again, there are no external marks of violence. I haven't got to the neck structures yet, but I'll venture the opinion that she was smothered." Simeon stepped out into the corridor. "I'd better phone this in to Wills before I continue."

I stood beside Simeon's desk while he tried to reach Wills, and then Granada. After a baffling five minutes, he hung up. "Can't reach either of them. Well, they're the ones who were in the hurry."

"Did she take the sleeping pills?" I asked him.

"There are indications of it. I should be able to tell you more about that later. Now I'd better get back to the lady. She may have something more she wants me to know."

Padilla glared at him from the doorway, outraged by his levity. Simeon appeared not to notice. He went out, and his rubber-soled shoes whispered away along the corridor.

I said to Padilla: "Let's go down to Secundina's place."

Evening light ran in the alley like red-stained water. The berries on the Cotoneaster tree were the color of nail polish and blood. Secundina's sister came to the door when we knocked. The baby was sleeping in her arm.

She looked at Padilla with hard eyes. "You again."

"Me again."

"What do you want this time?"

"Ask you some questions, Arcadia. Don't be like that."

"I answered all the questions. What's the use? The old woman says they wanted her dead in the hospital, they gave her knockout pills. Maybe she's right."

"They don't do things like that at the hospital," I said.

"How do I know what they do there?" She held the child away from me, with her lifted hand between my eyes and his face.

"This is Mr. Gunnarson," Padilla said. "He won't give the little one *mal ojo*. He is a lawyer trying to find out what happened here today." He turned to me. "This is Mrs. Torres, Secundina's sister."

Arcadia Torres failed to acknowledge the introduction. Her intense, dark gaze was focused on Padilla. "What happened today? Secundina died today. You know it."

"Did she do it herself, with sleeping pills?"

"She took the sleeping pills from the hospital, the whole bottle. The copper—the policeman—he said when he came back here, there wasn't enough pills to kill her. But she's dead, ain't she?"

"What would make her do such a thing?" Padilla said.

"She was crazy about that Gus of hers, I guess. And she was scared. When she got feeling like that, she'd drink down anything. Mrs. Donato said that she had *susto*."

"What do you mean by anything, Mrs. Torres?"

"Anything she could get. Sleeping pills or GI gin, they call it, or the cough medicine. They had her name on a list at all the drugstores. Indian list, they call it."

"Did she take other drugs when she could get them?"

Her beautiful drooping mouth set itself in stubborn lines. Her Madonna eyes took on the dusty glassiness that I had seen in her sister's eyes.

"I don't want to talk about it."

"Did she have a habit?" Padilla asked her softly.

"Not any more she didn't. She was off of it. Maybe she smoked a little marijuana, like on a party."

"You mentioned that she was frightened," I said. "What was she frightened of?"

"Getting killed."

"So she tried to kill herself? It doesn't make sense."

"You didn't know Secundina."

"But you did, Mrs. Torres. Do you honestly believe she killed herself, or tried to?"

"That's what the old woman says. She says that my sister is burning in hell for it now."

"Is Mrs. Donato here?"

Arcadia shook her head. "She went to the *albolaria*. She says there is a curse on the family which only the *albolaria* can take off."

"Were you here when they took her away in the ambulance?"

"I saw them."

"Was she alive then?"

"I thought she was alive."

"Who called the ambulance?"

"The policeman."

"Sergeant Granada?"

She nodded.

"What was Granada doing here?"

"He wanted to talk to her about Gus."

"How do you know?"

"She told me. He sent her a message by the corner grocery. But when he got here, she was out, lying on the bed. He went in and found her."

"Did you see them together?"

"After he called the ambulance, I did."

"And she was alive then?"

"She was breathing, I think. But she wouldn't wake up."

"Was she afraid of Granada?"

"I don't know. She was afraid of a lot of things."

Padilla spoke sharply to her. "Answer the question!"

She gave her head a violent shake which left it tilted on her neck away from me. She answered Padilla in Spanish.

"What does she say, Tony?"

"She doesn't want to talk to you any more, I'm sorry. When a bad thing like this happens we—I mean they turn against people, you know, people from uptown. Maybe if you let me talk to her?"

"Go ahead. I'll wait in the car."

I smoked a couple of cigarettes and watched the daylight dying on Pelly Street. Dark boys in twos and threes were prowling the sidewalk. The neon signs of the bars and cafés hung like *ignis fatuus* on the twilight. Jukebox music reached my ears like distant battlecries and lamentations. In competition with it, a chorus of voices rose behind the painted windows of a storefront church. "Telephone to Jesus," they were singing.

Padilla emerged from the alley. His movements were furtive, like a dog's that has been kicked. He looked up and down the street, pretending for an instant that he couldn't see me.

I got out of the car. "Did she do any more talking to you?"

"Yeah." He moved uneasily, on his toes, his left shoulder slightly raised. "I don't get it. She says it was Holly May that Secundina was scared of."

"Did she name her?"

"She didn't have to. It was her, all right. Secundina saw her with Gaines and Gus Donato the night before last, the night she disappeared. They had a reefer party up in the mountains."

"Where in the mountains?"

"Arcadia doesn't know that. She only knows what Secundina told her. Gus had marijuana contacts and he provided the weed. Secundina went along for the ride. It was quite a party, the way she told it to her sister. Holly was picking fights with people, yelling that she was the greatest actress in the world. Also, she had the most beautiful figure in the world. At one point she took off her clothes to prove it. Gus made a play for her, and Secundina stepped in, and Holly broke off the end of a bottle and went for her. I don't get it. She never acted like that on liquor."

Padilla dropped his protective left shoulder and stood back on his heels.

"Was Holly smoking marijuana?"

"She was certainly high on something."

"It changes people sometimes, Tony. It acts like a trigger on unstable people."

"Yeah. I know, I've tried it." He caught himself. "I mean, away back when." His eyes were shabby.

"Where?"

"When I was a kid."

"In town here?"

"Yeah." He looked up and down the street. "I didn't mean to tell you that, Mr. Gunnarson. It's something I'm not proud of. I ran with the ice-plant gang for a while, before I caught on to what it was all about. We used to smoke the stuff when we could get it."

"Did you know Gus in those days?"

"Him and Secundina, too."

"Granada?"

"Yeah. I was there the night that Gus and him had their big fight. I could have stopped them, I was boxing in those days. But, hell, I let them fight. I was hoping they'd knock each other off. No such luck."

"What did you have against them?"

The color left his face. After an ivory interval, he said: "Now wait a minute, Mr. Gunnarson. You wouldn't be trying to tie me in with all this." He glanced over his shoulder into the shadowed alley. "That was all years ago. I was just a crazy kid out of high school, looking for kicks."

"So was Granada, wasn't he?"

"Him and Gus was different. I've always hated the bastards, both of them."

"On account of Secundina?"

"Yeah." The blood rushed back into his face and turned it
cordovan. "I used to know her way back in Sacred Heart
School. She was in the third grade, I was in the sixth. She
was just a bright-eyed little kid, not a care in the world.
Her mother sent her in clean dresses, ribbons in her hair.
Christ, she played an angel in the Nativity. Look at her
now."

"You can't blame the men in her life. People grow up."

"Down," he said. "They grow down." He grimaced at the
sidewalk as if he could see hell under it.

"I want you to think about it, Tony. Could you be mistaken about Granada?"

"Yeah," he answered slowly, "I could be mistaken. I could
be wrong about anybody, I guess. I'm sorry if I gave you a
bum steer."

I didn't answer him. I was sorrier.

"I got carried away, maybe, too many things at once. I
get these days when my whole damn life rears up on its
hind legs and smacks me."

He threw a short left hook at an invisible opponent. His
fist completed its arc at the side of his own jaw. He
half turned toward the alley.

"Where are you off to, Tony? Shouldn't you be getting
back to work?"

"Arcadia wants me to stay with her. She put Torres in the
clink for nonsupport. Now she's scared to be alone herself.
She thinks maybe she's getting *susto*, too."

"What is *susto?*"

"Bad sickness. The doctor says it's psychological, like. My mother says it's from an evil spirit."

"Which do you say?"

"I dunno. They taught in high school there was no such thing as evil spirits. But I dunno." His eyes were like occulted lights.

He moved away into the mouth of the alley. I drove back to my office on automatic pilot. My thoughts remained with Tony and Arcadia, caught in the ambiguous darkness between two towns, two magics.

*chapter* 21

MY OWN NAME, WM. GUNNARSON, stenciled on the stucco wall at the head of my parking slot, reminded me where I was and what I was doing. I turned off the engine and used my key to the back door of the building. There was a light behind the office door.

"I've been trying to get in touch with you," Mrs. Weinstein said. She looked tired, and her smile was wan. "I believe I've located the place you're looking for. It's a small city called Mountain Grove, inland from here about sixty miles, in the Valley. More than half of the names check out, and I have their addresses for you."

She handed me a carefully typed list. There were street and telephone numbers for six of the names, including an

Adelaide Haines who lived on Canal Street. I felt a rush of satisfaction. I had been needing it.

"No Dotery?" I said, and spelled it out.

"No. It was an old telephone book, though, that they had at the answering service. While I was there, incidentally, some man called for you. Colonel Ferguson. He wants you to come out to his house, he said. He intimated that it was very urgent."

"How long ago was this?"

"Twenty minutes or so. I just got here."

"You're a treasure, Belle."

"I know. *Buried* treasure. Do you want to tell me what it's all about?"

"Tomorrow, perhaps, when I get back from Mountain Grove."

She looked at me with concern. "You're not leaving town without going home? Mrs. G. has a stiff upper lip, but you don't want to strain it."

"You've done me a big favor. Would you do me another?"

"I know. Spend the night with Mrs. G. I could see that one coming a long way off."

"Will you?"

"I'll be glad to, Bill." She seldom called me by my first name. "*You* take care of yourself. I like working for you, in spite of all the alarms and excursions."

The floodlights were burning outside Ferguson's house, throwing Chirico shadows along the cliff and up the driveway. A dusty late-model Ford stood in the turnaround. I thought I knew it, and looked in. It was a rented car, according to the registration slip. A light hat with a sunburst band lay on the front seat.

When Ferguson opened the door, the short and passionate man from Miami was standing close to his elbow. He said to Ferguson: "Who did you say this is?"

"Mr. Gunnarson, my local attorney. This is Mr. Salaman, Mr. Gunnarson."

"I know him."

"That's right," Salaman said. "At the Foothill Club, in the parking lot. Why didn't you tell me you were Ferguson's lawyer? We could of got things settled there and then." He smiled without showing his teeth.

Ferguson looked drained and miserable. "Let's not stand around in doorways, gentlemen."

We followed him into the big room that overlooked the ocean. Salaman took up a position in the middle of the room, like a proprietor. The swelling in his armpit was quite prominent in the light, radiating wrinkles across his gabardine jacket.

"What is this all about?" I said.

He nodded peremptorily at Ferguson. "Tell him."

Ferguson said in a husky voice: "Mr. Salaman is a businessman from Florida. He claims that my wife owes him a good deal of money."

"Claims is not the word. She owes it and she's going to pay it."

"But my wife isn't here. I told you I have no idea where she is."

"Don't give me that." Salaman wagged his head with sad tolerance. "You know where she is, you'll tell me. If you don't, we'll run her down. We got an organization behind us. But that would be doing it the hard way."

"I understood you were fond of the lady," I said.

"Not sixty-five grand worth. Anyway," he added delicately, "we won't go into the sex angle in front of her old man here. I don't wanna interfere with anybody's legal marriage. All I want is my sixty-five thousand."

"Sixty-five thousand for what?"

"Value received. That's what it says on the notes. Don't think she didn't sign notes."

"Let me see the notes."

"I don't carry them with me. But get it through your head, it's strictly legal. As you will find out if you make me go into court. But you don't want that."

"No," Ferguson said, "we don't want that."

"What did the money go for?"

Salaman flipped his hand palm upward, pointing the thumb at Ferguson. "Tell him."

Ferguson swallowed a bitter grin. It almost choked him. "Holly lost some money gambling shortly before we were married. She didn't have the cash to cover her losses. She borrowed from a finance company which is run by a Miami gambling corporation. Mr. Salaman is the major stockholder. The amount was less than fifty thousand, originally, but apparently the interest has mounted up."

"Interest and service charges. It's more than six months overdue. And it costs money to collect money. Now an op— a man in your position, Colonel, I'd think you'd want to pay up."

I said: "Would this be blackmail, by any chance?"

Salaman looked hurt. "I'm sorry you used that word, Mister. If you're smart, though, you'll tell your boss to pay up. It wasn't just the tables the lady blew her money on."

Ferguson had turned to the window. He spoke with his face hidden, but I could see his ghostly reflection forcing out the words. "Some of the money went for drugs, Gunnarson. If we can believe this man, she started gambling to procure money for drugs. She got in deeper and deeper."

"What drugs?"

Salaman shrugged his shoulders. "I wouldn't know. I'm no pusher." He smiled his sealed smile. "All I know is what I read in the papers. Like what it said in the columns about her and the lifeguard. *This* would make a nice splash in the papers."

Ferguson turned back to the room. He was as pale as his reflection. "What is this?"

"It sounds like blackmail to me," I said.

Salaman said: "The hell it is. Your boy here isn't too bright, pops. My advice to you is trade him in on another mouthpiece but fast. You need a boy that's hep to the public-relations angles, that's what makes and breaks. I got a right to protect my legitimate interests."

"I understand that," Ferguson said with a dismal look at me. "I don't have the money on hand."

"Tomorrow will do. Tomorrow at the latest. I can't sit around in this burg while you make up your mind. I got to get back to some action. How about this time tomorrow?"

"What if I don't pay then?"

"Your little doll won't be making no more movies. Maybe horror movies." Salaman showed his teeth. They were bad.

Ferguson said in a thin and desperate voice: "You're holding her somewhere, aren't you? I'll gladly pay you if you give her back."

"Are you nuts?" Salaman swung around to face me. "Is this a nuthouse? Is the old guy nuts?"

"You haven't answered his question."

"Why should I? It don't make sense. If I had Holly, she'd be here doing the asking. On her knees."

"You implied you could put your hands on her."

"Sooner or later, sure. I can send out a private circular to all the gambling spots, all the major bookies. Sooner or later she'll turn up at one of them. But the longer I have to wait, the more it costs. And it ain't only money I mean, bear it in mind."

"My client and I want to discuss this in private."

"Sure you do." Salaman flung out his hand in a generous arc. "Discuss it all night if you want. Just come up with the right answer by tomorrow. And don't try to get in touch with me. I'll be in touch with you." He saluted us with two fingers and walked out. I heard the Ford go up the drive.

Ferguson broke the silence. "What am I going to do?"

"What do you want to do?"

"Pay them, I suppose."

"Do you have the money?"

"I can phone Montreal. It's not the money I'm concerned about." He added after another silence: "I don't know what sort of a woman I married."

"You didn't marry a saint, that's evident. Your wife is having her troubles. She was having them before she became your wife. Have you considered cutting your losses?"

"I don't follow, Gunnarson. I'm not feeling myself."

He sat down on a long chair, his head resting limply on the back, one leg dragging on the floor.

"You're not responsible for her debts, unless you want to be."

"I can't let her down," he said weakly.

"She let you down."

"Perhaps. But I still care for her. I don't care about the money. Why is everything always put to me in terms of money?"

There was no answer to that question, except that he had

money, and had used it to marry a woman half his age. The question was addressed to the ceiling, anyway. He announced to the ceiling: "Damn it, I hate to give in to their dirty threats. But I'm going to pay them their dirty money."

"That may not be wise. It could lead to a long series of payments. It's possible, in fact, that you've paid them once already."

He sat up blinking. "How?"

"The money you delivered to Gaines and your wife today— it may be the first installment and this is the second."

"You think that Salaman is behind the kidnapping?"

"It wasn't a kidnapping, Colonel. That seems to be clear by now. I keep getting further evidence that your wife conspired with Gaines to collect that money. She may have needed it to pay these gambling debts, if these really are gambling debts. Did she ever mention them to you?"

"No."

"Or ask you for large sums of money?"

"She didn't have to. I provided her with ample funds for her needs."

"Maybe she didn't think so. A drug habit, for instance, can be terribly expensive."

"You may think I'm a fool," he said, "but I simply cannot believe that she is an addict, or ever was. I've been living with her here for six months, and never noticed the slightest indication."

"No peculiar-smelling cigarettes around the house?"

"Holly doesn't even smoke tobacco."

"Does she possess a hypodermic syringe? Have needle-marks on her arms or legs?"

"The answer is no to both questions. Her limbs were as clean as a peeled willow."

"Did she use barbiturates?"

"Very occasionally. I disapproved of them. Holly often said that whiskey was the only tranquillizer she needed."

"She drank quite heavily, didn't she?"

"We both did."

"Drinking doesn't often go with drug addiction. She may have stopped using drugs and started using alcohol as a substitute. Has she always been a heavy drinker?"

"No. When I first met her in Vancouver, she hardly touched the stuff. I suppose I taught her to drink. She was rather—she was frightened at first, in our relationship. Drinking made it easier for her. But she hasn't been drinking nearly so much in the last few weeks."

"Pregnant women usually do cut down."

"That's it." Ferguson's eyes were moist and bright in his craggy face. "She was afraid of injuring the child—Gaines's child!"

"How do you know it's his? It could be yours."

"No." He shook his head despondently. "I know where I stand, I won't try to blink the facts. I had no right to expect so much out of life. I tell you, it's a judgment on me. I've had it coming to me, all these years."

"Judgment for what?"

"My moral rottenness. Years ago I got a young girl pregnant, then I turned my back on her. When Holly turned her back on me, I was only getting my just deserts."

"That's not rational thinking."

"Is it not? My father used to say that the book of life is like a giant ledger. He was right. Your good actions and your bad actions, your good luck and your bad luck, balance out. Everything comes back to you. The whole thing works like clockwork."

He made a downward guillotining gesture with the edge

of his hand. "I threw that little girl in Boston out of my life, gave her a thousand dollars to shut her up. And when I did that, I condemned myself. Condemned myself to the hell of money, do you understand me? In my life everything comes back to money. But Good Christ, I'm not made of money. I care for other things. I care for my wife, no matter what she's done to me."

"What do you think she's done to you?"

"She's defrauded and betrayed me. But I can forgive her, honestly. I owe it not only to her. I owe it to that little girl in Boston. You don't know me, Gunnarson. You don't know the depths of evil in me. But I have depths of forgiveness in me, too."

He had been taking a moral beating, and wasn't handling it well. I said: "We'll talk it over tomorrow. Before you make any final decisions, you'll want all the facts about your wife and her activities."

He closed his fists on his knees and cried hoarsely: "I don't care what she's done!"

"Surely that will depend on the extent of her crimes."

"No. Don't say that."

"You still want her back, don't you?"

"If I can have her. Do you think there's a chance?" His hands turned over and opened and clutched air.

"I guess there's always a chance."

"You don't see any hope in the situation," Ferguson stated. "But I do. I know myself, I know my wife. Holly's a lost child who has done some foolish things. I can forgive her, and I feel sure we can make a go of it."

His eyes shone with a false euphoric brightness. It made me uneasy.

"There's not much use in talking about that now. I'm on my

way out of town. I'm hoping to find out something more
definite about her background and her connection with
Gaines. Will you hold off everything until tomorrow? Including too much thinking."

"Where are you going?"

"A town in the valley, Mountain Grove. Did Holly ever
speak of the place?"

"I don't believe so. Did she use to live there?"

"Possibly. I'll report to you in the morning. Will you be
all right tonight?"

"Of course," he said. "I haven't given up hope, not by a
long shot. I'm full of hope."

Or of despair so sharp, I thought, that he couldn't feel
its edge biting into him.

*chapter* 22

THE MOUNTAINS WHICH GAVE the town
its name lay on the horizon to the west and south like
giants without eyes. Against their large darkness and the
larger darkness of the sky, the lights on the main street
flung a meretricious challenge.

It was like a hundred other hinterland main streets,
with its chain stores and clothing stores closed for the night,
restaurants and bars and movie houses still open. Perhaps
there were more people on the sidewalks, more cars in the
road, then you'd see in the ordinary town after ten at night.
Most of the pedestrians were men, and many of them wore

the hats and high-heeled boots of ranch hands. The young men at the wheels of the cars drove like an army in rout.

I stopped at a gas station, bought two dollars worth of gas out of my last ten-dollar bill, and asked the proprietor to let me consult his telephone directory. He was an old man with a turkey-red face and eyes like chips of mica. He watched me through the window of his office to make sure that I didn't steal the directory off its chain.

It said that Mrs. Adelaide Haines lived at 225 Canal Street, which was the address that Mrs. Weinstein had set down. The red-faced man told me where it was. I drove across town at the legal speed limit, fighting down my excitement.

Canal Street was lined with trees and houses a generation old. Number 225 was a wooden bungalow with a light on the porch, filtered green through a passion vine which grew thick to the eaves. A card in the front window became legible as I mounted the front steps: VOICE AND PIANO TAUGHT.

I pressed the bell push beside it, but no audible bell rang. I knocked on the screen door. The holes in the screen had been ineffectually mended with what looked like hairpins. An aging woman, for whom the idea of hairpins had prepared me, opened the inside door.

She was tall and fine-boned and thin to the point of emaciation. Her face and neck were roughened by years of valley sun, and the fingers at her throat were conscious of it. In spite of this, she had some style, and a kind of desperate, willful youthfulness. Her thick black hair was coiled on her head like sleeping dangerous memories.

"Mrs. Haines?"

"Yes. I am Mrs. Haines." The cords in her throat worked like pulleys to produce the syllables. "Who are you, sir?"

I gave her my card. "I'm William Gunnarson, a lawyer from Buenavista. You have a son named Harry, I believe."

"Henry," she corrected me. "I called him Harry when he was a child. His grownup name is Henry."

"I see."

Threading her genteel accents was a wild and off-key note. I looked at her face more closely. She was smiling, but not as mothers smile when they speak of their sons. Her lips seemed queerly placed against the bone structure. They were open and stretched to one side, in an off-center leer.

"Henry isn't at home, as you probably know." She looked past me at the dark street. "He hasn't lived at home for years. But you know that. He's living in Buenavista."

"May I come in, Mrs. Haines? You may be interested in what I have to say. I know I'd like to talk to you."

"I'm all alone here. But of course you realize that. We won't have a chaperone."

A nervous giggle escaped the hand which she pressed to her mouth a second too late. Lipstick came off on her fingers. They were vibrating like a tuning fork as she unlocked the screen door.

Her perfume flooded over me as I entered. She was wearing so much perfume that it hinted at panic.

She ushered me into a fair-sized front room which was obviously her studio. An upright grand piano as old as the house stood against one inner wall. A Siamese cat jumped straight up into the air from a mohair armchair which was in process of being disemboweled. The cat hung in the air for a long instant, glaring at me with its hazel eyes, then reached for the arm of the chair with stretching legs. It landed on the piano stool with all four feet together like a mountain goat, struck one angry chord on the keyboard, and rebounded to the piano top. There it slunk and slalomed among metronomes and music racks, and crouched behind a old-fashioned photograph of a girl in a cloche hat.

On second glance, it was a very fine photograph. The arrogant good looks of the girl jumped to the eye like a mask of pride and pain.

"That was taken in San Francisco," Mrs. Haines said conversationally, "by San Francisco's leading photographer. I was very beautiful, wasn't I? I gave recitals in Sacramento and Oakland. The Oakland *Tribune* said I had great promise. Then, unfortunately, I lost my voice. One misfortune followed another. My second husband fell from a window just as he was about to make a killing on the stock market. My third husband deserted me. Yes, deserted me. He left me to support our infant son as best I could with what remained of my music."

It was a speech from a play, a shadow play in the theater of her mind. She stood by the piano and declaimed it without feeling or gestures, in a monotone.

"But you know all this, don't you? I don't want to borrow you—bore you with my sorrows. In any case, the clouds have silver linings. Hell has its hindrances." She smiled her disorganized smile. "Sit down, don't be bashful, let me make you some coffee. I still have my silver percolator, at least."

"No thanks."

"Afraid I'll poison your cup?" Perhaps it was meant to be a humorous remark. It fell with a thud, and she went on as if it had been uttered by someone else, a third person in the room.

"As I was saying, life has its compensations. Among my compensations, my voice is coming back, as happens in a woman's prime occasionally." She sang a cracked scale to prove it, sat down at the piano, and struck a cluster of notes as discordant as the cat's chord. "Since my pupils dropped away—none of them had any talent anyway— I've had an opportunity to work with my voice again, and even do some composing. Words and music come to me together, out of thin air. Like that."

She snapped her fingers, struck another discord, and burst into improvised song. "Out of thin air, I don't know where, You brought me a love so rich and rare. That's two songs in five minutes."

"What was the other one?"

"No chaperone," she said. "It started to sing itself to me as soon as I said those words." She raised her voice again to the same tuneless tune. "We're all alone, No chaperone, And no one to bother on the telephone."

She laughed and turned on the piano stool to face me. The cat drifted onto her shoulder like a piece of brown floating fur, and ran down her body to the floor, where it stationed itself between her high-heeled feet.

"He's jealous," she said with her nervous giggle. "He can tell that I'm attracted to you."

I sat on the arm of the disemboweled chair and looked as forbidding as I knew how. "I wanted to talk to you about your son, Mrs. Haines. Do you feel up to talking about him?"

"Why not?" she said. "It's a pleasure. I really mean it. The neighbors don't believe me when I tell them how well Henry is doing. They think I can't tell the difference between my dreams. In fact, I seldom have an opportunity to converse with a person of cultivation. The neighborhood has gone downhill, and I'm seriously thinking of moving."

"Moving where?" I said, in the hope of switching her mind to a more realistic track.

"Buenavista, perhaps. I'd like that, but Henry's opposed. He doesn't want me getting in his way, I realize that. And I'm not equal to the high-flying people that he has the opportunity to rub elbows with. Perhaps I'll just stay here and renovate the house." She looked around the shabby room. The rug was threadbare, the wallpaper was fading, spiders had fogged the corners of the ceiling. "God knows it needs it."

The dream was wearing thin at the edges. I chopped at it with the harshest words I could bring myself to speak to her. "What are you going to use for money?"

"Henry is generous with me, are you surprised? I hate to take money from him. He is, after all, a young man on his way up. He needs fluid capital, which is why I keep working at my little songs. One of them will be a hit, you know, and then I won't be a burden on Henry's shoulders. I fully expect to write a song which will sell a million copies. I'm not a stupid woman. And I recognize other intelligent people at sight. But you know that."

Her assumption that I knew whatever she knew was the most disquieting thing about her, of several disquieting things. I sat there caught between pity and something close to panic, wondering what Henry's childhood had been like. Had he walked on the walls of her fantasies and believed they were solid earth? Or doubted the earth itself when his feet broke through the wallboard?

"How does Henry make his money?"

"He's in business," she answered with satisfaction. "Buying and selling art objects to a private clientele. It's just a temporary thing, of course. Henry hasn't given up his own artistic aspirations, as I'm sure you are aware. But Mr. Speare told him the time wasn't ripe for him yet. He needed further study. So Henry went into business, he has a fine eye for value. Which it's only fair to say he inherited from his mother." Her smile was wide and toothy, a sudden manifestation which her mouth could hardly contain. "Do you know Henry well?"

"Not as well as I'd like to. Were you referring to Michael Speare the agent?"

"Yes. Henry hoped that Mr. Speare would represent him. But Mr. Speare said he needed more work before he made his professional debut. Art is a hard taskmistress, as I have good reason to know."

She spread out her fingers and flexed them several times. The cat rose on its hind legs and batted upward, playfully, at her hands.

"Down, Harry," she said. "I call him Harry."

I said from far left field: "Did Harry make contact with Speare through Hilda Dotery?"

"Henry," she corrected me. "I prefer not to discuss that. There are certain people I will not sully my tongue with. The Doterys are at the head of my personal blacklist."

"But Henry knows Hilda Dotery? They were in a high-school play together, weren't they?"

Without obvious alteration, her smile had become an angry grin. "I won't discuss her. She brought filth into my house. Henry was a good clean-living young man before she corrupted him. That Dotery girl was the source of all his terrible troubles."

"What did she to do him?"

"She attached herself to him like a succubus, she taught him wicked things. I caught them in the attic, right in this very house." The cat had begun to moan and pace, whipping back and forth like a bigger cat in a cage. "They pretended to be dressing up, trying on costumes for a play, but I knew what they were doing. She had a bad name already at that early age. I picked up a piece of rope that was on the wall, and I drove her out of here half dressed as she was, down the attic stairs and out the back door. I'm not a violent woman, you know that. But Christ drove the money changers out of the temple, didn't he? You know your Bible, I'm sure, a man of your brain power."

Her flattery, if that is what it was, had a quality of sardonic mockery. Her most affirmative statements seemed to be expressions of dreadful doubt. I was conscious of a darkness in her, a hidden self operating her smiles and gestures like a puppeteer. But the strings were tangled.

"'Harry,' I said to him, "he was Harry then: 'Your mother loves you as no one else will ever. Promise me on your bended knee you will never see her again.' I told him about the awful things that can happen to a boy, the disasters and the diseases. He was very meek and mild. He cried in my lap, and he promised that he would be a good boy forever. But he betrayed me, betrayed my confidence in him."

The cat stood still, like a cat in a frieze, transfixed by her high, thin voice. Its moaning changed to a snarling, and its long tail erected itself.

"Be quiet, Harry. I had the same trouble with you until I had you fixed. Didn't I, boy?" she asked liltingly. "But you still love your mother, don't you, boy? Eh, Harry?"

She crooked her finger. The cat jumped into her lap and rolled itself into a ball, perfectly still. She stroked it, talking to it in infantile language.

I broke in on their conversation. "You mentioned some trouble Henry had, Mrs. Haines. What sort of trouble?"

"Yes. They blamed things on him, incredible things, things he didn't do and would never have done. Those nights they said he broke into the houses, he was safe at home with me. Or else he was down at the library, or going to the movies to study acting techniques. He never drank or anything. The one night he came home with something on his breath, it was because some men forced him. They waylaid him in an alley and forced a bottle of whisky to his mouth. He spat it out and told them what he thought of them. And those things they found in the little room in the basement which I fixed up for him, he bought them fair and square from a boy he knew at school."

Her hands were stroking the cat rapidly.

"I know why they blamed him. I understand it only too well. It was his running around with that Dotery girl. Bad associations make bad reputations. The rumors were flying around about him, and what could I do with a fatherless boy and a living to make in this godforsaken hole? Could I go out on the streets and argue with them? Or stand up in court to defend him?

"His lawyer said he might as well confess, or they wouldn't admit him to Juvenile Court. They'd judge him as a man and send him off to the penitentiary. So he naturally confessed. He told me that very night it was all lies. He wasn't the cat burglar, he swore to me that he wasn't. But how could he prove it? A man is guilty until he's proved innocent. You're a lawyer, you know that. And there was the stuff in the basement which he'd bought from that nasty boy who ran away from school.

"I went to the principal and I told him the facts in the

case. He flatly refused to have the boy tracked down, the boy who really was the burglarizer. He flatly refused, and I began to see that the principal and the chief of police were covering up the real villains for reasons of their own. I could guess their reasons from what I learned of the white-slave traffic when I was a young girl. The chloroformed handkerchiefs, the whited sepulchers. I wrote a letter to the governor, and when he didn't answer, I telephoned him personally. I told him who I was, my father was one of the founders of the Mountain Grove Water District, a wealthy man in his time, and a good party worker all his life. But in the modern world there's no loyalty up or down.

"All I got for my pains, they sent a man to threaten me. He threatened to lock me up in an asylum if I brought pressure on the governor. That's how high the conspiracy went, as high as the State Capitol. I saw that it was no use. They sent my son to reform school, and he was gone for years. Nothing was done to the actual criminals. It's the same old story—after all, they crucified Christ."

Her fingers were tight on the cat, and tightening. It exploded out of her lap, crossed the room like long brown vapor, and settled in the corner behind my chair. She got down on her knees beside the chair, reaching for it, calling seductively: "Come to Mother. Come on now, Harry. Mother didn't mean to hurt you, boy."

It stayed out of her reach. Looking down at her nape, I could see the gray tendrils that the dye had missed. Her perfume rose to my nostrils like the odor of funeral flowers over the scent of corruption.

"Is the Dotery family still in town?"

"How would I know?" She sat back on her haunches and looked up at me angrily. "I assure you that I have nothing to do with people like that. My father was a respectable man, a monied man in his day. He was a member of an old Ohio family. Where do the Doterys come from? Nobody knows. They're people without a history."

She went back to calling the cat. "Come now, Harry. Don't be silly, lover. Mother knows you're just being coy. She didn't mean to hurt hims."

She crawled into the corner. The cat walked away from her clutching hands disdainfully, and went behind the piano. It was a game, perhaps a nightly one. But the knowing cat and the crawling woman with the twisted stockings were getting me down.

"Where do the Doterys live?"

She must have heard the impatience in my voice. She got to her feet and returned to the piano stool, sitting down with prim politeness as if I'd interrupted her housekeeping.

"The Doterys," I said. "Where do they live?"

"You're angry. Don't be angry. Everyone gets angry with me and then I want them to die, another sin on my conscience. You're a lawyer, you should understand. They used to live over a store on the other side of town. They used the store as a front for their activities. I don't know if they still do, I haven't ventured out that way for years. Sometimes I see a woman in the market who resembles Mrs. Dotery in appearance. She may be someone sent to trap me into admissions. So I never speak to her, of course, but I watch her to see if she steals anything. If I could catch her, just once, it would reveal the whole conspiracy."

"There is no conspiracy." I didn't know if it was the right thing to say, but I had to say it, before the entire room was fogged by spiderwebs.

She was shocked into silence for a long moment. "I must

have misunderstood what you said. I understood you to say there was no conspiracy."

"There isn't, in the sense you're talking about."

She nodded. "I see. I see what you are. I took you for an intelligent man of good will. But you're another false one, another enemy of my son."

I got to my feet. "Mrs. Haines, have you ever discussed these matters with a doctor?"

"What would a doctor know about it?"

"He might be able to give you some good advice."

She knew what I meant, I think, and even considered it for a little. But she couldn't contain her anguished rage in the face of reality. "Are you casting aspersions on my sanity?"

"That wasn't what I meant."

"Don't lie to me." She struck her thigh with her fist. "I was talking to you in good faith, while you've been sitting there thinking false thoughts about me. Henry knows the truth of what I've been saying. They sent him to reform school on a trumped-up charge. They've been hounding him and harrying him for over seven years now. Ask him if you don't believe me. Ask him."

"I would if I knew where he is."

"Henry said he was coming—" She clapped her hand over her mouth.

"Coming here? When?"

"Next week. Next month. You're not going to worm and wangle anything more out of me. I don't know what you're doing coming here denying facts as plain as the nose on your face."

"I may be mistaken, Mrs. Haines." There was no point in arguing with her. I moved toward the door. "Thank you for your hospitality."

She rose and stood between me and the door. From the awkward fierceness of her movement, she might have been on the point of attacking me. But there was no harm in her. The harm she was capable of had long since been done. The rage that lived in her vitals had died down, and left her eyes empty and her mouth slack. The lipstick which her hand had smeared was like blood on a wound.

She showed herself to me for the first and only time. The woman who lived in her central desolation, obscured by sleight of mind and shadow play, said: "Is it bad trouble he's in?"

"I'm afraid so. Do you want to talk about it, Mrs. Haines?"

"No. No. My head."

She clutched her dark head as if it were an animal that had to be subdued. The cat came out from behind the piano, and rubbed its flank on her leg. She got down on her knees to speak to it: "*There* you are, Harry. He's a great comfort to his old mother, isn't he? He loves his muzzers, doesn't he?"

The cat permitted itself to be stroked again.

*chapter* **23**

I BOUGHT A CUP OF COFFEE and a piece of pie, for energy, in a restaurant on the main street. It was crowded with young people. The jukebox was playing rock —music for civilizations to decline by, man. The waitress who served me said yes, they had a business directory somewhere. She found it for me.

James Dotery was listed as the proprietor of the North

End Variety Store. His residence was at the same address. I got directions from the waitress, tipped her fifty cents, which seemed to surprise her, and drove out that way.

The store was in one of those badly zoned areas which clog the approaches to so many cities and towns. Grocery and liquor stores and taverns were intermingled with motels and private houses. The buildings had an improvised air, though most of them were old enough to be dilapidated.

James Dotery's store was on the ground floor of a two-story stucco shoebox. Its windows were sparsely furnished with warped hula hoops, packages of pins, fluorescent socks, plastic ice cubes containing flies, and other unlikely merchandise. A hand-lettered sign taped to the glass announced that everything was reduced twenty-five per cent.

There was a light on the second story. The door that led to it was standing partly open. Climbing the dark stairs, I felt a lift of excitement. You would have thought Holly May herself was waiting for me in an upstairs room.

The aproned woman who opened the apartment door came very near to sustaining the illusion. I didn't have to ask her if she was Holly's mother. She had the same facial structure and the same coloring except for her graying brown hair. She was very good-looking, and well-preserved for a woman of forty or more.

"Mrs. Dotery?"

"That's me."

I handed her my card. "My name is William Gunnarson."

"If it's Dotery you want, he ain't home. You'll probably find him down at the Bide-a-Wee." She studied my card in a puzzled way. "I warn you, though, he hates insurance salesmen. Dotery hates anything that reminds him he ain't gonna live forever like God Almighty."

"I'm not a salesman of any kind, Mrs. Dotery. I'm a law-yer."

"Yeah. I can see that for myself." She held my card up to the light and laboriously spelled out the word "attorney." "I don't read so good without my glasses."

I doubted that she read any better with them. "I would like to talk to you husband later—"

"He's down in the Bide-a-Wee lapping up liquor. We get a dollar or two ahead, and he goes off the wagon."

"At the moment there are some questions I'd like to ask you. Have you ever heard of a Hilda Dotery?"

"You kidding? All she is is my oldest daughter."

"How long is it since you've seen her?"

"Couple of weeks or three." Then she remembered some-thing, perhaps merely the fact that I was a lawyer. She seemed to be a simple-minded woman, and her feelings showed on her face. Her expression was one of dubious alertness, as if she was on an elevator going down to some unimaginable basement. "Is there a beef out on her?"

"Not that I know of. What kind of a beef do you have in mind?"

"Nothing special." She retreated clumsily from her ex-posed position. "I just thought, you being a lawyer and all —I mean, I thought maybe there was a beef out on her."

"No, but she is being looked for. Where did you see her two or three weeks ago?"

"Here, right here in the flat. She ran away, not that I blame her, five-six years ago. Then all of a sudden she turns up all dressed up in expensive clothes, wearing a ton of jewelry. You could have knocked me over with a sledge, like Dotery says.

"He jumped on her like a ton of bricks. He always hated

her anyway, and he never likes to see anyone get ahead. He started to cut and pick at her with that sleering way of his, asked her what racket she was in that she could afford to dress like that."

"What did she say?"

"She didn't say. She put him off with some story about her being an actress, that she hit it rich in the movies like. But she didn't tell him where the money come from. So where did the money come from? What is it they want her for?"

"Why do you take it for granted that she's wanted?"

"You said you were looking for her, didn't you?"

"That's because I don't know where she is."

Her mind refused to be derailed from its track. "Besides, that wasn't Woolworth jewelry, she didn't get it out of corn-flakes boxes. And I know darn well she didn't earn it acting in the movies."

"Are you sure of that?"

"I know Hilda, and she didn't change in those years she was away. She always was a play actor and a liar, putting on airs, pretending to be something she wasn't. What chance would a girl like that have to get into the movies?"

"They don't hire people for their moral qualities, Mrs. Dotery. Prepare yourself for a shock."

"She's dead, eh?" the woman said dully.

"That I doubt. Your daughter really was a movie actress, doing pretty well until she retired to get married."

"So she was telling us. I suppose," she said with heavy irony, "she married a millionaire."

"That's right, Mrs. Dotery."

"My God, you mean it's true? She wasn't lying?"

"Not about that."

"Well, what do you know?" she said with a kind of awe. Her daughter had enacted the American dream: become a movie actress and married a millionaire.

Mrs. Dotery looked down at her body, the source of all these marvels, and rubbed her aproned hip in a congratulatory way. "She always was attractive to men, I'll say that much for her. Dotery didn't like it, but he was mainly jealous. He was jealous of all the girls when they got bigger— drove them all out of the house, one way or another. Just wait until I tell him this!"

There was an edge of malice in her joy, and a certain hollowness, too. She seemed to be trying to make the most of her good news before it turned out, as her news usually did, to be not so good after all.

"What brings you here, may I ask?" she said formally, as if a genteel question would force a lucky answer. "I mean you say she's well-fixed and all, and she didn't steal those jewels she was wearing. So how does the law come into it?"

"It's a long story." Not so very long, but I was tired of standing in the hallway, and I wanted a more intimate impression of Holly May's background. "May I come in?"

"I guess you can come in. I warn you, the place is a mess. I'm always getting behind, trying to run the store in the daytime and do my housework at night."

She backed into the apartment removing her apron, as if this might work a transformation in her or in the room. The room needed some drastic change. It was a pink wallboard box jammed with cheap furniture and cluttered with the detritus of hard living: torn newspapers, overflowing ash trays, clouded glasses. The central feature of the room was a television set. On top of it was a lamp with a porcelain base in the shape of a nude woman. Through broken

Venetian blinds the neon sign of a bar across the street winked like a red peeping eye.

"Sit down."

She cleared a chair which was covered with dirty laundry. Carrying it out of the room, she paused beside the television set and dusted the porcelain figure with her apron. I wondered what dream of beauty and freedom its red-tipped breasts represented to her mind.

The chair growled under my weight, and its springs tried to bite me. I heard water run in the next room, then the clink of a bottle. Mrs. Dotery came back carrying two glasses full of brown liquid.

"This calls for a drink. I hope you don't mind cola. I never serve no hard stuff when I can help it. I never did. With young people growing up, I tried to set them a decent example, even if Dotery didn't. At least one of the kids turned out okay, which is more than you can say for some families."

She handed me my glass. I sensed that she was trying to postpone the inevitable moment when the good news turned bad. And I went along with her. "How many children do you have?"

She thought about this. "Five all told, four living. I hope they're living." She ticked them off on her fingers. "Hilda, June, Frank, Renee, Jack. Frank was the middle one, the one that got himself killed in the accident. Hilda was fond of Frank, the same way she hated June. You know how the first one is with the second one. She almost broke down the other week when I told her Frank was dead in a wreck. He wasn't even driving. I told her that's what happens when a girl turns her back on her family the way she did. You try to come back, and they're not there any more. The same

thing happened with me and my family, when I—when I
married Dotery, and we came out here to California to live."
She added without changing her tone: "It's some life he
led me, with his Chinchilla rabbits and his doughnut spas
and his variety stores. And all the time lapping up the
liquor."

"What happened to your other children?"

"Renee and June took off, the same as Hilda did. June
picked up with a salesman staying at the Star Motel. A
nylon-stocking salesman, he came to the door, a man old
enough to be her father. When Dotery found out about it,
he beat her with a hammer handle, but that didn't seem to
stop her. The last I heard of her, she was selling stockings
from door to door in Compton. That grieved me. June was
the one I thought would turn out best, I always favored
her. But if it had to be Hilda, it's the will of Providence."

"What about Renee?"

"Renee went away and got a job, soon as she was legal
age. She's working someplace around San Francisco. Waitress.
I heard from her at Christmas, only she forgot to put the address on the envelope."

"And Jack?"

"He's my youngest, just sixteen. I guess his age is a bless-
ing, considering he's in Juvenile. The policeman told me if
he was a little older they'd of sent him up to the pen for
stealing that car he stole."

It was a depressing rundown. Coming on top of Mrs.
Haines and her immense evasions, it left me undecided
whether to laugh in Mrs. Dotery's face or weep into her
cola. I asked myself what I was doing sixty miles from home
probing among the ruins of lives that meant nothing to me.
I amended the thought: lives that had meant nothing to
me until now.

Sipping the cola, lukewarm now, and watching Mrs. Dotery's passive face across the rim of the glass, I had a sense of the largeness of the earth spinning in light and darkness, and what it meant to bring children into life. Something moved like an earthquake in a part of my mind so deep I hadn't known it existed. It was an unspoken prayer for Bill Gunnarson, Jr.

"May I use your telephone, Mrs. Dotery?"

"Don't have one up here. There's one down in the store if it's important." She hesitated, and took the plunge. "You were going to tell me about Hilda."

"Yes. She's dropped out of sight, under suspicious circumstances. Her husband is deeply concerned about her. I represent him, by the way."

"How do you mean, suspicious circumstances? Has she done something wrong, after all?"

"That's not impossible. But it's possible she hasn't. She seems to be mixed up with a man named Harry or Henry Haines."

"You mean to tell me she's still messing with *him!*" A red flush surged up from her neck almost to her eyes.

"It looks very much like it. You know Haines, do you?"

"Know him? I should say so. He was the one that got her started."

"Doing what?"

"All the things a girl shouldn't do. I remember that first night she came home with liquor on her breath—a girl of fifteen-sixteen, so woozy she couldn't walk straight. 'Have you been lapping up liquor?' I said to her. She denied it and denied it. Then Dotery came in roaring drunk and started in on her. They had a terrible scrap. He would of beat her bloody, but I went and got the butcher knife and told him to lay off of her. 'Lay off of her,' I said to him, 'if you want to go on living.' He saw I meant it, and he laid off of her.

"But it was too late, we had no control after that. Dotery he blamed me for being too soft. But I dunno, you can't beat a girl to death. Or lock her up in her room. She would of jumped out the window anyway, that's how wild she was. Drinking and tearing around in cars and shoplifting in the stores and probably worse. And Harry Haines was the one that got her started."

"So they've been running together for quite a few years?"

"I did my best to nip it in the bud. They were in some show together at the high school, and he used to come in the doughnut spa. That was when we had the doughnuts, and Hilda and June waited on customers after school. June saw them smooching in the kitchen, and drinking vanilla extract out of pint bottles. The next time he come in, I was laying in wait. I tell you I sent him packing. And I told Hilda he was poison for her, poison for any girl. I know that lofty look that some of them have. They think that nothing's good enough for them. They'll take what they can from any girl and leave her empty-handed." She seemed to speak with the bitterness of personal experience.

"Have you seen Haines recently?"

"Haven't seen him for years. The last I heard of him they sent him off to Preston, where he belonged. They picked up Hilda, too—apparently he snitched on her—but they didn't send her away. She went away on her own a year or two later, and that was that. Till she turned up here last month."

"Did she mention Haines?"

"Not in my hearing. She talked a blue streak about this rich oilman husband of hers, but neither of us believed her. She seemed to be kind of flying, know what I mean? What sort of a fellow is he?"

"He seems to be a pretty good man, and a very successful one. But she likes Haines better."

"She always was stuck on him. Sometimes I think a woman only needs two things to make her happy—a hatchet and a chopping block. She lays her head down on the block and gets somebody in pants to chop it off with the hatchet and then she's satisfied."

"Why did Hilda finally come home?"

"Show off her glad rags, I guess. She was disappointed none of the others were with us any more. There always used to be rivalry between the sisters. Seiberling rivalry. And, like I said, she wanted to see Frank. She got real upset when I told her Frank was dead. I thought for a while there she was blowing her top, crying and storming around and blaming us for things we never done. Frank wasn't even driving that car, it was another boy name of Ralph Spindle."

"Did Hilda have emotional problems?"

"How do you mean, emotional?"

"You said that she was flying, on the point of blowing her top. Was that a new development in her?"

"No. I wisht it was. She always had a terrible temper, back to when she was a little girl. Mostly she kept it hid pretty good, but then it would flare out. Frank was the only one she got along with. She never got along with the other girls. Like when June snitched on her that time in the doughnut shop, Hilda picked up a pan of grease and was gonna throw it in her little sister's face. Boiling grease, you know how hot it gets, lucky I got there to stop her. The lady from downtown said she was severely adjusted."

"Maladjusted?"

"Maladjusted, severely maladjusted. They said Hilda was going through like a storm, and maybe she'd outgrow it and maybe she wouldn't. I guess she must of, eh? You don't get to be a movie actress without plenty on the ball. Did she make many movies? We don't go to the movies since we got TV."

"I've never seen her on the screen, either. I think just one or two of her pictures were released before she retired."

"It's a young age for a girl to retire," she said dubiously.

"How old is Hilda?"

"Let's see, I was eighteen when I had her. That was some of your teen-age storm like they were talking about. I'm forty-three now. That would make her, let's see—" She tried to count on her fingers and lost track.

"Twenty-five."

She nodded. "Yeah. You got a good head for figures. Dotery has, too, if he'd only use it. *He* could have been a lawyer, with his brains. No disrespect intended, Jim really is a smart man. That's one of the reasons he couldn't stand the kids. They were all dumb, like me. I guess you couldn't say that Hilda was dumb, but it sure looked like it for a while the way she handled herself." Her mental detour converged with her original line of thought. "I still think twenty-five is a young age to retire. Or did they fire her?"

"No. I've talked to her agent. They're eager to get her back."

"You mean she's really good?"

"She has what they need, apparently. But they don't have what she needs." Whatever that is or was.

"Hilda always was a good-looking girl," her mother said. "You ever see her?"

"Not in the flesh."

"I got some pictures of her someplace. I'll see if I can find them."

Before I could remonstrate, she had left the room, moving eagerly, as if it might still be not too late to put salt on the tail of the ruby-breasted dream.

A man in a sports shirt came in from the hallway without knocking. At first glance he was handsome and young. Then I saw the muddy blur in his eyes, the gray dusting his wavy blond hair, the smile like a fishhook caught in one corner of his mouth.

"I didn't know we had visitors."

"Just the one. And I'm not exactly a visitor. I'm here on business."

Business was a bad word. He said with hushed fury: "Get something straight—I do the business for this family. I handle the money. What you been trying to sell the wife behind my back?"

I stood up, into the zone of his breath. It was as foul as his temper.

"Gold bricks," I said. "She decided to take a dozen."

"Wise guy, eh?" Teetering on his heels, he reconnoitered me from a safe distance. "I want to know what you're doing in this flat."

"Your wife knows what I'm doing here. Ask her."

"Where is she?" He looked wildly around the room, then heard the rustling noise she was making on the other side of the wall. He rushed through the door like a rescuer or invader.

There was a muffled interchange, and then his voice rose uncontrolled in a queer, high, continuous yammering. "Once a dumbhead always a dumbhead what you think you're doing giving away the family secrets make him pay for them if the husband's wellheeled let him put up some money you goddam fool."

"I didn't think of it."

"I'll do the thinking you let me do the thinking you take my orders that way we'll get somewhere what you think you're doing giving him pictures these people pay money for pictures you sell 'em information so much a word I've had experience in these matters the girl's worth money alive or dead you don't just give it away."

"Hush now, Jim, he'll hear you."

"Let him hear let him realize he isn't dealing with country bumpkins I'm no booby even if you are you lousy deadhead dragging me down all my life I could of gone to college made something of myself but you had to make me get married I carried you twenty-five years like a body on my back and now when one of the house apes looks like paying off for all the money we spent on her education you want to give it away for free what'd he do butter you up a little tell you you still had a figure you bloated hag?"

"You mustn't talk like that," she said behind the wall. "You ought to have more pride."

"Pride for what I live in a hole with a hag and every time I turn my back you throw away another opportunity I should feel thankful no doubt but I say you're the one you hag you should get down on your knees and thank me for putting up with you you hag."

The sound of a slap came through the wallboard, followed by the woman's grunt of pain. I went through the door into the kitchen, where they were facing each other. An old carton spilling papers and pictures stood on the drainboard beside them.

The woman had her hand to her cheek, but it was Dotery who began to sob.

"Forgive me Kate I didn't mean it."

"It's all right, I'm not hurt. I know things never worked out for you. I'm sorry."

She put her arms around him. His face went like a child's to her breasts. She stroked his dusty gray hair and looked at me serenely from a standpoint beyond grief.

"You shouldn't lap up so much liquor," she said. "It isn't good for you, Jim. Now go to bed like a good boy, you'll feel better in the morning."

He stumbled in my direction. His eyes came up to my face, with a flash of the unquenchable anger that kept him almost young. But he went out without speaking.

The woman smoothed her dress down over her bosom. Except that her eyes were a little darker, the scene had not affected her.

"Dotery is a hard man to live with," she said. "Lucky for me I'm easygoing myself. Live and let live is my motto. You start pushing too hard, and what happens? Everything goes to pieces in a nutshell."

I didn't quite follow the sentence, but it seemed appropriate. "You were going to show me some pictures, Mrs. Dotery."

"So I was."

She took a handful of pictures from the carton and shuffled them like a fortune teller's deck. With a sudden gleeful smile she handed me one of them. "Guess who that is."

It was an old snapshot of a girl just entering adolescence. Her budding figure showed through her white tulle dress. She was holding a broad white hat by its ribbon, and smiling into the sun.

"It's your daughter Hilda, isn't it?"

"Nope," she said. "It's me, taken back in Boston thirty years ago, the Sunday I was confirmed. I was a good-looker for a kid, if I do say it myself. Hilda and June took after me."

The rest of the pictures illustrated this, and removed any possible doubt that Holly May was Mrs. Dotery's daughter. She said nostalgically: "We used to pretend we was sisters, me and the two oldest girls, until the trouble started in the family."

The trouble in the family had not yet ended. Dotery called through the wall in a voice that trembled with self-pitying rage: "You gonna stay up all night? I got to get up in the morning and work, even if you don't. Come to bed now, hear me?"

"I guess I got to go," she said. "He'll be out of there in a minute, and God knows what will happen. Anyway, Hilda's a lovely kid to look at, isn't she?"

"So were you."

"Thank you, sir."

Dotery raised his voice. "Do you hear me? Come to bed!"

"I hear you. I'm coming, Jim."

chapter 24

DOWNSTAIRS IN THE STREET, I found a public telephone booth outside a drugstore that was closed for the night. I stepped inside the glass cubicle and placed a collect call to my home in Buenavista. After repeated ringing, the operator said: "Your party does not answer, sir. Do you wish me to try again later?"

Fear stabbed me, twisting and turning into guilt. In the

last few weeks Sally had given up going out at night. It was unlikely that she was visiting the neighbors at this hour. The Perrys and our other neighbors were all early risers.

"Do you wish me to try again *later*, sir?"

"Yes. I'm in a public booth. I'll call again in a few minutes."

I hung up and looked at my watch. It was just a few minutes short of midnight. Of course, Sally was asleep. She'd been sleeping heavily lately. The bedroom door was shut, and she hadn't heard the phone.

Then I remembered that Mrs. Weinstein was supposed to be there with her. Death in his distorting mask slipped into the booth, to my right and a little behind me, just outside the angle of my vision. When I turned to look at him, he moved further behind me.

I tried my home number again. No answer. I called the Buenavista police, but the line was busy. I opened the door of the booth to breathe. Laughter and music came in gusts from the bar across the street. Bide-a-Wee, its flashing red neon said.

To hell with biding, I said to myself. To hell with Mountain Grove and its broken pasts, to hell with the Ferguson case. I wanted no part of it. The only thing I wanted was Sally safe in my arms. I could be home in an hour if I drove fast.

I ran back to my car and started the engine. But the case wouldn't let me go. A man said behind me, under the engine's roar: "Keep your hands where I can see them, Gunnarson. On the wheel. I have a gun pointed at the back of your head."

I turned and saw his face in alternating reddish light and reddish darkness. It was secret and handsome in the half-

light, with liquid-glinting eyes and metal-glinting hair. I recognized Haines from his photograph.

He was crouching in the space between the seats with my
car blanket over his shoulders. He lifted his hand from
under the robe and showed me a heavy revolver. "I'll use this
if I have to. Bear it in mind."

There was no real menace in his voice, no feeling of any
kind. Its emptiness was the alarming thing. It was the voice
of the man from space who owed no human allegiance any-
where. Harry Haines, self-conceived out of nothing, a fatherless man with a gun, trying to steal reality for himself.

I could feel his breath on the side of my neck. It made me
angrier than a blow would have. "Get out of my car. Go back
to one of your women, Harry—Larry. Snuggle up under a
skirt, you won't feel so anxious."

"Why, damn you," he said. "I'll kill you!"

"Mother wouldn't like it."

"You keep my mother out of this. You had no right to force
your way into her house. She's a respectable woman—"

"That's right, she wouldn't like it if you shot me. Right
here in Mountain Grove, the scene of your early triumphs.
Local boy makes good, again."

"I'm doing better than you are, Gunnarson."

His voice was painfully high. He didn't take pressure
well. I gave him another notch of it. "Sure, as a two-bit gun-
man you're doing fine. I have about seven dollars in my wallet. You're welcome to it if you're that hungry."

"Keep your money. You'll need it for a down payment on
a tombstone."

He was a poor imitation of a storm trooper. But so were
most of the originals. I'd read enough criminology to know
that the cat burglars, the night walkers, were the really dan-

gerous ones. They killed for unknown reasons at unexpected times. The reality they stole was ultimately death.

Gaines came over the back of the seat in a swift feline movement. He squatted on his knees beside me, thrusting the gun at my side. "Get going, straight ahead."

"What did you do to my wife?"

"Nothing. Get going, I said."

"Where is she?"

"Out on the town, for all I know. I never saw your frigging wife."

"If she's harmed in any way, you won't last long. Do you understand that, Gaines? I'll attend to you personally."

I was stealing his lines and it made him nervous. He stammered slightly when he said: "S-shut up. G-get going now or I'll b-blast you."

He urged the gun into my side, handling it with more bravado than caution. Perhaps I had a fifty-fifty chance of taking him now. I wanted a better chance, something like ninety to ten. I had more to lose than he had. I hoped. I desperately hoped. And I got going.

The road ran northward out of town, straight as a yardstick through dark fields. I pushed the speedometer needle around past seventy, nearly to eighty. Whatever was going to happen, I wanted it over.

"Don't drive so fast," he said.

"Does it make you nervous? I thought you liked going fast."

"S-sure. I used to d-drag-race, here on this very road. B-but right now I want you to slow down to sixty. I don't want the HP on my tail."

"Maybe you'd like to do the driving."

"Oh, certainly, and let you hold the g-gun."

"Is it such fun holding the gun?"

"Shut up!" he cried in a sudden yapping rage. "Shut up and slow down like I said."

He pressed the muzzle of the revolver into the soft place below my ribs. I slowed down to sixty. There were lights ahead, an island of bleak color on the darkness, where the road joined the east-west highway.

"You're g-going to make a left turn here. I don't want any funny stuff."

I slowed still more as we approached the intersection, and stopped for the red light. Two cars were being gassed at a bright, bare all-night station. In the adjacent lunchroom, people sat at the counter with their backs to me.

"You heard me, d-didn't you? No funny stuff. Let me know you heard me." He thrust the gun into me with all his force. He was no longer interested in self-protection. The light had turned green. He was interested in imposing his will on me. "Let me know you heard me."

I remained silent.

"Let me know you heard me," he said urgently.

I sat with my teeth clenched, my hands turning white on the wheel. The moment stretched out like rotten elastic. A pair of headlights plunged up out of the fields of night behind us. The traffic light turned red again.

One of the cars left the gas station and rolled out onto the highway. It passed in front of us going east, gathering speed. I felt invisible. The hot valley wind blew through my bones like the breath of nothingness.

"What are you trying to do?" Gaines said. "Are you trying to make me k-kill you?"

I was trying to gather the animal courage to open the door of my car and get out and walk over to the gas station. The thought of what I had to lose held me paralyzed. The plunging headlights on the road behind were nearer and brighter. In a few more seconds they'd be on me like a spotlight, making a zone of safety that I could walk through.

They filled the car with sudden shadows. Though the traffic signal was still against us, they swerved to pass. I heard the squeal of tires and caught a glimpse of a pale adolescent face at the wheel. A girl clung like a huge blonde limpet to the driver's body.

He made a grandstand turn in front of me, double-clutched his hot rod, and fled eastward down the highway trailing noise. No use to me, no use to anybody.

I made a left turn on the green.

A late moon had risen over the mountains, blurred large by thin clouds. The highway climbed through foothills toward it, then rose in sweeping arcs into the pass. I could feel the pressure in my ears.

We passed the sign that marked the summit. I caught a glimpse of the curved aluminum sea far ahead and below. A long beam flashed out from its edge, possibly from the lighthouse on Ferguson's cliff.

"Are we going back to Buenavista?"

"You'd like that, wouldn't you? But you're not going back there, now or any time. You can k-kiss the place good-by."

"To hell with you and your cheap threats."

"You think I'm cheap, eh? You called me a two-bit g-gunman. Think again. My g-grandfather had a summer place up here, a real showplace. In addition to the spread he had in the valley. I'm not the b-bum you think."

"How does your grandfather prevent you from being a bum?"

"I have background, see? You're stupid for a lawyer. My g-grandfather was loaded. He had two houses, b-big ones."

"Why tell me?" A plague on both his houses.

"I wouldn't want you to d-die in ignorance. You better slow down. We'll be coming to the turnoff in a minute."

It was marked by a boulder which jutted out of the cutbank. Some crank or prophet had scrawled on the boulder in whitewash: "We die daily."

I turned into a gravel road worn bare by the rains of many winters. The bank above it was crenelated by erosion. Below in the canyon, moonlight drenched the treetops. An owl hooted softly and mournfully.

I was keenly aware of these things, their strangeness and their beauty. I thought of turning hard left over the edge, holding on and taking my chances, letting the deep trees catch me if they could. I must have given away the thought somehow. Gaines said: "Don't do it. You're a d-dead man if you try it. Just keep on driving until we reach the g-gate."

I did as I was told. My patience was wearing thin, though, and my time was running out. I wished that I could read Gaines's mind as he had just read mine. Apparently he had cast me for a role in his fantasy. He wanted to hurt me, and he wanted to impress me. Both halves of the double role were dangerous.

Coming out of a long climbing curve, the headlights flashed on gateposts of squared stone. The gates themselves had rusted off their hinges and leaned crazily.

"Turn in here. This is it, James. The ancestral acres." There was a weird, sardonic sorrow in his voice.

The driveway was half overgrown with weeds which brushed against the underside of the car. On either side, eucalyptus trees hung in the moony air like shapes of mist congealing into cloud. The house loomed dark at the end of the avenue.

It was a two-storied house with walls of stone and a

round stone tower at each end. It had been built to resist time, but time and weather were winning out against it. Mountain winds had torn off shingles and left ragged holes in the roof. The windows on the upper floor were smashed; the windows on the lower floor were boarded up. There was a light behind one of the boarded front windows.

"My mother used to live here in the summers when she was a girl." As if it were the conclusion of the same line of thought, Gaines added: "G-get out now, I'll be right behind you. One false move and I fire, see?"

His voice was small in the silence. Drifts of leaves and fallen branches and twisted strips of bark littered the ground. They crackled under our feet. The moon peered down through flimsy cloud like an acned blonde roused behind her curtains by our noise. Our shadows fell jerkily across the veranda and lengthened up the door into the darkness under the veranda roof.

Gaines thrust his leg out past me and kicked the ancestral door. A woman's voice answered, its brassiness hushed by alarm. "Who is it?"

"Larry. Open up. I brought a friend with me."

A bolt squealed. The door opened an inch, and then a foot. The woman who called herself Holly May looked out. "What friend? You got no friends."

She slouched in the doorway, narrow-eyed. A dead cigarette hung down from the corner of her mouth. Her body gave off a sense of sleeping danger, immediate as an odor.

"It isn't exactly a friend," Gaines said. "It's the lawyer Ferguson hired."

"Why did you have to cart him up here?"

"I p-picked him up in Mountain Grove. I couldn't let him run loose."

"Well, don't just stand there, bring him in."

Gaines ushered me in with the gun. The woman bolted the door behind us. We went down a vast dark hallway into a vaster room.

One end of the room was lit by a gasoline lantern which stood in the nearest corner. Its hissing circle of brightness fell with shuddering violence on the very light housekeeping arrangements which Gaines and the woman had set up: a canvas sleeping bag on the bare floor, a rustic bench blanched by rain and sun, a few glowing coals in the great stone fireplace, bread and cheese and an open can of beans laid out on a page of newspaper which carried the picture of Donato, under his sheet.

I wondered when they planned to start spending Ferguson's money. Or had they involved themselves in crime merely to reduce themselves to this? To make a brief impossible marriage in a corner of the wrecked past.

"Stand b-back against the wall alongside the fireplace," Gaines said to me. "On the far side away from the lantern. And stand still, you hear me?"

I stood against the wall in silence.

"You hear me?" Gaines said. "Let me know you hear me."

I could see him clearly for the first time. He was a good-looking man, if you didn't look too closely. But his eyes were small and brilliant with trouble. They moved like ball bearings magnetized by the woman. Her presence seemed to focus his personality, and also to diminish it.

He stood with one hand on his hip, the other holding the gun. He might have been posing for a photograph: rebel without a cause years later and still without a cause; or actor in search of a role, looking for the crime that would complete his nothingness. I guessed that his life was a series of such stills, forced into the semblance of action by fits and starts of rage.

"Let me know you hear me, G-gunnarson."

I stood silent. He glanced down anxiously at his gun, as if it might suggest an action to him, turn in his hand like a handle and open the door on manhood. The gun jerked. A bullet tore the floor in front of me and sprinkled my legs with slivers.

Among the dying echoes of the shot, the woman said: "Don't get gun-happy, Larry. We're not the only people in these hills."

"You can't hear it outside, the walls are too thick. I used to come up here when I was a kid and shoot at targets."

"Human targets?" I said. "Was that your boyhood hobby?"

The woman tittered like a broken xylophone. Unkempt as she was, her bleached hair stringy as hemp, her hips bulging in a pair of men's jeans, she dragged at the attention. Her eyes were blowtorch blue in a white, frozen face.

"Have yourself a good look, lawyer. It's going to have to last you a long time."

"Are you going someplace, Hilda?"

"Hey," she said to Gaines, "he knows my real name. Did you have to tell him my real name, stupid?"

"D-don't you call me stupid. I can think rings around you any day of the week."

She moved toward him. "If you have such a brilliant brain, what did you bring him here for? He knows me. He knows my name. It's a hell of a note."

"Your mother and D-dotery told him. I don't know how he got to them, but I caught him outside their store in the G-grove."

"What in merry hell are we going to do with him now? We're supposed to be hitting the road tonight."

"We'll knock him off. What else can we do?" His voice was shallow, almost devoid of expression. He glanced down at the gun and said more forcefully: "Knock him off and burn the frigging place down. We can d-dress him in some of my clothes, see, we're about the same size. Once he's cremated, nobody will know the d-difference. Even the Rover boys won't know the d-difference."

"You're going to cut them out, then?"

"I always did intend to cut them out. It isn't a big enough melon to slice so many ways. It's why I wanted Broadman out, why I tipped off the cops on D-donato." He strutted at the edge of the light. "I'm not so stupid, bag. Anyway, what contribution did the Rover boys make? I'm the brains, they're nothing better than errand boys."

"They did your dirty work for you."

"That's what I mean, I'm the brains. They'd crucify their g-grandmothers for a stick of H. Let the k-kill-crazy bastards stay here and take the rap. I'll send them a postcard from South America."

Her blue gaze jumped like a gas flame at his face. "You mean we will, don't you?"

"We will what?"

"Send them a postcard from South America, stupid. We're going there together, aren't we?"

"Not if you g-go on calling me stupid."

"What in hell is this, Larry?"

"You keep a civil tongue, talking to me."

"Oh, sure. The mastermind. The big brain." She snarled at him: "Let me see those tickets."

"They're not here. I don't have them."

"You went down to the Grove to pick them up. Didn't Adelaide buy them?"

"Of course she did. They're in my car. Everything's in my car."

"How do I know there are two tickets?"

"I'm telling you. Do you think I'd stand you up at this late date?"

"If you thought you could get away with it. Only you can't."

It resembled a conversation on a lower floor of merry hell, where two dead souls re-enacted a meaningless scene forever. It was the meaninglessness that made it hell. I dug deep for the most meaningful words I could find. "Listen to me. Hilda. Ferguson's very fond of you, he's ready to forgive you. Why throw yourself away on thieves and psychos? You still have some kind of future if you'll take it."

Gaines moved on me jerkily. His boot soles thumped the floor as if he had poor contact with reality.

"I'm no psycho, d-dad." He offered the gun in evidence, leveling it at my middle. "Take it back or I k-kill you now. I'm going to k-kill you anyway. I'd just as soon k-kill you now."

Hilda stepped between us. "Let the man speak his piece."

"What the hell for?"

"He's funny. He gives me kicks." She was looking at me like a lost soul out of hell.

"You've had your k-kicks." He smiled at her malignly.

"What's on your mind? Are you taking Adelaide with you instead of me? I wouldn't put it past you, mother lover."

One of his sudden rages went through him like a hemorrhage. It drained his face of color. "D-don't call me that. You want to d-die, too?"

"Christ, you're the one that's kill-crazy. You better give me that gun."

"I wouldn't trust you with it."

"Hand it over, little man," she growled. Her breasts were thrust out under her shirt, aggressive as nose cones.

"D-don't give me orders."

The gun wavered toward her. She reached for the muzzle. Gaines looked horribly torn, ready to faint. He raised the gun and struck her with it on the side of the head. She went to her knees like a supplicant.

I stepped around her and hit him in the soft place below his ribs. He opened his mouth to grunt. I smashed it with my right fist. He ran rapidly backward across the room and slammed into the wall on the far side. The gun clacked on the floor and skittered away into shadow.

I went after Gaines. He didn't come to meet me. He stayed against the wall, gasping for breath, until I was almost on top of him. Then he moved very quickly. His fist came out from under his windbreaker with a blade projecting upward from it.

I rushed him and got both hands on the arm behind the fist. We were face to face for an instant, static and straining. Before the instant was over, I knew that I was stronger than he was. The knowledge made me grin.

He struck and scratched at my grin with his free hand. I concentrated on the wrist behind the knife. I forced it up to the level of my chest, ducked under it, turning, and twisted it with the whole torque of my body. Something gave. The knife fell between us.

I picked it up, but it did me no great good. The woman was crawling away from the light into the deep shadow. She found the gun and sat on the floor with it. Resting the barrel between her pulled-up knees, she sighted along it and fired.

The bullet hit my shoulder, turned me, and set me in motion. She fired again, but I felt no second wound. I didn't need one. I waded to the doorway in the floor's dissolving surface and fell slack. My head must have struck the **door** frame. I dropped across the threshold of consciousness.

**((❖((❖((❖((❖((**
**((❖((❖((❖((❖((** *chapter* 25
**((❖((❖((❖((❖((**

INTO THE LANDSCAPE of a hundred dreams. I was out in the orchard sailing chips in the creek. The rolling hills on the far side supported white cumulus clouds. Above them the sun soared, brightening. It blasted my face with heat. The creek dried up. I covered my eyes. When I looked up again, the sun was red; the hills were black as lava, except where barns were burning. The apples turned black on the trees and dropped in the black grass. I went into the house to tell my father. "He's dead," said an old brown woman I didn't know. "They flit by the window, and what's become of Sally?"

The thought of her took hold of me and jerked me out of dream country. I felt floor against my face, hot air on the back of my neck.

"There's a Santa Ana blowing," I said. "Somebody left a window open."

No one paid any attention. I lifted my head and saw the firelight dancing on the wall. It was a pretty sight, but it annoyed me. With the desert wind blowing, it made no sense to build up the dying fire.

I rolled over and sat up. One side of the room was alive with flames. They fluttered toward me like ribbons in a fan

draft, and toward the woman lying on the floor. I thought
with something approaching awe that Gaines had included
her in his plan of destruction. Her clothes were disarrayed as
though she had put up a struggle. A blue bruise spread from
her temple across one eye.

I started to crawl toward her, and discovered that my
right arm wasn't working. Before I reached her, a tongue of
flame licked at her outflung hand. Her fingers curled up
away from it. Her whole body stirred sluggishly. She wasn't
dead.

Which meant I had to get her out of there. I scrambled to
my feet. Fire flapped like flags around her. I twisted my
good hand in the tails of her shirt and heaved. The shirt tore
and came away from her body.

She was becoming very important to me. Holding my
breath against the heat, I caught hold of her limp wrist and
dragged her into the hallway. It was like a wind tunnel. Air
poured through the open front door. I pulled her out into the
blessed night.

The fire was beginning to sing and surge behind me. In
no time at all it would be a roaring furnace. I looked for my
car. It was gone. I maneuvered the unconscious woman to
the edge of the veranda, hauled her up to a sitting position, crouched in front of her, and lifted her by the wrist
across my good shoulder.

Somehow I got my knees straightened out under her
weight, and started down the driveway. I had a fixed idea that
I must get her as far as the road, in case the trees caught
fire. It wasn't likely, after the winter rains, but I wasn't
thinking too clearly.

The trees on either side swayed mystically in the moonlight. I swayed not so mystically. My faint and hunchbacked

shadow mocked my movements. The soft burden on my back seemed to increase with each step I took. Then it began to slip.

Before she slithered from my grasp entirely, I went to my knees at the side of the drive and let her down carefully. We were still under trees, a hundred feet short of the gate, but this would have to do. She lay like a marble torso fallen from its plinth, waiting for someone to lift her back into place.

I sat down heavily in the weeds beside her. I couldn't have been so very far gone, because her bare breasts disturbed me. I got my jacket off and covered her with it.

The right side of my shirt was dark and clammy. I felt the dark goo with my fingers and only then recalled the shocking image of Hilda sighting across her knees and firing. With my left forefinger I found the hole she had made, just under my collarbone. It was wet and warm. I balled my handkerchief and held it against the wound.

The woman whimpered. Faint coppery lights were moving on her face. I thought for an instant she was coming to, then realized it was the fire's reflection. The upstairs windows of the house were rectangles of twisted orange and black. Black smoke boiled up toward the moon in clouds whose bellying undersides were flame-lit and peppered with flying sparks.

The Forest Service would be sure to sight it or get a report of it. They were probably on their way now. I might as well relax until help arrived.

It arrived sooner than I expected. A single pair of headlights fanned up the winding road, turned in at the gate without pausing. I got up onto my feet and stumbled into the middle of the driveway.

The headlights stopped a few feet short of me. Behind

them I recognized the bulky shape of an ambulance. Whitey and his partner Ronny climbed out on opposite sides of the cab and converged on me.

"You got here fast, boys."

"That's our job." Whitey looked me over in the glare of the headlights. "What happened to you, Mr. Gunnarson?"

"I have a shoulder wound that needs attention. But you better look after the woman first."

"What woman?"

"Over here," Ronny said from the side of the road. His voice was vaguely familiar, though I didn't remember hearing him speak before. He switched on a flashlight and examined her, turning up her eyelids, sniffing her breath.

"She may be under drugs," I said.

"Yeah. It could be an overdose of morphine, or heroin. There's needle marks on her arm." He indicated several dark pinpoints in the white flesh of her upper arm.

"She was talking and acting as though she was high on something."

"Whatever it is, she's mighty low on it now."

"You mean she talked to you?" Whitey said. "What did she say?" There were dancing orange gleams in the centers of his eyes, as if he was burning up with curiosity.

"She said a lot of things. They'll keep. Let's get a temporary dressing on this shoulder."

He answered slowly. "I guess we better do that. Ronny, leave the pig lay for now. I may need your help with Mr. Gunnarson."

The hinges of my knees were as loose as water. I barely made it to the ambulance. They hoisted me up into the back, turned on the roof light, and let me down gently on a padded stretcher. As soon as I was horizontal, my head began to swim and my eyes played tricks. Whitey and Ronny seemed to hover over me like a pair of mad scientists exchanging sinister smiles.

"Strap his wrists," Whitey said.

"That won't be necessary, I won't fight you."

"We won't take any chances. Strap his wrists, Ronny."

Ronny strapped my wrists to the cold aluminum sides of the stretcher. Whitey produced a triangular black rubber mask attached to a narrow black tube.

"I don't need anesthetic."

"Yes you do. I hate to see people suffer, you know how I am."

Ronny snickered. "I know. Nobody else knows, but *I* know."

Whitey shushed him. He fitted the soft rubber mask over my nose and mouth. Its elastic strap circled my head.

"Pleasant dreams," he said. "Breathe out and then breathe in."

A sense of survival deeper than consciousness made me hold my breath. Behind my eyes, broken black pieces were falling into place. I had heard Ronny's snicker on the telephone.

"Breathe *out*. Then breathe in."

Whitey's face hung over me like one of the changing faces you see between sleeping and waking at the end of a bad day. I raised my head against the downward pressure of his hand. The end of the black tube was wrapped around his other hand. Using both hands, he forced my head back down.

"Listen," Ronny said. "There's a car coming up the hill." After a listening silence: "It sounds like a Mercury Special."

"Cop car?"

"Sounds like it."

"You should have been monitoring the police calls. You goofed, man."

"You said you needed me in here."

"I don't any more. I can handle him."

"How's the patient doing?"

"He'll be gone in a minute. Get out there and give them a story. We pulled him out of the fire, but he died of asphyxiation, poor fellow."

He leaned hard on the mask. I was far from gone. One of my sports was diving without a lung.

Ronny leaned over to look at me. I doubled up my right leg and kicked him in the middle of his face. It felt like stepping on a snail.

Whitey said: "You devil!"

I tried to kick him. He was beyond the reach of my flailing legs, bending over my face with his full weight on me. The dark wheel of unconsciousness started to spin in my head. I tried to breathe. There was nothing to breathe.

The sound of a motor whining up the grade detached itself from the whirring of the dark wheel. Before the two sounds merged again, headlights filled the ambulance with light. The pressure was removed from my face. I caught a blurred glimpse of Whitey standing over his prostrate partner with a black automatic in his hand.

He fired it. The ambulance interior multiplied its roar like an echo chamber. The single sharp crack that followed was more than an echo. Whitey bowed like a performer at the footlights, clasping his abdomen.

Pike Granada came into the ambulance and took the rubber thing off me before I followed Broadman and Secundina all the way into darkness.

## chapter 26

SPOTLIT ON A BLACK, jagged landscape, Sally was being carried away by a gorilla who was wooing her in Spanish. I caught them and tore off the gorilla suit. Then I was wrestling with a man whose name I couldn't remember. I opened my eyes and saw Lieutenant Wills scowling at me through bars.

"You can't keep me in jail," I think I said. "Judge Bennett will give me a writ of habeas corpus."

Wills grinned at me balefully. "It will take more than that to spring you out of this."

I sat up swearing. My head took off from my shoulders and flew around the big dim room, bumping into empty beds. It looked more like a dormitory than a jail.

"Take it easy, now." Wills leaned on the barred side that turned my bed into a sort of cage. Grasping my good shoulder, he pressed me back onto the pillowless sheet. "You're in the recovery room in the hospital. You just got out of the operating room."

"Where's Sally? What happened to Sally?"

"Nothing happened to her, except in the course of nature. She gave birth to a little girl last night. Six pounds ten ounces. The two of them are right here in this same hospital, down on the third floor. Both doing well."

"Is that where she went last night?"

"This is where she went. What bothers me is where you

went, and why. What were you doing up in the mountains there?"

"Hunting deer by moonlight out of season. Arrest me, officer."

Wills shook his head curtly. "Get off the pentothal jag. This is serious, Bill. You ought to know how serious. Pike Granada says you were within seconds of getting smothered to death. It he hadn't been keeping an eye on those ambulance drivers, you would have been a goner."

"Thank Granada for me."

"I'll do that, with pleasure. You owe him personal thanks, though, and maybe an apology, eh? Just for good measure, he gave you a pint of his own blood this morning."

"Why would Granada do that?"

"He happens to be your blood type, and the bank was out of your type and you needed it. You needed it in more ways than one, maybe. You could do with a little Spanish blood in your veins. And a little cop blood."

"Rub it in."

"I don't mean to do that. But you gave me a bad ten minutes yesterday, until I had a chance to talk to Pike. You know what you are, don't you? Prejudiced."

"The hell I am."

"Prejudiced," Wills repeated. "You may not realize it, but you don't like cops, and you don't like Spanish people. If you want to practice law in this town, do it effectively, you're going to have to get to know *la Raza,* understand 'em."

"What does *la Raza* mean?"

"The Spanish-American people. They call themselves that. It's a proud word, and they're a proud people. You don't want to undersell them, Bill. They have a lot of ignorance, a lot of poverty, a lot of crime. But they make their contribution to this town. Look at Granada. He came up out of the gangs, sure, but you don't judge a man by what he did in his crazy teens. You judge him by his contribution over the long hike."

"I get the message."

"Good. I thought I'd get my oar in while you were still feeling no pain. You were pretty hot against Granada."

"I was half convinced that he killed Broadman."

"Yeah. We all know different now, thanks to Granada. He figured out for himself that Whitey Slater and his partner Ronald Spice were the guilty ones. I didn't buy it myself at first, so Granada followed through on his own time. After Doc Simeon told him Mrs. Donato was killed the same way Broadman was, he stuck to Spice and Slater like a leech."

"Why didn't he arrest them?"

"Premature. He wanted them to take him to their leader."

"Have you caught Gaines?"

"Not yet." Wills sat down solidly, and crossed his legs. "I was hoping for some help from you on that, and other matters."

"I don't want to be inhospital—inhospitable," I said. "But I happen to have a wife and a new baby that I'm eager to see."

"Forget them for now. You'd never make it down to the third floor anyway. And I have some things I want to ask you about. There's been a lot of talk about a kidnapping. Was there a kidnapping?"

"Technically, yes. Gaines kidnapped me in Mountain Grove last night. He took me to the mountain lodge where Granada found me. Gaines and I had a fight there, which he more or less won."

"He shot you?"

"I was shot, yes, and out for a while. He set fire to the house, probably by smashing a gasoline lantern, and left me to burn."

"And Mrs. Ferguson? He left her to burn, too?"

"Evidently he did. I came to in time to get her out. Is she all right?"

Wills answered carefully. We were fencing, and both of us knew it. "It's hard to tell. Her husband is having her privately looked after. He says he doesn't trust the hospital, with all the shenanigans going on. I'm wondering if he doesn't know more than I do about the shenanigans going on."

"Have you talked to him?"

"Just for a second, when he picked up his wife in the emergency ward. He wasn't communicating, and I can't force him to. He hasn't done anything criminal, that I know about. The wife is another matter, now. I can't figure what she was doing up in a mountain hideout with a wanted man. Was she there voluntarily?"

"I don't know."

"You must have some opinion on the subject. You saw her there with Gaines, didn't you?"

"I saw her."

"Was she tied up, or confined, or under duress?"

"I don't know."

"How can you help knowing?" Wills said sharply.

"There are various forms of duress, including the psychological."

"Was she conscious?"

"Yes."

"Did he threaten her?"

"Yes. As a matter of fact, he hit her with a gun."

"Same gun he shot you with?"

"Same gun," I said, but I was beginning to sweat. I hardly knew why I was framing my answers so as to protect the woman. I was in no condition to work out a conflict of conscience. The worst of these conflicts is the tendency they have to crop up when a man isn't equal to handling them.

Wills sensed my indecision. "This psychological duress you mentioned, it's an interesting idea. What does it boil down to, the fact that he had something on her?"

"I don't know."

He said as if at random: "Poor kid, they had to walk her for nearly two hours. She was loaded to the gills with morphine, did you know that?"

"I suspected she was drugged, yes."

"Is she an addict? Is that what Gaines had on her?"

"Your guess is as good as mine."

"I doubt that. You've had opportunities to talk to them, her and her husband both. I understand you've been seeing quite a bit of him in the last day or two."

"I saw him once or twice. He's pretty good man, in case you're in doubt about that."

"Would you vouch for the wife, too?"

"I hardly know her." The sweat was soaking through my hospital gown. Unless I concentrated on my vision, I tended to see Wills in duplicate. One of him was too many at the moment. "Why don't you go away and let me enjoy my misery in peace?"

"I'm sorry, Bill, honestly. But these are questions that need answering. Ronald Spice's unsupported statement isn't worth the paper it's written on. He confessed crimes that never even occurred. And some that did, of course."

"I'd like to see that statement."

"I'll show it to you, soon as we get copies. I also wanted to show you a statement we got from a better witness than Spice—manager of the local Bank of America. It says that Ferguson drew a lot of cash out of his savings account yesterday. So much cash they had to borrow from their Los Angeles branches. Do you know what Ferguson did with all that cash?"

"I know what he told me."

"What did he do with it?"

"Ask him."

"I'm asking you, Bill. You're a rash young fellow, but you're basically sensible, and you're building a position in this town. You wouldn't lie there and try to sit on a major crime at this late date."

"There have been several major crimes. Which one are you referring to?"

"Kidnapping. Spice says Gaines ran out with his and his partner's share of two hundred thousand dollars. Two hundred thousand dollars which Ferguson paid to Gaines as ransom for Mrs. Ferguson. He says she was snatched from the Foothill Club while he and his partner stood by, monitoring our calls on their short wave so we wouldn't get in the way. Which incidentally they've been doing all through this wave of burglaries. It was a neat little system they had, passing along information on hospital patients and then keeping track of our movements while Gaines and Gus Donato burglarized their houses.

"According to Spice, they did the same thing yesterday noon when Ferguson made the money-drop. They were supposed to get a cut of it, twenty-five grand apiece for services rendered. But Gaines ran out on them with the whole bundle. You can understand why Ronald Spice is spouting like a whale. Of course he's trying to cheat the fireless cooker, too. Not that we'd make a deal with scum like that."

Wills was hoarse with anger. "Scum of the earth, masquerading as public servants, using their position to knock off injured people. You know what they are. They almost did it to you."

"Has Spice confessed the Broadman killing?"

"In effect he has. He didn't know he was confessing. He thought he could blame it on his dead partner. Whitey Slater did the actual murder, apparently, while Spice was driving the ambulance to the hospital. But Spice shared the knowledge and intention, which makes him equally guilty, as you know. Gaines is equally guilty, too. Broadman was killed on his orders."

"Why?"

"Broadman was an ex-leader of the ring, with emphasis on the ex. He was at the point of turning them all in. I think he knew they were on their way to capital crime, and he wanted to cut himself clear of them. The purchase of that diamond from Ella Barker was a small thing, but when he reported it to us, it served notice on Gaines. Gaines turned Donato loose on Broadman. Donato fumbled the job. Slater and Spice were standing by, and they stepped in and finished it. Next day they did the same to Donato's wife, for the same reason."

"Was Secundina a member of the ring?"

"I doubt it. But she knew who was, and she was about to talk to us. Granada thought she was, anyway. And apparently Gaines and his ghouls thought so. When she panicked and took those sleeping pills, it gave them a chance at her. They didn't want her waking up."

"Nice people."

"Yeah. All nice people. What I don't understand, Bill, you've got a chance to help us wind up the case, put the rest of them behind bars. But you won't take it. What does this Ferguson woman mean to you?"

It was a hard question. The cliché phrases like "beauty in distress" didn't answer it. Neither did the answer I gave him. "Ferguson is my client. He retained me yesterday."

"Mrs. Ferguson isn't."

"Ferguson retained me for the specific purpose of procuring information about his wife. The information is privileged."

"Her husband doesn't trust her either, eh?"

"That's your conclusion."

"It sure is. What did you find out about her? I'm not asking you to talk for the record, just for checking purposes. Spice's story got pretty fantastic at certain points, and I can't afford to make any false moves."

"You'll be making one if you try to force me to give you privileged information. You can't force Ferguson to talk about her, either."

Wills sat with his chin in his hand, and pondered the situation. I tried to do some consecutive thinking about the rule of privilege, but my line of thought was invaded by images: my wife in childbirth, Secundina dead, a rose-tipped body fallen in fire, in weeds; and a woman firing across her knees at me. Whatever else was covered by the rule, that shooting wasn't, and I knew it. I was holding back on my own responsibility, for reasons that wouldn't stand up under examination.

Wills looked up from his deep thought. I suspected that it had been partly assumed, to give me time to consider.

"I know," he said in a soothing voice, "you want to be fair

to your client, and you want to be fair to the law. I'll tell you a funny thing, it may help you to decide. Ronald Spice came up with quite a snapper when we pressed him. He claims that the kidnapping at the Foothill Club was a phony, something cooked up between Gaines and the woman to extort money from her husband. He claims that she co-operated with them all the way, that she even drove the car for Gaines when he picked up Ferguson's box of money. That she deliberately showed herself to her husband at that time so that he wouldn't know what action to take. Does that fit in with your information about her? Or was Spice just trying to get off the hook as accessory to a snatch?"

"I wouldn't know."

"I don't believe you, Bill. I talked to a waiter in a bar and grill where you and Ferguson had a pow-wow yesterday. He heard some mighty queer snatches of conversation. Privilege or no privilege, bullet wound or no bullet wound, you're on shaky ground if you're trying to cover up a kidnapping."

"I thought your theory was that no kidnapping occurred."

"I don't have a theory. I don't know what occurred. I believe you do. I'm asking you to tell me."

"When I find out, I'll be glad to."

"It can't wait. Don't you see, if this Hollywood floozie is in cahoots with Gaines, she probably knows where he is, or where he's headed. Don't you want him caught?"

"As much as you do. Get that straight, at least." From the jumble of images in my head, I dredged up a fragment of a scene in merry hell. "I remember something that was said last night. Gaines and the woman are headed for South America. Gaines's mother was supposed to buy tickets for them."

"Gaines's mother?"

"She lives in Mountain Grove. Why don't you question her?"

Wills stood up abruptly, crossed the room to press the elevator button, and came back to me. "This is the first I heard of a mother. Who and where is she?"

"Her name is Adelaide Haines. She lives on Canal Street in Mountain Grove."

"How did you get a line on her?"

"Through Ella Barker. Incidentally, it should be plain by this time that Ella Barker's involvement was innocent."

"You're probably right. Spice's statement pretty well clears her."

"Don't you think she ought to be released?"

"She went home this morning. I got the D.A.'s office to agree to reduced bail and a friend of hers, a Mrs. Cline, put up a property bond."

The elevator took him away. I let the images in my head whirl out centrifugally. The pentothal sleep came back like soft and sudden night.

*chapter* 27

WHEN I WOKE UP AGAIN, the elevator was taking me down to a room on the fourth floor. Dr. Root, the bone surgeon, came along and watched the orderlies transfer me from the rolling cot to the bed. He said when the door closed behind them: "I ordered you a private room because you need rest and quiet. Is that all right with you?"

"If you say so, Doctor. I don't expect to stay long."

"You'll be in for a few days, at least. I understand there's nobody at home to look after you."

"But I have things to attend to."

"What you have to attend to," he said firmly, "is letting that shoulder knit. By the way, I have something for you. Thought you might like to keep it as a memento." He produced a small plastic pillbox and rattled it at me. "It's the slug I removed. It will make an interesting conversation piece. Pieces, rather. It's in several pieces."

He showed me the distorted fragments of lead. I thanked him, because it seemed the thing to do.

He shook his gray head. "Don't thank me. You should be thanking your lucky stars. It was providential for you that your collarbone deflected it upward. You could have come in here with a bullet in the lung. Who shot you, by the way?"

"I don't remember."

"Your wife?" Perhaps his narrow smile was intended to be jocular. "I'd hardly blame her, for taking the chances you took. I hope you've learned to leave these matters to the authorities. What were you trying to do?"

"Get myself shot. I succeeded. Next question."

My unpleasantness failed to deter him. "There may be more to that than meets the eye. I've seen young men do some wild things while their wives were having babies. It isn't only the women who suffer from parturient pangs."

"What is that supposed to mean?"

"Think about it. How are the wife and baby doing, by the way?"

"Fine, they tell me. Is it all right with you if I go down and see them? I'm feeling pretty good myself."

"Tomorrow, perhaps, if your temperature stays down. I

want you to remain in bed today. Can I trust you to do that?"

I grunted something noncommittal at him.

I asked the nurse's aide who brought me breakfast to see if she could dig up pencil and paper. While I was waiting for her to come back, I composed a note to Sally in my head. Perhaps composed is not the word:

> *Dearest. I apologize, to you and Her, for getting shot. I did not plan this. It happened. You should have married a policeman if all you wanted was security. But you had to go and marry the slowest draw in the American Bar Association.*
>
> *They are holding me incommunicado in Room 454. But I will foil them. I will put on the faded burnoose which was a gift from an old Bedouin riding companion, darken my skin with a little walnut juice, and pass through their lines like a phantom. Be on the lookout for me. I will be the one with the inscrutable smile. Burn this.*

When my writing materials arrived, I wrote it down quite differently. The pentothal had worn off, and I wasn't feeling so funny. I put the plastic pillbox in a drawer of the bedside table where I couldn't see it.

I noticed for the first time that there was a telephone sitting on a lower shelf of the table. I picked it up and tried to call Sally. The switchboard operator told me acerbly that maternity had no telephones. I called Ferguson's house instead.

He answered himself, in a hushed and wary voice. "Who is calling, please?"

"Gunnarson."

His voice rose in pitch. "But I thought you were in the hospital."

"I am. Come and see me. Room 454."

"I've been planning to, naturally. I'll try to drop by tomorrow. Or is tomorrow too soon for you?"

"It isn't soon enough. I want you out here this morning."

"I'd like to come, but I simply can't make it today. Please don't think I'm unappreciative of all you've done for us. I'm profoundly grateful, really, and so is Holly."

"I want something more than gratitude. The police have been bearing down on me. You and I need an exchange of views, to put it mildly. If you're not here by noon, I'll assume that our professional relationship is dissolved and act accordingly."

Somebody was knocking softly at my door. It seemed like a good time to hang up. The door opened inward, and Ella Barker peeped around the edge of it:

"May I come in, Mr. Gunnarson?"

"Please do."

The girl approached me tentatively. Her eyes were very large and dark, with semicircular imprints under them. She had on hospital shoes and a clean white uniform, but no cap. Her black hair was brushed gleaming, and she was wearing fresh lipstick.

"I wanted to thank you, Mr. Gunnarson. I came over here as soon as I heard. To think that you got yourself shot on my account."

"It wasn't on your account. Put the thought away and forget about it. Anyway, it's not a serious wound."

"You're just being nice." She leaned above me, her eyes brimming with inarticulate feeling. "You've been awful nice to me. Would you like a back rub? I give a very good back rub."

"No thanks."

"Did you have a nice breakfast? I can get you some fruit juice if you're thirsty."

"You're very kind. But I seem to have everything I need."

She moved around the room, setting it straight in small, unobtrusive ways. I don't know exactly what she did, but the place began to seem more comfortable. She picked up an empty glass vase that stood on the bureau, straightened the runner under it, and set it down again in the exact center.

"I'm going to get you some flowers," she announced. "You need some flowers to brighten up the place. What kind of flowers do you like?"

"Any kind. But please don't send me flowers. You can't afford them."

"Yes I can. I'm starting back on duty tomorrow morning at seven." She turned with a slight dancer's lilt, and smiled at me across the foot of the bed. "The hospital is taking me back."

"No reason why they shouldn't."

"But I was so afraid they'd fire me. After all, I was in *jail*. I ran around with some terrible people."

"Next time you'll be more careful."

"Yes. I guess I'm lucky to have a next time." The marks of iron were showing on her face. It would take time for them to dissolve away. "Did Larry Gaines shoot you?"

"I can't discuss that with you, Ella."

"He did, though, didn't he? And he got away."

"Don't worry about him," I said. "He won't be coming back to hurt you."

"I'm not afraid of him. I just don't want him to get away."

"Forget about him, too."

"I'm trying. It is like a sickness, just like you said. Well. I don't want to wear out my welcome. If there's anything I can do for you, day or night—" She completed the sentence by adjusting my sheets.

It wouldn't be long, I thought, before she'd be making some man a good wife. It was the first satisfaction that I derived from the case. She came around to the side of the bed and leaned over me again. Before I could guess her intention, she kissed me lightly on the corner of the mouth and made for the door.

It was not the kind of kiss that goes to your head, but I was feeling very susceptible. I got out of bed and found a striped cotton bathrobe hanging behind my clothes in the closet. I more or less got into it, and reconnoitered the corridor.

The elevator doors were beside the nurses' station. I went in the other direction, down the fire stairs. On the third floor I found an orderly with gray hair and a paternal expression, to whom I explained my problem, omitting salient details. He escorted me to the door of Sally's room.

She was lying there with her bright hair spread on the pillow. She looked pale and wan and wonderful.

I kissed her smiling mouth, and she kissed me back. Her arms came around me, with the warmth of reality itself. Then she pushed me back to look at me.

"I got your note. It was sweet. But you're a wild man, a positive wild man. Are you all right, Bill?"

"Fine. It was only a flesh wound," I lied.

"Then why is your arm in a sling? And who shot you, anyway?"

"I don't know. It was dark."

"Also," she said, "you have lipstick on your face, and I'm not wearing lipstick. Have you been kissing the nurses?"

"No, they've been kissing me. Ella Barker came by to thank me."

"She better." Her hand tightened on mine. "Bill, will you

promise me something—just one thing? Promise me you won't take criminal cases and rampage around the countryside and all."

"I promise." But I had mental reservations.

My wife may have sensed them. "You have a family to think of now, not just me. She's beautiful, Bill."

"Like her mother."

"Not this morning I'm not beautiful. I'm all washed out this morning. On the other hand, have you noticed my abdomen? It's getting quite flat already. I can actually see my toes."

She demonstrated this, wiggling her toes under the covers.

"You're as flat as a pancake, darling."

"Not *that* flat, I hope. Bill?" She turned toward me, pushing her hair back. Her eyes were deeper and softer than I had ever seen them. "Do you mind awfully the fact that our joint product is not a boy? You like little girls, don't you?"

"I like girls of all sizes."

"Don't try to be funny. We have a serious problem."

"You're okay, aren't you?"

"Oh, *I* feel pretty good. Kind of empty, though, like an elevator shaft after the elevator went down. Except when they bring her in. Then I feel full."

"Is there something the matter with her? Where is she?"

"Don't get panicky now. She's in the nursery, and she's physically perfect. Not to mention precociously intelligent and aware. I can tell by the way she nurses. That makes the problem even more urgent. We have to give her a name, for her to start forming her personality around. We can't simply go on calling her Her, like something out of H. Rider Haggard."

"How about Sally?"

"Negative. One Sally in a family is enough. Do you like Sharon for a name, or is Sharon Gunnarson too cosmopolitan? Rose of Sharon Gunnarson is even more unwieldy, but that is the way I feel about her. Rose of Sharon Gunnarson," she said dreamily.

"Negative. Rose Sharon Gunnarson, maybe."

"But Rose by itself is such a florid name. Do you like Sarah? Susan? Martha? Anne? Elizabeth? Sandra?"

"Strangely enough, I like them all. How about Nancy?"

"I like Nancy. But let me think about it. We'll both think about it. Now you go back and rest, Bill, you look tired. Maybe I can visit *you* tomorrow. Dr. Trench says my pelvis was formed for motherhood and I should get my strength back very rapidly."

I told Sally that I adored her pelvis. She bumped it at me under the covers feebly.

I met Dr. Trench outside the door. He was a short man of forty with horn-rimmed glasses and a quick, intelligent smile. A little too intelligent at the moment.

"Well, well, the prodigal husband himself. The wanderer returns."

"Go ahead and have your bit of vaudeville. Everybody does. Then I want to talk to you seriously."

"Sally's in fine shape, if that's what you're worried about. You're fortunate to have a secretary who knows what labor pains are."

"It isn't Sally I'm worried about. Can you give me a few minutes in private?"

"I have patients to look after. Including your wife."

"This concerns one of your patients."

He consulted his watch. "All right. Five minutes. Where can we talk?"

"Up in my room."

I was shaky and sweating again when I reached my bed. I sat on the edge of it.

Dr. Trench remained standing. "I suppose the patient you mean is Mrs. Ferguson?"

"Yes. Have you seen her since the—accident?"

"I attended her, yes. Her husband requested me not to discuss her condition with anyone." His eyes were stern.

"Good. Ferguson has retained me as his attorney. Anything that you tell me will be privileged."

"What do you want to know about her?"

"I'm interested in her mental condition, for one thing."

"It's not too bad, considering what she's been through. She seems to be blessed with a good strong nervous system. I was afraid she might lose her child, but there seems to be no danger of that now."

"Is she at home?"

"Yes. She doesn't seem to require hospitalization. I found that her injuries were superficial."

"Is she in fit shape to be questioned?"

"It depends on the questioner, and the nature of the questions. She's resting quietly, at least she was two hours ago. I'd leave it for a few days, if I were you. You can use the rest yourself."

"It won't wait, Doctor. I have to get a statement from her about the events of last night. Not to mention the night before and the night before."

"I don't see how she can help you much. She was unconscious, as you know, literally dead to the world."

"Is that what she told you?"

"Yes, and I have no medical reason to doubt it. She was in a state of drugged sleep throughout her period of—ah—

detention. It's lucky for her the kidnappers knew how to handle drugs. They could so easily have killed her."

"*They* gave her drugs?"

"Who else? I gather from her fragmentary memories, and from the medical indications, that she was forcibly drugged at the actual moment of the kidnapping. It occurred in the parking lot of the Foothill Club. She was lured out there by a telephone call from someone purporting to be a relative. They seized her at the door of her car and gave her an injection of pentothal or some other quick-acting anesthetic."

"Do you believe all this?"

"I know it sounds melodramatic, but the marks of the needle are on her arm. Later, to keep her under, they evidently gave her spaced shots of morphia or demerol. I suppose their idea was to keep her quiet and make it impossible for her to identify them later."

"What if I told you that I talked to her last night?"

"Around what time last night?"

"It must have been about one o'clock when I got to the mountain house. Your patient was very much alive and kicking."

"What did she say?"

"I'd hate to repeat it."

Trench took off his glasses and polished them with a handkerchief. Under cover of this business, he was studying my face. "I'd say that one of you was lying, or hallucinating. Mrs. Ferguson was still in a drug-induced coma when she came into my hands early this morning. When she did rouse out of it, she had no memory of the previous forty-eight hours or so. Her physical condition supported her subjective account."

"You should have seen her last night. She was moving around like a cat on a hot stove, and spitting like one. It occurred to me at the time that she had been taking drugs. Is it possible she took an overdose and it suddenly caught up with her?"

"Took an overdose of her own accord?"

"Yes. There are indications that she is an addict."

The doctor's eyes widened. He put on his glasses as though to protect them from seeing too much. "You must be mistaken. She's been visiting me biweekly for two months. I've noticed no—" His voice broke off. He looked up sideways at a corner of the ceiling and stayed with his eyes fixed in that position.

"Have you remembered something, Doctor?"

He answered in a rather flustered way. "I'm sure it's of no great significance. In one of her visits to me, Mrs. Ferguson did bring up the subject of drug addiction. It was a purely academic discussion—at least it seemed so to me—having to do with the effect of drugs on an unbalanced mind. I told her that most addicts probably have some degree of mental or nervous illness to begin with. That's what makes them addicts. She seemed very interested in the subject."

"Personally interested?"

Trench looked up at the ceiling again, as if he were balancing pros and cons on his chin.

"I'd say so, yes. I gathered, from another discussion we had, that some friend or relative of hers is a psychopath—what the psychiatrists call a severely maladjusted personality. She was very much concerned with the question of inherited character defects. I assured her that such things weren't inherited. That isn't entirely true, of course, but we know so little about the genes as they affect mind and emotions, there's no use worrying a pregnant woman about it."

"Is she psychopathic herself?"

"I've observed no signs of it." But a deep cleft of concern had appeared between his eyebrows. "I wish I knew where your questions are leading."

"So do I. Consider this possibility. This friend or relative she blames things on—couldn't it be her way of referring to her own alter ego? A second personality that gets out of control and jumps out at her when she's disturbed?"

"If so, I've never seen it. I understand—books and movies to the contrary—that a true case of multiple personality is rare. Of course I don't pretend to be a psychiatrist." After a pause, he added: "You may be interested to know that I've asked Mrs. Ferguson to have a neuropsychiatric examination. Perhaps she'll agree to share the findings with you, if it really is so important."

"Why did you suggest it?"

"Simply as a precautionary measure. She seems to have come through her ordeal without brain damage. But it's dangerous to spend such a long period under drugs, even in *good* hands." He looked at his watch impatiently.

"You mentioned her interest in heredity. Was there any thought of her not having her child?"

"She's very eager to have it. So is the father, now that he knows about it. It's true, with an older father, the probability of mutation rises, but not to the point of negative indication."

"Ferguson is the father, then?"

"I have no reason to doubt it." Trench gave me a queer, cold look. "In any case, I'm sure your client wouldn't authorize you to ask that question about my patient."

"Is that intended to be a negative answer?"

"Absolutely not. The question doesn't deserve an answer. You seem to be trying to rake up any dirt you can about Mrs. Ferguson."

"I'm sorry it looks that way to you, doctor. It's true I have to know the worst about her, if I'm going to do anything for her."

"What are you trying to do for her?"

"Give her the legal protection she's entitled to. She's likely to be arrested some time today."

"On what charge?"

"I prefer not to name it. If the police or the D.A.'s men try to ask you any questions about her, tell them you've already communicated your information to me. Tell them if charges are laid, I expect to use you as a witness for the defense. And don't tell them a damn thing else."

*chapter* 28

FERGUSON APPEARED shortly after lunch. He hadn't shaved. He looked frowzy and harried, a Quixote who had tilted at windmills once too often and found out they were giants after all.

"You're late."

"I came at all because I owe you a great deal—Holly's life. But you should not have forced me to leave her. Her life is still in danger. I couldn't possibly leave the house until Dr. Trench got there."

"Trench says she's in fairly good shape."

"Physically she is, thank God. She's emotionally upset. We had a most disturbing phone call this morning. That Florida jackanapes, Salaman, insists on seeing her."

"Don't let him."

"How can I stop him? I have no recourse to law."

"Are you going to pay him?"

"I don't know. Holly tells me she owes him nothing. She never heard of the man until today."

"And you believe her?"

Ferguson came unconsciously to attention. "I believe my wife implicitly."

"How does she explain the alleged abduction?"

"I resent your use of the phrase."

"That's your privilege. How does she explain it?"

"She has no knowledge of it. Her mind is a blank from the time that she left the Club."

"She'll have to do better than the old blackout gambit. You saw her in Gaines's car when he picked up your money."

"I was mistaken. It must have been someone else." He cupped his hand protectively around his bulbous nose.

"Is that what Mrs. Ferguson says?"

"We haven't discussed the incident."

"Don't you think you better? She can fill you in on a lot of interesting facts, about Gaines, and about herself."

He stood above me shivering. It wasn't a cold enough day to make a Canadian shiver.

"Damn you, I resent this, bitterly. I'm going to have to ask you to retract."

"What exactly do you want me to retract?"

"The whole allegation that she was involved with him in any immoral way."

"I got the idea from you."

"I was mistaken, tragically mistaken. I misunderstood their relationship—exaggerated it. It was simply an old man's jealousy."

"What about the child she's carrying?"

"The child is mine. She had nothing at all to do with Gaines, in that sense. She was simply giving the fellow a helping hand. My wife is a remarkable woman."

His eyes had taken on a euphoric glare. I began to feel the dimensions of the dream that held him. It included his passion for his wife, his hope of a second youth, and now the belief that she would give him a child. I knew precisely how he felt about that.

But the dream had to be destroyed, and I was the one elected to destroy it. "Your wife's real name is Hilda Dotery. Does the name mean anything to you?"

"Not a thing."

"It does to some other people. I have witnesses to prove that Hilda Dotery has been mixed up with Gaines for the last seven years, ever since they were high-school delinquents together. His real name, incidentally, is Henry Haines."

"Who are these witnesses?"

"Their parents, Adelaide Haines, James and Kate Dotery. I talked to all three of them last night in Mountain Grove."

"They're lying."

"Somebody is. I assure you that I'm not. There's no doubt at all in my mind that the kidnapping was a phony one, and that your wife was Gaines's partner in it. That's not the worst of it. She shot me last night. Assault with intent to commit murder is a very ugly charge, but there's not much use beating around the bush. You can't keep her shut up at home and expect this thing to blow over. I want complete co-operation from both of you, starting now."

Ferguson shook his fist at me. The light in his eyes was dancing out of control. "You're like all the rest. You think you have me on the hip, that you can bleed me for money."

I sat up and slapped his fist away with my good arm. "You're pretty fouled up on the money angle, aren't you? The man with the Midas touch. You may be right at that, Ferguson, in reverse. If you weren't loaded, nobody in his senses would come within a hundred yards of you. You're merely trouble that walks like a man. Stupid trouble. Stupid, ignorant trouble. You're so morally stupid you don't know where you're hurt, or what's hurting you."

I was hurting him now. He blinked and shuddered under the impact of the words. They seemed to strike through to his knowledge of himself. He walked away from the bed and sat in a chair in the corner behind the door, nursing his hurt.

He spoke after a time. "You're right about the money—the idea of money. It's been a root of evil in my life. My father died poor, and he was a better man than I shall ever be."

I asked him about his father, partly because I was interested, but mainly because it was a way in. I'd begun to understand that it wasn't happenstance that Ferguson had been victimized by a pair of young criminals. He was one of those victims whose natures, whose whole lives, set them up for a particular crime.

The elder Ferguson had been a sheep rancher who came out from Scotland around the turn of the century and homesteaded near a hamlet named Wild Goose Lake. He went back overseas with the Scots Grenadiers and died at Vimy Ridge.

"I tried to follow him," Ferguson said. "Though I was underage, I managed to enlist in 1918. But I never got out of the country, in that war. It was just as well: Mother needed me to help run the ranch. We had hard sledding for nearly ten years, until oil and gas were discovered on our section.

"You mustn't imagine that it was a bonanza, not at first.

But enough money began to come in so that I was able to go to college, finally. By the time I finished my degree in Edmonton, we had more money than we knew what to do with. Mother decided that I should have some specific training in business.

"She sent me, more or less against my will, to take a course at Harvard Business School. I didn't do too well there. For one thing, I was worried about Mother: she hadn't been strong the last few years; the years of struggle had been too much for her. And then I got involved with the girl I told you about, the one I betrayed.

"It's a wretched thing for a man to have to confess. It's still hard for me to relate it to myself. I'd never been in the States before, you see. Whatever happened below the border seemed unreal to me, like life on Mars. My actual life was back in Alberta, where Mother was slowly dying and dictating long letters to her nurse telling me how to conduct myself.

"I conducted myself very badly, as it turned out. I was in my late twenties, but I'd never had a girl, in the physical sense. I realized before long that I could have the girl if I wanted her. I had all the money I needed, and she came from a desperately poor family. They lived in a crowded flat somewhere in the wilds of South Boston."

"How did you meet the girl?"

"She was a salesgirl in Filene's. I went there to buy a gift for Mother. She was very helpful, and it went on from there. It took me a week to get up the nerve to kiss her, and then that very night she let me have her. I took her to a hotel off Scollay Square. I shouldn't have done that. She wasn't a prostitute, she wanted to marry me. When we faced each other in that shabby hotel room, I realized that I was using her. I threw her down on the bed."

His voice cracked like an adolescent's through his aging mask. It was a strange conversation, and getting stranger. I'd had a few others of its kind. In the tension of a legal contest, or the aftermath of a crime, old springs of emotion stir. Unsuspected fissures open into the deep past.

"She's been on my mind this past year," Ferguson said. "I haven't been able to stop thinking about her since I met Holly again."

"Again?"

"I don't mean 'again.' It's just that Holly reminded me of her in so many ways. I believed I was being given a second chance—a second chance at happiness. When I didn't deserve the first chance."

"What exactly did you do to the girl?"

He didn't answer directly. His eyes were turned downward, fixed on the past, like eyes watching underwater movements, a drowned girl or a swimmer or a monstrous shape compound of both. Like an insubstantial colloidal web, the truth or something near it formed between us slowly as he spoke.

"Mother died that winter, and I had to go home for her funeral. I'll never forget her face the night she said good-by to me in Boston Station. She was three months pregnant, unmarried and still working, but she looked so damn *hopeful*. She ate a dozen cherrystone clams, for the good of the child, she said, and assured me that she'd be fine while I was gone. I promised her I'd be back as soon as the estate was settled, and then we could be married. She believed me.

"Perhaps I believed myself. I didn't know certainly that I would never go back until the afternoon we buried Mother. It was a bitter day in the middle of February. The gravediggers had to use pickaxes and blowtorches to break through the crust of the earth. The lake below the graveyard was nothing but a flat place under the snow. The wind swept down from the Arctic Circle across it.

"They covered the chunks of frozen earth with that imitation green grass they used in those days: a little rectangle of horrible fake green in the middle of the flat white prairie, with wooden oil rigs standing on the horizon. I could never think of going back to Boston and marrying the girl. I couldn't even imagine her face without the blackest feeling of melancholy. As I think I told you last night, I arranged with a lawyer in Boston to give her a thousand dollars."

"You could have gone in person, at least."

"You don't have to tell me that. I've had it on my conscience for twenty-five years."

"Weren't you concerned about the child?"

"I'll be honest. My main concern was fear that she would search me out, turn up on my doorstep with the child in her arms. Or sue me. I was a rich man, you understand, and on my way to becoming richer. She was a girl from the Boston slums who couldn't speak proper English. I was afraid that she would stand in my way."

"Your way to where?"

He didn't try to answer that question. It was rhetorical, anyway. I lay there wondering how much weight his conscience was able to bear. Though I felt sorry for the man, I couldn't see any way out of telling him what I suspected. Perhaps it was in him already, unrecognized and unadmitted, but eating away at his marrow like moral strontium.

"Why did you marry Holly?" I said.

"I've told you why. When I saw her on the screen, then met her in the flesh, she was like my youth come back to me —a second springtime." He broke off, shaking his head. "I must sound like a romantic fool."

"I think you were looking for something impossible. The

worst of it is, when you want something impossible, you often get it. You married Holly because she resembled a girl you knew in Boston twenty-five years ago. Did you ever think of questioning that resemblance?"

"I don't understand you."

"What was the girl's name?"

"Mulloy. Kathleen Mulloy. I called her Katie."

"Did Holly ever tell you who her mother was?"

"No." He got up and came to the side of the bed. He walked with his eyes down, slowly, watching each step. "What sort of a woman is her mother? You mentioned that you spoke to her last night."

"She's not a bad sort of woman, and quite good-looking. She looks like your wife twenty-five years older. Her name, as I think I said, is Kate Dotery. I don't know what her maiden name was, but I can guess. She came originally from Boston, and she told me that Hilda was her eldest daughter. She also said something suggesting that Hilda was not a legitimate child."

Ferguson hung over me like a man falling through space at the end of a long tether. He reached the end of the tether. His head came up with a jerk.

He walked mechanically to the window and stood with his rigid back to me. My room was four stories up. I hoped he wasn't thinking of taking the final fall. Then the first deep shock hit him.

He let out a coughing groaning grunt: "Augh!"

I sat up with my legs over the edge of the bed, ready to go for him if he opened the window. He made a stumbling run for the bathroom door. I heard him being sick behind it.

I got up and started to put on my clothes. I was half dressed when Ferguson came out.

He looked like a man who had passed through a desperate

crisis, a nervous breakdown, or an almost mortal illness. His eyes in their deep cavities were very bright, not with hope. His mouth was like blue iron. "What are you doing?"

"I have to talk to your wife. Take me to her, will you?"

"I will, if it has to be. Forgive my outburst. I'm not myself."

He helped me on with my shirt and jacket, and tied my shoelaces for me. He spoke like a supplicant from his kneeling position. "You won't tell her, will you? What you just told me?"

"No."

"It would drive her out of her mind."

Perhaps it already had.

*chapter* **29**

SHE WAS SITTING UP in the long chair by the window, with the sky and sea behind her. The sea was ruffled and burnished by wind. Spinnakers stood on the horizon, as still to the eye as traveling moons.

She looked like a young barbarous queen. A scarf worn like a turban and held in place by jeweled pins concealed the places where the fire had scorched her hair. Jeweled dark harlequin spectacles hid her eyes. A silk robe covered her legs and the lower part of her body.

"I thought you were never going to come back," she said to Ferguson. "Who's your friend?"

"This is Mr. Gunnarson, Holly. The man who rescued you from the fire."

"I'm very pleased to meet you, Mr. Gunnarson."

She held out her hand in a rather regal gesture and kept it out until I took it. It was limp and cold. What I could see of her face had a pale and lunar look.

Her voice barely moved her lips. "I've been wanting to thank you in person for all you did. You really plucked me burning, didn't you? Like in that poem which my husband bought me a record of. By T. S. Eliot. I never heard of the label before, but the poem certainly sent me."

Except for the last line, the little speech sounded rehearsed. The expressionlessness of her face gave it a ventriloquial effect. The entire scene had a staged quality.

If I had been feeling stronger, I'd have gone along with it for a while. But my knees were shaking with weakness and anger and doubt. "We've met before, Mrs. Ferguson."

"I guess you could say we have, in a way. I wouldn't remember, drugged like I was. The dirty ba—the dirty beggars drugged me."

"You don't remember shooting me?"

The room was silent for a long moment. I could hear the susurrus of the waves like whispering at the windows. The woman tipped up her chin to Ferguson, carefully, so as not to destroy the beauty of her pose. "What is he talking about, Ian?"

"Mr. Gunnarson claims you shot him last night." He was watching her like a photographer, ready to click the shutter of his judgment. "There's no doubt he was shot."

"I didn't shoot him, for gosh sake. Why would I shoot the man that was trying to help me?"

"That's one of the questions I came here to ask you."

"Are there others? You keep on pitching low curves at me like that one, I'll ask my husband to chuck you out on your ear."

Ferguson shook his head at her.

I said: "Why did you shoot me? You know perfectly well you did."

"I don't know anything of the sort. And don't stand over me, I hate people standing over me." A thin edge of hysteria had entered her voice.

Ferguson picked up a chair and placed it for me, a safe distance from her long chair. "Please sit down. There's no need to stand, after all."

I noticed as I sat down that Dr. Trench had slipped in behind me and was standing quietly just inside the door. The woman appealed to her husband, holding up both hands to him with the fingers stiff and spread. "Tell him he's making a mistake, Fergie. You know I couldn't have done it, I was out like a light. It must have been somebody else shot him. Or else he's nuttier than a fruitcake himself."

"Was somebody else there, Mrs. Ferguson?"

"I don't know, honest. I don't know who was there. They had me drugged, and I lost two whole days. You don't have to take my word, ask Dr. Trench." She craned her pretty neck to look past me.

The doctor stood there polishing his glasses. "This is no time to try to settle anything. Why don't you let it lie for now, Gunnarson? Mrs. Ferguson's had a rough two days."

The third day was turning out to be no less rough. I heard a car coming down the lane and thought it was Wills, arriving on cue. I went with Ferguson to the door. It was Salaman.

"I want to talk to the lady in person," he said.

"Say whatever you have to say to me. My—wife is far from well."

"She'll be farther from it unless she pays her bills."

Ferguson said in an old, weary voice: "I'll pay you. I'll give you a check on the Bank of Montreal."

"Don't you do it, Fergie." The woman had come up behind us in the hallway. She brushed past me and leaned on Ferguson's arm. "This character knows we're in trouble, he's trying to shake you down. I don't owe him or anybody else any sixty-five thou. I don't owe him sixty-five cents."

"She's lying her little head off," Salaman said. "She thinks she can gamble my money away and lie herself out of it."

"I never gambled in my life. I never even put a dollar in a slot machine."

"You've never even been in Miami, I bet."

"That's right, I haven't."

"Liar. You slept with me in Miami two months running last summer. What's more, you liked it. Maybe you want to forget it, now that you're married to Pops here, but I'm here to tell you that you can't."

"Which two months last summer?" I said.

"July and most of August. I wasn't planning to bring this up, but the lady forced me to."

"I was in Canada all through August," she said.

"That's true," Ferguson said. "I can vouch for it."

"It takes more than that. I don't like using muscle, but why are the ones with the most the hardest to collect from?" Salaman's voice was rising. His hand went under his gabardine jacket, as if he felt a pain there, and came out holding an automatic. "Make with the checkbook, Pops. And take my advice, don't try to stop the check."

"I don't know what goes on here," the woman said, "but we're not paying money we don't owe."

Salaman leaned toward her. "You're Holly May, ain't you?"

"That's my name, little man. It gives you no right—"

"You're the movie actress, ain't you?"

"I used to be in the movies."

"You remember me, don't you? Hairy-legs Salaman with the loving disposition?"

"I never saw you before in my life and I wouldn't touch you with a ten-foot pole."

"I hear you saying it. You used to tell it different."

Ferguson looked at her in bitter doubt. She answered his look. "This boy has got me tabbed for somebody else. It happened another time last year, before I went to Canada. Some stores in Palm Springs sent me bills, and I hadn't been in Palm Springs all winter."

"Aw, cut it out." Salaman reached for her face in a sudden movement and snatched off her harlequin glasses.

"Don't you dare, you!"

"Hey!" Salaman said. "Come out in the light. I want to look at you."

He took hold of her wrist, not roughly, but with an easy assumption of superior force, and pulled her out into the sun.

"Let go of my wife," Ferguson cried. "I'll break your bloody neck."

Ferguson started to move on him. I tried to hold him. A bullet in the bowels was all he needed to complete his disaster. I couldn't hold him with one arm. He tore himself out of my grasp.

The woman swung her body between her husband and the gun. She jerked her wrist free and grabbed her dark glasses out of Salaman's hand. Salaman's eyes remained intent on her face. Then he looked around at us. The gun muzzle followed his glance.

"What are you trying to pull on me? She ain't Holly May. Where's the real McCoy?"

"How would I know? There's thousands of people look like

me. They used to send me their pictures in the mail." The woman let out a laugh of savage enjoyment. "Too bad, lover-boy, some gal conned you good. You better get out of here before somebody steals your wallet. And put that firearm away before you hurt somebody."

"That isn't a bad idea," Trench said at my elbow. He walked toward Salaman with a double-barreled shotgun in his hands. "Put the cap pistol away and get out of here. I happen to be a skeet shooter, and this shotgun is loaded. Now get."

Salaman got.

I noted his license number, and telephoned it in to the police station. If he had a criminal record, as he almost certainly had, concealed-weapons charges would keep him out of mischief for some time. This pleasant duty accomplished, I asked for Lieutenant Wills.

Wills was on his way in from the mountains. The desk sergeant said if it was urgent he could direct him by radio to Ferguson's house. I told him it was urgent, and went back to the big front room. Meeting Trench in the hall, I asked him to absent himself for a while.

The moony spinnakers were strung out down the sea, ballooning home. Ferguson sat on a stool beside the woman's chair, holding her hand. Or perhaps she was holding his hand. She was a powerful woman, whoever she was.

"Take off your glasses again, Mrs. Ferguson. Would you mind?"

She made a mouth at me. "I hate to. I look awful with this black eye."

But she removed the harlequin glasses and let me look at her. The bruise was an old one, already turning green and yellow at the edges. She couldn't have received it within the past fifteen hours. Besides, it was on the wrong side. Gaines was right-handed. The woman in the mountain house had been struck on the left side of the head by his revolver.

There were other, more subtle differences between that woman and the one in front of me. She had had a frozen face, as hard as a silver mask, and eyes like blowtorches which had burned holes in it. The face I was looking at was mobile and lively, in spite of the damage to it. The eyes and mouth were smiling.

"You'll remember me."

"For more reasons than one. Has somebody been masquerading as you?"

"It certainly looks like it."

"And you say it's happened before?"

"At least once, maybe other times. That would explain a lot of things."

"Do you have any notion who's been doing it to you?"

"I know darn well who did it that time in Palm Springs. Mike Speare hired a detective to find out."

"Who was it? Your mother?"

"Don't be ridic. Momma's no great moral figure, but she wouldn't do a thing like that to me."

"One of your sisters?"

"You're sharp." She said to Ferguson: "This boy is sharp."

"Which one? Renee or June?"

She emitted a burst of laughter. It was a queer, high, bitter, rowdy laugh, hyphenating the tragic and the comic.

"My God," she said, "I'm beginning to get the picture. Who do you think I am?"

"I know who you are, Hilda."

"You may think you do, but you don't. I happen to be June. Hilda was the one who used my professional name to run up bills in Palm Springs. I guess I should have done something about her then. But you sort of hate to sick the law on your own sister. I certainly wasn't going to sick that hoodlum on her.

"I can't blame her too much," she added in a softer voice. "She always wanted to be a big name, an actress. If the truth be known, I caught the bug from Hilda. It must have driven her crazy when she saw me on the screen, and realized I was her little sister June."

"You're a generous woman to feel that way about her."

"I can afford to be generous. I was the one that made it. And when I made it, I found out I didn't want it. I wanted Fergie here. Thank the Lord I've got him."

Her smile resembled her mother's. It lit up her face like a ray which had traveled through light-years of darkness to this moment. She turned it on Ferguson, and he tried to respond. His mouth only grimaced. He was sweating out his own darkness.

"Hilda's your oldest sister?"

"That's right, she's the oldest one, and I'm the second oldest. Hilda's only our half-sister, though."

"Do you know that for a fact?"

"I ought to." Her smile faded. "It was no secret in our family. There were never any secrets in the Dotery family— the old man saw to that. When we were kids, he brought it up about three times a day, at mealtimes, that Hilda wasn't his, or anybody's. It was very nice for all of us, especially for Hilda."

"She must have been somebody's."

"She was Momma's. The father was some guy that Momma knew in Boston before the old man married her. The jerk ran out on her. He sent her a thousand bucks, which Dotery used to buy a car to come to California. That's all I know about it."

It was enough. Ferguson's teeth were set like a wounded man's biting on a rag.

His wife told her story to Wills when he arrived. I sat and monitored the interview, ready to suppress hearsay evidence and irrelevancies. I was Ferguson's lawyer, after all, and Hilda was his daughter.

Wills sat slumped in a chair and listened without arguing. He looked very tired. There was a black smear of char on his right cheekbone. He shook his head at her when she had finished. Ashes fell from his hair, filling a shaft of sunlight with their particles.

"I wish you'd spoken up this morning, Mrs. Ferguson. Time is of the essence in these matters, and your sister could have traveled a long way since early this morning. In addition to which, we put out the word that Gaines is traveling alone."

"But I didn't know that Hilda was in it this morning."

He looked at her unresponsively. "How could that be, Mrs. Ferguson? It was her phone call that decoyed you out of the Foothill Club and set you up for the sna—for the abduction."

"I know that now," she said. "I didn't then. When Hilda phoned me the other night she said that she was Renee, my youngest sister. She just got in from San Francisco, she said, and she was down at the bus station. She said she was in trouble, and needed help. I believed her."

"The girl's in trouble, all right," Wills muttered.

"You won't be too hard on her, will you? Hilda isn't too responsible, and Gaines has always led her around by the nose."

He disregarded her question. "That's another thing I don't understand, Mrs. Ferguson. You knew what kind of a character Gaines was, going back to early days of childhood. You knew that he was using a false name. Yet you've been fraternizing with him these last months. No offense intended, but you must have been aware you were putting yourself in danger."

She looked at her husband, rather guiltily. He looked guiltily back at her.

She said: "I was a damned fool, frankly. He told me he was reformed, that he was trying to live down his past and earn an honest living. I felt so lucky myself, I gave him the benefit of the doubt." She changed the subject quickly. "What are you going to do to him and Hilda?"

"Find them." Wills hunched his body forward, heavily, and held out his hands as if he was getting ready to receive a weight. There were lines of grime across his palms, and his fingernails were dirty. "Then it's out of my hands." He let his arms drop to his sides.

"Will Hilda go to jail for a long time?"

"She'll be lucky if that's all that happens to her. There's no use beating around the bush, Mrs. Ferguson. This is a case of multiple murder. You know the penalty for premeditated murder."

"But Hilda didn't kill anyone herself."

"She didn't have to, to be guilty of murder. Ronald Spice says she was the one that phoned them and told them to knock off Secundina Donato. Even if Spice is lying, she's tied to another murder, one we didn't know about. We've been doing some digging at the scene of the fire, and we found human remains. There isn't much left of whoever it was—"

Holly cried out, and turned her head away. She had reached her limit. Dr. Trench stepped in and ended the interview. As Wills and I left the room, she began to wail.

I couldn't keep up with Wills, but he was waiting for me in his car. I got in beside him. "Whose body is it, Lieutenant?"

"You can't call it a body—a piece of skull and some teeth and a few charred bones. I was hoping you could tell me who they belonged to. Who else was up there, besides you and Gaines and the sister?"

"Nobody else that I saw. Are the remains male or female?"

"I can't tell for sure. Simeon probably can, but he hasn't seen them yet. They look like a man's teeth to me. Do you have any suggestions on the subject?"

"Not unless it's Gaines himself."

"That doesn't seem too likely. As I see it, he and the woman made a clean getaway in your car. The Mountain Grove P.D. picked up your car about a block from his mother's house. Apparently he had his own car stashed in her garage. There's fresh oil spots on the floor, and she has no car of her own."

"Did Mrs. Haines go with them?"

"Not her. The Grove police brought her in for questioning, but she claims to know nothing about them. She says she had a headache and took some sleeping pills, slept right through until the police woke her up. The chief there says she's been off her rocker for years, in a harmless way. Ever since her boy got into trouble the first time." Wills sighed. "Why can't people stay out of trouble and lead a natural life?"

"You'd be out of a job."

"Gladly. Dr. Root tells me, by the way, that he gave you

the slug extracted from your shoulder. He shouldn't have done that. It's evidence."

"Take it up with him."

"I already did. Do you have it with you, Bill?" He was calling me Bill again.

"It's in my room at the hospital. Do you want to drive me back there? I was intending to ask you for a lift."

"Sure thing. You look as though you could use more hospital. As a matter of fact, you look like the wrath of God."

I caught a glimpse of my face in the rear-view mirror, and concurred. I'd been going on nerve ever since Ferguson's Boston adventure shocked me out of bed. I leaned my head against the back of the seat and dozed all the way to the hospital.

The nurse in charge at the third-floor station opened her mouth to upbraid me. She closed it again when Wills stepped out of the elevator behind me. I was probably being arrested. I certainly deserved it, her look said.

I opened the drawer of the bedside table and handed him the pillbox. He dumped its contents into his hand, growling over them. "Fragmented. We probably can't do anything with it."

"What do you want to do with it?"

"Just hold it in readiness," he said, "until we get our hands on the gun. Who shot you, Bill, Gaines or the woman?"

"She did."

"And then she dragged her unconscious sister out and changed clothes with her?"

"Apparently."

"That's what I guessed. You thought you were covering up for Mrs. Ferguson. The girl you were actually covering for may turn out to be the most vicious killer of them all. There's a hole in that piece of skull we found, looks like a bullet hole, spang in the middle of the forehead. She left three people to burn up in that fire, you and the sister and a third party who was probably dead already. Who was the third party, Bill? You must have some idea."

I remembered the second shot Hilda had fired, just before I knocked myself out on the door frame. I'd assumed it was aimed at me.

"There was no third party, unless he or she was out of sight with the unconscious sister. You may have turned up the victim of an old killing."

"That's possible, too."

Wills went away at last. I undressed with shaking hands. The head nurse came in to fix my bed and give me hell. Dr. Root dropped by and gave me hell. Sally came up in a wheelchair and gave me hell.

Very mild hell. She had the baby with her. I passed out more or less content, wishing my little nameless girl a better fate than some.

((⟨⟨⟨((⟨⟨((⟨((
((⟨((⟨((⟨((⟨((⟨((   *chapter*  30
((⟨((⟨((⟨((⟨((

FERGUSON HIRED DETECTIVES. The FBI entered the case on the grounds that Gaines and Hilda were in unlawful flight. In two days the various agencies established that the pair had crossed no borders, taken no planes; and were not walking the streets of Los Angeles, San Diego, San Francisco, Portland, Seattle, Salt Lake City, Reno, Las Vegas, Phoenix, Albuquerque, New York, Miami, or Boston.

Dr. Root let me out of the hospital on the afternoon of the

third day. I found Ferguson's check for two thousand dollars waiting in my office mail, and later used it to make a down payment on a house.

That same afternoon I asked Mrs. Weinstein to place a second call to Michael Speare in Beverly Hills. I was remembering things.

Speare hadn't been in his office all day. His secretary, if that is what she was, finally relinquished his private number. I reached him there at seven o'clock at night.

He greeted me over the wire like a long-lost brother. "Good to hear from you, Bill. I've been following your adventures in the newspapers. Greatest thing since Pearl White in *Plunder*."

"Thanks. I want to talk to you as soon as possible. Tonight."

"Go right ahead."

"In person."

"What about?"

"Certain phases of my adventures involving you."

"You mean Holly and this Gaines character? I've been thinking maybe I made a mistake about them. They probably weren't as close as I imagined, you know how it is."

"I know how it is, Speare. That's just one of the things we have to discuss."

He was silent for nearly a minute. Then he said in a chastened tone: "As a matter of fact, I've been wanting to talk to you. How's about coming over for a drink?"

"You come here. I'm not driving yet."

I told him how to find my office, and he agreed to be there in an hour. Shortly after eight o'clock I heard a racing motor die coughing in the street. Something told me it would be Speare. Through the window I watched him disembark from a low-slung silver car and take off his helmet and goggles.

In the full light of the anteroom I saw that he was a worried man. He had been treating his worry with alcohol, more alcohol than he could have drunk in an hour. When I ushered him into my private office I could smell his breath. He sat down as if he had eggs in his pockets. I shut the door. The sound of it made him jump.

"About those little discrepancies, Bill, you got to understand. I had a lot at stake in Holly's career. Things have been tough in my business the last five years. And you got to admit I was only telling you what you wanted to hear."

"Just don't tell me any more lies."

His face crumpled and uncrumpled. "Is this room bugged?"

"No."

"How do I know you're telling me the truth?"

"That's not our problem. How well did you know Larry Gaines?"

"You don't expect me to answer that one, do you? He's wanted for a list of crimes as long as your arm. I'm not responsible for the morals of people I do business with."

"You did business with Gaines?"

He caught himself up. "No. He came to me, wanted me to represent him. I didn't think he had it. Besides, I didn't like his looks. I wouldn't touch him."

"I heard different."

"Oh?" His webbed eyeballs rolled. "Who from, Bill?"

I left his question hanging. "Why did Gaines pick you out to represent him?"

"It's a long and sordid story. I don't mean I did anything out of line. I was only trying to protect my client."

"Then you don't have any reason to suppress it. And you might as well tell the truth the first time around. If we have to go around a second time, we'll do it up the street at the police station."

"That's a hell of a way to treat a man, when I came here willingly to co-operate."

"Then co-operate."

His eyes, his entire face, even his bald spot, had a fine glaze on them, like well-fired pottery. He rose and took a few steps away from me and then came back. He leaned on the top of my desk. "I came here to co-operate. I'm in a worse bind than you know. The whole thing started early last spring before Holly left me. That sister of hers, the one you're looking for, ran up some bills in Palm Springs stores, using Holly's name. I hired a detective to track the sister down. If she got into the papers, it wouldn't be good. The sister was traveling with Gaines at the time—he was the one who put her up to the con game—and they gave my gumshoe quite a chase, all the way across the country.

"I kept the gumshoe after them because when he found out what they were doing, it looked pretty serious.

"He traced them to San Antonio and dug up a dentist there who'd put crowns on Hilda's teeth, Hollywood style. The dentist led him to a crooked plastic surgeon who specialized in fugitives from justice. He'd given Hilda a nose bob and some other touches, working from a photograph of Holly. From San Antonio the two of them went to Houston, where she promoted herself a wardrobe. Then on to sucker-land.

"The suckers in Miami weren't having any, not the respectable ones with the big money. Hilda looked like Holly, but she lacked the class. She had to settle for fringe benefits, using Holly's name to gamble on. She fell into the hands of a cookie named Salaman—the hood they arrested in L.A. the other day. When my man caught up with her finally, she was living with Salaman, paying off the interest on the money that she owed him. She was still using Holly's name, and

Salaman thought he was sleeping with a star, bragging around town about it. I flew to Miami the end of August to put a stop to it."

"Why didn't you put a stop to it?"

"I did. At least I thought I did. I gave her twenty-four hours to crawl back into the woodwork and stop damaging my client."

"Holly wasn't your client at the end of August."

"I know, but I was hoping to get her back. And I anticipate what you're going to say, that I was too soft-hearted. I should have turned Hilda and Gaines over to the police, and saved us all a lot of tragedy. I've always been too soft-hearted where women—"

I cut him short. "What happened after that?"

"Nothing. I paid the detective off, with my own money, and flew on home."

"Will he confirm your story?"

"Certainly, if you could reach him. Only, he's retired to Honolulu."

"What's his name?"

"Smith. I forget his first name."

"I know a police detective named Wills," I said. "If I can't get the truth out of you, he can."

"The truth is all I've been telling you."

"Tell me more of it."

"You can't get blood out of a stone, Bill."

I picked up my phone, dialed the police station, and asked for Lieutenant Wills. The desk sergeant said I could probably get him at home.

Speare seized my arm and spilled whisky-flavored words over my face. "Listen, no cops, the publicity would ruin me. Hang up."

He spoke with the sincerity of panic. I hung up.

"You got to understand, Bill. How could I tell it was going to turn out the way it did? I thought I was acting in Holly's best interests. She married an old man for his money. I thought she'd be better off working, in fact I know it. I know my clients like a book, better than they know themselves."

"What did you do? I think I know, but I want to hear it from the horse's mouth."

"Nothing much. I brought Gaines and Hilda back here and kept them on the hook for a while, wondering what to do with them. Some way or other they got the idea that I'd be pleased and happy if Holly's marriage didn't work out too well. I talk too much sometimes when I've been drinking—"

"I'll translate that. You blackmailed Gaines and Hilda into coming out here and trying to break up Holly's marriage."

"That's a rough way to put it, Bill. Gaines needed no urging. He had his own ideas about Holly May. I think he got delusions of grandeur traveling with her double. He told me one night when he was high that he was going to take her away from Ferguson and marry her himself."

"What was he high on?"

"Heroin. They both take heroin when they can get it."

I stood up behind my desk. Speare sat down quickly, for fear I was going to hit him. I almost hit him anyway, with my left hand. "That was a fine plan you had, turning loose two hopped-up criminals on your ex-client."

"It wasn't such a good idea, Bill. I didn't know it was going to turn out this way." His face had broken up like crackleware. "Look. I'll make a deal with you. Forget about this little business, keep my name out of it, and I'll give you something you *really* want."

"I have everything I really want."

"You don't have Gaines and the woman," he said softly.

"You know where they are?"

"I might."

"Let's have it."

"I said a deal. If this thing spills in the L.A. press, I'm a nothing man, I'm dead. I'm back selling stockings from door to door."

"Have you sold stockings from door to door?"

"Not in recent years, but my uncle does. I guess I can always get my old job back, if you insist on ruining me." He watched me through his pathos. He was sobering up. "Do I deserve to be ruined, Bill?"

"Stop calling me Bill."

"Whatever you say. Do we make a deal?"

I gave it some thought. It didn't take much thought, with the entire country being ransacked for the pair.

"It's a deal. Give me Gaines and the woman, and I'll forget you. With pleasure."

"I can't guarantee Gaines for sure. Hilda says he ran out on her. But she should be able to lead you to him."

"Have you talked to her?"

"Oh yes. I've talked to her. You think *I* blackmailed *her!* *She's* been blackmailing *me!*"

"What for, or need I ask?"

He hung his head. His bald spot shone like a wet egg. He covered it with a hand that was pocked with droplets of sweat. "She threatened to wreck my reputation unless I gave her money. I guess she's afraid to spend the ransom money. Or else Gaines really did run out on her. I've been putting her off with peanuts for the last two days, and incidentally slowly going crazy. She's sitting there like a ticking bomb. Last night she threatened to shoot me—"

"Sitting where? Where is she?"

"I'll tell you. Is it a deal?"

"I said it was."

He raised his eyes to my face and studied it. "I guess I can trust you. I got to trust somebody. Anything to get her off my back. She's holed up in a beach shack between the Palisades and Malibu, on 101 Highway." He gave me the address. "It's a brown shingle shack on the right-hand side of the highway, just a few hundred yards past a drive-in named Jack's. I was supposed to meet her there tonight, with five thousand dollars."

"What time tonight?"

"Now. I'm supposed to be there now."

"I'll go with you."

"All right. Whatever you say. Now that we've got this business settled, how about a short one to celebrate?"

"I don't keep liquor here."

"Do you mind if I run out for a quick one? I need a drink but badly."

"Go ahead."

He scuttled out. I telephoned Ferguson.


Speare never did come back. His silver racing car was still parked in front of my office, helmet and goggles on the seat, when Ferguson and I left. Ferguson drove, and I talked, from Buenavista to Malibu.

Beyond the deserted beach, the ocean was the color of iron. The moon had shrunk to a sliver of itself. At Zuma we could hear the surf thundering in like doom.

"It's a beastly situation," Ferguson said.

"They get that way sometimes when you let them lie for a quarter of a century."

"Please don't moralize. I've had the whole thing out with

myself. There's nothing you can say that I haven't already thought."

"Have you had it out with your wife?"

"Yes. She's going to stay with me whatever comes. This thing has brought us closer somehow—closer than we were. I know now that she loves me."

"You're lucky to have such a woman."

"I realize that, Gunnarson. Both Holly and I have realized a number of things. I thought I could start a brand-new life at the age of fifty-six, as if I hadn't already had a life. Holly was doing the same thing in her way. She tried to turn her back on everything, her family, the whole past. But the past has its revenges.

"It has its compensations, too," he added. "We went to see Holly's mother yesterday, in Mountain Grove. I imagined that she'd spent her life hating me. She hasn't. She forgave me years ago. It's good to be forgiven."

"Has she had any word from Hilda?"

"Not recently. Hilda showed up there several weeks ago. She managed to convince her mother that she was the one who had become an actress and married—a wealthy man." He was embarrassed by this reference to himself.

"Tell me, Ferguson, does Hilda know that you're her father?"

"I'm not certain. Kate Dotery said she told her my name when Hilda was a young girl. The chances are that Hilda doesn't remember."

"If she does remember, it may explain the crime—I mean the crime she attempted against her sister. There's no question she left her to burn."

"I know, and it wasn't her first attempt. She attacked Holly several times before, once with a butcher knife, once with a pan of hot grease. I think that's the basic reason why

Holly severed connections with her family. The butcher-knife episode occurred just a day or two before she ran away. She took off with a stocking salesman named Sperovich when she was sixteen. Holly's had a hard life, too."

There was nothing in his voice but sympathy, and an undertone of sadness. The jealousy and the rage, the desperate hopefulness, had burned out. He drove at a steady sixty toward whatever final revenge the past was going to take.

"Did you bring your gun, Ferguson?"

"I did. I don't intend to use it, unless Gaines is there. I have no compunction for him."

The highway climbed away from the sea among coastal hills. The hills were dark and barren. There was very little traffic. Ferguson let the long grade slow the car. He was driving mechanically.

"Do you believe this Speare is telling the truth? She's actually there?"

"She's there, all right. Speare had nothing to gain by inventing the story."

"What am I going to say to her, Gunnarson?"

"Nothing that you can say will change the situation very much. Tell her you're her father, you want to help her."

"But what good can I do her?"

"We'll be helping her simply by bringing her in."

"And after that?"

"She'll need the best criminal lawyer and the best psychiatrists your money can procure. They won't be able to get her off, of course, but they can save her from the extreme penalty. No one with strong financial backing is ever executed."

"Money again, eh?"

"Be glad you have it, for your daughter's sake."

"I don't know. If it hadn't been for my money, me and my

money, Hilda would never have been born—never con-
ceived. Or else she'd have had a father, a decent bring-
ing-up."

"How do you know? You can't second-guess the past. All
you can do is learn to live with it."

"You have a good deal of understanding, Gunnarson."

"More than I had a week ago, anyway. We all have."

We were near the top of the grade. Ferguson had slowed
to thirty-five or forty. A pair of headlights came up behind
us rapidly. A low-slung car went by like a silver bullet. I
caught a glimpse of a goggled, helmeted head.

"I think that's Speare," I said. "He may be planning to
double-cross us. Can you drive faster?"

Ferguson pressed the accelerator to the floor. The heavy
car gathered speed and soared over the crest of the hill. Below, the road curved back toward the sea. At the end of the
curve a red sign flashed: JACK'S DRIVE-IN.

Speare's silver car swung wide on the curve and almost
went off onto the left-hand shoulder. I saw it pause, incredi-
bly, like a bird in flight, and heard the screech of its brakes.
A tiny skirted figure, black in the headlights, was running
across the highway. She stopped in the middle, facing the
weaving car with something in her hand. The something
spurted fire. The car flung her off the road before I heard
the shot, and slewed on for another hundred feet.

We got to her before Speare did. I knew her by the shape
of her body. Ferguson went to his knees beside her. He
touched her ruined head.

Speare came trotting, throwing off his goggles as he ran.

"I didn't mean to do it. You saw her run out in the road.
She tried to shoot me. I did my best to avoid her, but I
couldn't. You're a witness, Bill."

His eyes were headline black. He clutched my arm, bab-

bling and shaking. People began to gather, like Martians
dropped from the pierced sky.

Ferguson had the dead woman in his arms.

"Who is she? Do you know her?" somebody said.

He looked up at the Martians and their sky. A shudder
went through him, violent and unwilled as the spasm that
had engendered her. "She's my daughter," he said in a clear
voice. "My daughter Hilda."

The Highway Patrol found the gun in the ditch. It turned
out to be Gaines's revolver, and it held three empty shells
and three loaded shells. A dentist from San Antonio, Texas,
identified the charred jawbone Wills had dug out of the
ashes. It was the jawbone of a man he had done some fillings
for the previous May. The name on the charts and X rays
was Larry Grimes.

Hilda's second shot had not been aimed at me.

In due course the bones of her son were released to Adelaide Haines for burial. Wills attended the funeral, he told
me later. He was interested in the fact that Mrs. Haines had
paid thirty-five hundred dollars for a bronze casket with
silver embellishments.

Wills followed her home after the service to ask her a few
questions. She tried to buy him off with ten thousand dollars in cash. He found the rest of the money her son had left
with her inside the case of her upright grand piano. He
found also a first-class airline ticket to Rio de Janeiro, made
out in the name of the Reverend Cary Caine.

As for the diamond brooch, the nurse who undressed Mrs.
Haines in the psychiatric ward of the Mountain Grove Hospital discovered that she was wearing it pinned to her slip
under her black mourning.

Printed in the United States
by Baker & Taylor Publisher Services